Fortunes
Alane Hotchkin

Fortunes

Alane Hotchkin

Affinity
eBook Press
NZ
2017

Fortunes
© 2017 by Alane Hotchkin

Affinity E-Book Press NZ LTD
Canterbury, New Zealand

1st Edition

ISBN: 978-0-947528-42-3

Editor: Angela Koenig
Proof Editor: Alexis Smith
Cover Design: Irish Dragon Designs

Acknowledgments

There are so many to thank as always. Where would I even begin and not forget anyone. Thank you as always to the betas and editors. They find the "whoops" that I miss and fix the dreaded commas that cause me such headaches. Of course they also have to tell me when a scene goes off on a tangent and just doesn't read properly.

Kudos of course to Nancy, Mel, and Julie for believing my story was good enough for the public.

A side thanks goes to the fantastic friends I have that listen to my ramblings over a meal, whether it be pizza or sushi. All of you are awesomesauce!!

Above all, I have to give the largest piece of the pie to my wife. She is my lifeline and keeps me grounded. She makes sure I remember to get enough sleep, and shoves food in front of me if I'm too engrossed in whatever I happen to be working on at that moment. She also, of course, gives me a reality check if ever I need one. She is my world.

Dedication

We as a society have progressed so far yet we still have so many miles to go. While some have never been subjected to one moment of unpleasantness in their lives, others have to endure relentless anguish that at any moment they could be a target of a homophobic confrontation.

This story is for those who have to live with that constant worry. Keep fighting, keep your head held high because there is a way. There is always a way.

Be true to yourself and never hide the real person living within you. Those close to you will always have your back, they will fight for you and beside you. If they don't they are not worth knowing.

To you, I say, find your path, no matter how hard it is. In the end it is worth it.

Be strong, you will prevail.

This book is for you and the warrior with in you.

Love & Hugs,
Alane

Table of Contents

Also by Alane Hotchkin

Once Upon a Time

The Ball

Beginning of the End

My Everything

Prologue

Here we are once again on Valentine's Day. Some love this holiday while others not so much. I, even with being the romantic I am, can see both sides. I am in agreement, though, that over the last couple of decades, holidays have become too commercialized. Even with that being said, I still believe in the romance of the holiday they call a day for lovers. Maybe it's the fem in me that makes me romantic.

Maybe though, it is the writer in me that loves romance. I've almost finished my current writing project. The only obstacle now is the ending. For some unknown reason, the true ending has eluded me for over two months. Not one idea I have had has rung true. The voices in my head that whisper the words I put on paper seem to have gone on holiday to Disneyland and don't plan on coming back any time soon.

I write under a name other than my own; H.R. Lemming is my pen name and Remmy my given name. Don't get me wrong, I'm not ashamed that I write lesbian novels or lesbian erotica. Why should I be? I've been out since my early teen years and refuse to hide in any closet. I mainly do it because I do not want some psycho following me or terrorizing me because of who I am. I vowed to myself never again would I be at the mercy of a madman.

Of course, though, what is in a name? Not one person would think to look for a female with my name. I was named Remmington after my grandfather; my father really, really wanted a boy you see. Instead, thirty-three years ago I was born. My father got his wish two years later with the birth of my brother, Jacob. I teased Jacob his whole life that he was born a day late and a dollar short, that I got the better of the two names.

What I wouldn't give to be able to tease him now, to be able to just hug him one more time. It seems the last decade has brought such change to the world around me.

Could this be the reason I can't find the ending to my current manuscript? My mind has flittered in so many directions these past months.

I sat at my computer this morning and into the afternoon, staring at the screen, lost in thought. Could this newest idea to pop into in my head be the ending to my novel, a novel I have been writing for three years now? I have published four other novels and many short stories in that time, yet for some reason can't finish this one novel. I can't seem to put this story to bed.

My doorbell rings; taking a deep breath, I pray to any goddess that is listening to give *her* the courage and bring her to my doorstep. Opening the door, my heart pounds out of my chest and tears come to my eyes. Never before have I felt happier.

But I am getting ahead of myself. My story began two years ago with a chance meeting…

Chapter One

In Lethbridge, in a hospital room on the twelfth floor, Remmy stood looking out the rain-streaked window at the city below. She didn't see the city; her mind's eye saw only white-hot anger. Emotions raged within her, driving her to the brink of insanity.

As she watched, lights blinked on as dusk descended upon her hometown. The darkness slowly crept along the street, just as it had into her heart. She knew the sun would rise in the morning and lighten the day once more. Her heart was another matter altogether.

The war on terrorism had finally descended upon this city, her home, her world, and it would never be the same. Friends passing her in the street would look at her differently now. There had been sympathy in their eyes for her over the past three years since her girlfriend's death; now there would be pity at the loss of her brother.

Her reflection in the window glared back at her. She looked worn out. Her shoulder-length, curly, molasses-brown hair stood out in every direction and there were heavy bags under her copper eyes. Even the extra few pounds on her

3

body, baby fat as her father called it, seemed to betray her and triple in size.

She did not like what she saw. Looking back at her was the face of a middle-aged woman that had been broken by life, not a woman of twenty-nine years who had yet to begin to live.

Taylor, her father, had tried since her teens to convince her she held within her features the classical beauty of actress Nastassja Kinski, while at the same time all the feistiness and grace of the actress Julie Newmar. At that moment, she saw not a shred of what he saw. Her eyes were puffy from crying non-stop and she felt defeated, not confident and feisty. The woman she saw did not reflect the woman she truly was.

With slumped shoulders, she laid her tired head against the window, as she quietly sobbed for all that was lost. Startled by a rustling sound behind her, she jumped and tried to compose herself. She needed to be strong for her father, just as he had been for her.

Taylor had been her rock three-and-a-half years ago. She'd sunk to the edge of oblivion after Haley's death and he brought her back. She hadn't cared whether she lived or died and he had made her see that life did go on, even if she didn't feel it deep in her heart.

Taylor made her see the beauty in being alive once more. He had lost sight of it once in his life when he lost his wife, and upon finding it again, had never let go. He cherished both of his children more than anything in life. His son's birth, robbing him of the love of his life, had brought about his darkest moment when it should have been one of his happiest.

Wiping her face on her sleeve, she turned around. "Oh Daddy, what am I to do now…"

✝

Less than twenty-four hours earlier the two of them had been cleaning up after their lunch. Remmy had been helping her father plant his tomatoes. Their time in the garden had been cut short when the rain started. While in the kitchen relaxing a moment after their meal, a knock at the front door drew their attention.

The intrusion startled the weathered older man. "Who the hell could that be?"

"Why don't you see who's at the door? I'll bring our beers into the den and turn on the Steelers game." Wiping her hands on the dishtowel, Remmy closed the dishwasher.

She took two ice cold Labatt's from the refrigerator, popped off the tops, and walked into the hallway. Her father opened the front door as she rounded the corner.

There, standing on the other side of the screen door, was what he thought of as his enemy. All the color drained from Taylor's face as he took a step back from the door. "No! You have the wrong house! You must have the wrong name."

Hearing her father's distressed voice, Remmy set the bottles on the hallway table and rushed to the front door. It was then that she fully saw who was there. A Marine captain in full uniform. Their eyes met and she knew. For a brief moment, Remmy couldn't get enough air into her lungs. The dread and fear she had lived with since her brother had enlisted closed around her heart and squeezed tightly. She now knew what an animal felt when trapped within barbed wire.

Gathering courage, she didn't know she had, she stepped forward. "Daddy, let me handle this."

She opened the screen door. "Please come in, sir, what may I do for you?"

Her father's trembling hand grasped her arm. "No, child, I'll deal with this. Why don't you go to the kitchen and make some coffee?"

Despite being dismissed, she refused to move.

"No, I'll stay right here." She turned her attention back to the officer in front of them. Remmy studied him a moment, noting the sadness in his eyes. He was a nice-looking, rugged young man and towered over her own five-nine height.

Remmy surmised that he could more than hold his own in hand-to-hand combat. However, his task of informing families of their loved ones passing on was taking its toll on him. She knew that vacant look that his eyes held. It was the same she had in hers three-and-a-half years ago on a cold and dreary day when her life had been ripped in two, the good half of it gone forever.

"Mr. Garrick, I am Captain Jenkins. Do you think we could sit? I have some..." The older man before him clutched his chest in pain.

"Sir...sir...excuse me, ma'am, but please call 911, your father is ill." He moved to catch the falling man.

✝

Brought back from her mind traveling and reliving that few moments in time from the previous day, she heard her name called.

"Remmy..." Her father's voice was only a mere whisper.

The only light in the room came from a dim fixture over his bed, causing most of the room to be cast in eerie shadows. The machines monitoring her father's heart beeped quietly at regular intervals. Remmy wiped her face a second time and quietly stepped over to her father's bedside.

Once again noting his pale features, she felt her heart leap back into her throat. Dr. Morgan had told them it was a mild heart attack; there would be no long-term effects. The hospital, however, still wanted to keep him for monitoring.

Remmy straightened the thin blanket covering him. She could never understand why the blankets in hospitals where always so pathetic. She made a mental note to ask the next nurse that came in if she could please bring an additional blanket to keep him warm through the night.

"I'm right here, Daddy. What can I get for you?"

Taylor partially opened his eyes and looked at her. She saw tears forming in the corners of his eyes.

"I'm sorry, Remmy. I should've tried harder to talk Jacob out of joining the Marines."

Remmy carefully picked up his hand, holding it between hers. "Daddy, you couldn't have done anything different. Jacob was headstrong and as stubborn as a bucking bull. He wasn't about to listen to either of us."

He squeezed her hand. "You two were so close up 'til Haley's death. What happened? You never told me, sweetie."

She couldn't believe he was concerned about her problems. Straightening her shoulders, Remmy went on the defensive and tried to steer around the question. "Dad, you have more important things to think about right now. You have to get well and remember to take your medications, not rehash old shit."

Even ill, he was still strong, not just in presence but in muscle from years in the construction business. He pulled her closer. "Bullshit. Tell me what happened. You've ne'er lied to me, nor hid nothin' from me 'til she was killed. Please, sweetie, talk to me."

Remmy became perturbed with her father's insistence. He didn't need to worry himself with things that were beyond anyone's control now. As annoyed as she was, she let none of it show. "Daddy, we can talk about it later, okay?"

Remmy received Taylor's best *I don't think so* glare.

"No, not this time kiddo, you always say that. Then we ne'er discuss it."

Taylor's heart monitor beeped a little faster, which alerted Remmy that he was getting agitated. "Dad, calm down, please."

"Remmington Victoria…"

Using her full name was all the pushing that she needed to break. She crumbled, spilling what had happened between brother and sister three years ago.

She pulled the reclining chair closer to her father's bed. "There's really not much to it. Jacob was just being Jacob. He never did like what Haley did for a living and he told her every chance he ever had."

Taylor's larger hand covered Remmy's smaller one. "I ne'er knew that. Why didn't you say somethin'?"

Remmy sighed and sat farther back in the chair. Maybe it was time to unburden some of her inner turmoil to her father. She and her father had always been so close and had no issue with talking about everything that came to mind. Remmy knew his guilt surfaced from time to time and now she was watching it wash over him.

"Maybe if your mama had been alive none of this would ever've happened."

"Daddy…dad, please don't. Mom died giving birth to Jacob. There was nothing you could have done; back then, almost all women who hemorrhaged during childbirth died. She gave her life so Jacob could live."

She herself had no memories of the woman. All she knew about her mom came from her father. She had no aunts or uncles either since both of her parents had been only children. As much as she would have loved to know her mother, she would never have given up one moment of her precious time with her brother to wish otherwise.

"Remmy, let's not dwell on what can't be changed. I think you were going to tell me something?"

Remmy sighed again; she wasn't going to get out of the conversation. She figured she might as well jump in with both feet. Maybe it was time she told him.

"What would you like me to say, Dad, 'my brother's a hardhead and thinks my girlfriend likes to live dangerously'? No, it was between him and me. I love...loved him to pieces but, boy, could he be a jackass sometimes. He hated that she was a corrections officer..." She stuttered as memories flooded back as well as the pain.

She felt her father grip her hand tighter, offering her a lifeline. She began again with renewed strength. "When she was killed, he was so angry. At first, I thought it was something I had done. Then he stopped by the house one night. He was drunker than a skunk."

Remmy felt herself travel back to that night. She could smell the alcohol now just as clearly as she could that night. It wafted off him as she opened the door. She no longer was in her father's hospital room but standing beside herself in front of her drunken brother.

When she spoke, her voice came from far away, from three years in her past. "He started yelling, cursing her for getting herself killed. I realized his anger was at her, not me. He told me he actually hated her for hurting me. We talked through the night, but no matter what, I couldn't get him to understand, that she died trying to make a difference." The words caught in her throat.

"Our parting words that night were him telling me that at least I was now filthy rich because of the settlement with the state. I told him I'd rather be piss-poor and have her back, but it wasn't going to happen and I had to somehow find a way to go on, even though I really didn't want to. And if he couldn't understand that, then he needed to get out and never come back." She closed her eyes and felt the heat of her brother's words sear through her.

Remmy stood, moving to the windows once more. "I'll have to live with the loss of both of them. That... and...and the knowledge that they did make a difference. Right now, though, it doesn't seem all that significant."

Night had fully set and fog had rolled in, making the streetlights cast an eerie glow. "If I had known it would be the last time I was going to see him...maybe I would have let him win the argument for once."

Remmy could feel the anger at him boiling within her. "Damn him! He belonged home with his family. Not some place he wasn't wanted. He only had one week to go before coming home. Then he would have been out in six months. Damn him!" She pounded her fist against the window, not caring if she broke the glass or not.

From the darkness behind Remmy, her father's voice told the truth.

"Remmington, there was nothin' you could have done to convince him. He had to see the light for himself. As for damning him...he too, was doing what he thought was right. Would you hold him to a different set of rules than you held your Haley? No, I don't think so. You and I will get through this too, just as we did before. We're strong, you and I, we'll make it."

She sighed. In the recesses of her mind, she knew he was right. They would survive and go on, but at what cost? Even though her heart told her differently, she would be strong for her father.

"Yes, Daddy, we'll be okay. I remember you telling me something when Haley died. You said that Nietzsche said it best, 'That, which does not kill us, makes us stronger.' You said it was Mama's favorite saying. By now both of us should be able to lift Lady Liberty with one finger." Remmy smiled as she always did with the memories of Haley.

"Honey, you've seen and felt too much pain in such a short life. Out there waiting for you, is a woman just as wonderful as Haley was, but in her own special way. Someday, sweetie, she'll come. You'll have no choice but to love her and fight for her."

Remmy turned quickly. "What are you talking about, Daddy?"

When she approached the bed, she found him sound asleep. "What the hell are you talking about, Daddy? There could never be anyone else."

She spoke to the darkness of the night, but how could her father think she could ever fall in love again? "It's too preposterous a thought to even consider."

She pulled the thin blanket up over him, kissing him goodnight on the forehead. Brushing his thinning hair off his forehead, she noticed for the first time how old he looked. Surely, he had not looked so weathered before this.

"I should have noticed. Oh, Daddy, when did you age so much? There's white in your hair and it's starting to thin some." She studied the wrinkles on his face.

To Remmy, he'd always been a handsome man. She inherited her height from him and the rest of her features from her mother. She remembered growing up that his six-six frame had always caused problems for him when he would visit other people's homes. He had built their home to accommodate his taller stature.

Looking down at him, Remmy still saw, under the paleness, the man that was her father. She always told everyone he was the most handsome man in the world. He had the same striking features, domineering personality, and strength, as her idol Clint Eastwood. Never once had Taylor Garrick ever had one problem with any of his crews on the construction sites. They feared him yet at the same time had the utmost respect for him. There was only one man who didn't get along with her father - her cousin Ronald.

Shit, he better stay away from Daddy. Knowing that leech though, he'll come sniffing around fast to see if he can get control of the company.

Her father moved slightly beneath the sheets as he snored softly. She thought back to his last words. "How could you think that? Sometimes, Daddy, I think your mind is slipping a little." Sure, she had met a couple of nice women, but fall in love again? She couldn't even comprehend the idea.

The thought of letting anyone else touch her soul was foreign to her. The two that she did have sex with in the past couple of years were only that - sex. Even then, she'd felt nothing. She told herself that she felt more when she made herself come than with either of them.

Jack Sheridan was her best friend and had been practically since birth. They were each other's rock in the bad times and instigators in the good. Her friend teased her relentlessly that when she did find that someone special, as he put it, *you're going to explode like confetti.*

"Night, Daddy, I'll see you in the morning." She passed the night nurses on the way out and asked them for the additional blanket, then bid them good night as well.

✝

While sitting in the hospital parking garage, Remmy pulled out the journal that she always kept with her and put her thoughts of the past hours in the hospital with her father and of her brother's passing, down in words.

The cycle of life is at times too short, just as for others it is too long. When it is brutally and unjustly cut short, it changes the reality of all it touches. Death is the only mystery remaining to humanity. Try as one might, it can never be prevented.

Every living creature is affected by death; it is how they react that is different. Animals and humans alike. After all, aren't humans just animals in disguise?

Except, of course, humans have a tendency to destroy all they touch while rationalizing their decisions. Mankind cannot even live together without demolishing each other. Young men and women sign their lives away with the idea that they can be the one who can make the difference. They believe they can stop the madmen.

Do they not think of the ones they leave behind? Who will comfort the ones who open the screen door to find a man in full-dress uniform standing on the other side? No one, because there is no comfort. There is only anger and terror for those left behind.

If one wish could be made in the whole world, would it not be for all the brutality to end?

✝

Pulling her black, fully loaded Ford F-350 truck into her driveway, Remmy didn't bother to park it in the garage. Her door opener was broken and she was too tired to put the door up manually. Looking at the clock on the dashboard, Remmy realized it was still early. "It's only nine-thirty, Jack should still be up." Remmy patted the dashboard. She loved her new truck with all the little gadgets in it.

Her father had been more than a little miffed when she'd driven up to the house four months ago in the new truck. He was a Chevy man through and through and it rattled him when his own daughter bought a Ford.

He still gave her a hard time any chance he got, which always gave her a chuckle. "I wonder what he would have done if I had bought a Honda?" She laughed. He would have disowned her for buying what he considered foreign.

She stopped herself. "Shit! I'm freakin' talkin' to myself now." Laying her head against the steering wheel, she sighed. *Okay, time to get the ass moving.*

Shutting her truck door behind her and locking it, she slowly walked into the house. After throwing her keys on the kitchen counter, she took a beer from the fridge, and shuffled into the living room. She knew she should eat something but she wasn't the least bit hungry.

Standing in the middle of the living room, she looked around, then closed her eyes. It was so quiet she could hear herself breathing. Listening for the creaking the house made, she heard none.

In her mind, she could hear voices in the house from long ago, pulling her back to a happier time. It was when the house was filled with laughter and love.

Remmy open her eyes and scanned the room. She was in the past, an outsider looking in.

In the middle of the living room sat the extra-large blue folding table and eight chairs. On it sat Haley's favorite deck of cards, the ones with an assortment of Harley-Davidson bikes on the back. Beside the deck sat the tray of poker chips and the box of expensive Cuban cigars.

Remmy stood facing the stone fireplace just beyond the table. Behind her, she heard Haley rooting around in the bottom of the liquor cabinet for a new bottle of Scotch. She knew the two fingers left in the current bottle would only last five minutes.

Remmy watched as she herself came in from the kitchen carrying the new bottle but not giving it to Haley without first getting the payment of a kiss. Her eyes traveled from the table to the left, surprised when she saw herself lounging on their brown leather sofa. Remmy forced herself to look back at the table. She stumbled backwards into the end table when she saw all of them sitting in the room. It played out before her as it had many times in her nightmares.

Jacob, Haley, Jack, Brett, RJ, and Taylor were sitting at the card table, each with a cigar and scotch, trying to out-bluff each other at poker. It was the night Jac wasn't able to make the game. Usually Ronald would arrive when they were on the second or third hand with beer and more food. Ronald was the grandson of her grandmother's sister. She didn't like him, but she tolerated him because he was the only other living family she had.

Behind her, she heard Ronald arrive, late as always. She assumed it was to piss off Taylor, who had no tolerance for lateness, especially when it came to the Friday night poker games. She watched as they got into their usual argument.

Remmy smiled. It always amused her how the players would always get into a fight sometime after midnight, only to make up and continue playing until well into late Saturday morning.

She turned, seeing herself sitting and reading. She only joined them occasionally for a hand or two. As Remmy watched, a typical Friday night played out before her. Tears filled her eyes. They were not from sadness; they sprang from love - the love that flowed through her as the memories flooded her senses. Remmy could smell the cigar smoke and taste the homemade pizza that she would make for them at midnight.

The room looked as it had for many years, before she had Colin strip the house two years ago. During that time Colin had become more than just an employee, he became a good friend. Making over of some of the rooms gave it a fresh feeling at a time when she had thought of selling it in order to remove the reminders of what she had lost. She reconsidered, however, when she walked into the living room and saw that he had kept the leather sofa and chair that she had purchased as gifts for Haley.

It was still the same home, even with the new paint and new items. She liked the pale sage color of the walls better now. The tone was unlike any she had seen before, bringing out the warm brown of the leather furniture and the oak of the mission-style end tables and coffee table. Colin had even hung several of the portraits he found in the attic, pictures of her parents and grandparents.

Whenever she walked into the room, it smelled of leather, wood, and the essence from the fireplace. It smelled as a home should smell - lived in and loved.

Her mind was drawn back to the table once more, into the past, where she saw herself urging Haley to call it a night. On the Saturdays that Haley had to be up early for work, Remmy would have to harp on her that she needed to get some sleep. On the Friday nights that Haley had to work, they would move the game to Saturday.

After Haley was killed they tried to continue having the weekly Friday night game, but it just wasn't the same. Everything had changed, as if the very life had gone out of the house itself. After trying two more weeks of failure, they stopped altogether. It was then that Remmy had lost touch with Haley's friends. They had promised her they would forever be there for her; however, she just could not bear to be reminded of what she had lost. Maybe it was time to start thinking of getting back in touch with them.

Remmy now sat on yet another Friday night, lost in her memories. She came back to the present to find herself sitting in the soft, brown-leather recliner. It matched the sofa she had bought for Haley the Christmas when Haley had proposed to her.

"Wow, I seem to be reliving the past lately. This can't be a good thing." She held up the beer bottle, only to find it empty.

When had she done that? She couldn't remember drinking any of it. *Damn, I must really be losing it! I need another then.* She looked across the room at the mantel above the television and saw the framed photos.

One photo was of her and Haley that Christmas Day. She had on her favorite holiday sweater with the beautifully decorated Christmas tree on it, including the tiny bells that jingled. Haley loved that sweater. She had threatened once to put bells on all of Remmy's clothes so that she couldn't sneak up on her. It was the only thing Remmy did that drove Haley nuts. She would never hear Remmy until it was too late and Remmy would scare the wits out of her.

17

In the picture, Haley was at her most handsome. She'd gone out the previous morning and got a haircut just for the occasion. Her black wavy hair was cut just above the ears, and so short in the back it was to the point of being shaved. Haley liked it that way, all she had to do in the morning was run her fingers through it and she was done.

For the special occasion, Haley had worn her favorite long-sleeved, Boston Red Sox jersey and the pair of stonewashed denim jeans that Remmy loved because they were so tight that Haley had to pour herself into them. They not only showed off her perfect ass, but her long legs as well.

Wearing the jersey though had been risky. The fact that she was a Red Sox fan never sat right with any of them. Haley, after admitting which team she liked, had found herself in a house full of Yankees fans. She had worn it on their first date and the fact that she had been allowed back for a second date had proved that it was love.

The other photo was of her and her brother. She picked up the picture and clutched it to her chest. The picture gave her comfort as she carried it with her. Since the refrigerator was against the wall between the dining room and kitchen, Remmy cut through the dining room to get there. She opened the stainless steel door, retrieved another ice-cold beer, and returned to the living room.

Sitting in the chair, she tapped the bottle to the picture. "Here's to you, little brother. Is it my fault? I feel like it is." She swallowed half the bottle in one gulp. The beer was so cold that for a moment it gave her a pain in the eye.

"Ah, nothing beats an ice cold beer to clear the brain of its cobwebs. Isn't that what both you and Haley used to say? Dang, it's cold." She rubbed her temple as it throbbed.

She picked up the phone from the table beside her and pressed the speed dial for Jack. What was she going to tell him? All three had been friends since childhood. They were the three amigos, or as Taylor had always called them, *the three biggest damn troublemakers in the world.* It rang twice. "Hey baby, was she a good fuck?" Jack loved to personalize his hellos.

Remmy suddenly remembered she was supposed to have had dinner that evening with someone she'd met a few weeks ago. She couldn't even remember her name, not that it mattered anyhow.

When she didn't answer immediately, Jack continued, "Ah, she was that bad, huh?"

Remmy's mind returned to why she had called him. It was at that moment that everything she had lost crashed down upon her. "He's dead and Daddy's in the hospital..."

She dropped the phone to the floor, curled into herself and sobbed.

Remmy heard Mr. Bubbles, the midnight black feline, meow from the top of the stairs. She remembered how for weeks he had walked around the house crying out for Haley after her death. He was very sensitive to Remmy's moods and would know something had happened.

Mr. Bubbles pranced down the steps and onto the arm of the chair to rub his furry face against hers. He purred as he wiped away the tears with his fur. Mr. Bubbles gave her unconditional love and understanding.

Remmy reached up and stroked his fur, taking comfort in how soft and silky he was, still amazed to this day that he was so skinny for an adult cat. Any other cats she'd had in the past had acquired the middle-age spread when they were a couple of years old.

However, Mr. Bubbles was different. He was six years old and thought he was still a kitten. He quite literally pranced through the house as if it was his kingdom. Everything about him was different, right down to his personality. Remmy wondered sometimes if he didn't think he was a human.

"Oh, Mr. Bubbles..." She quietly cried, pouring all her sadness onto the shoulders of her feline friend.

Chapter Two

Jack pulled the phone away, looking at it as if it were a foreign object. "Shit!" He put the phone back up to his ear. "Remmy? Remmy!"

His only answer from the other end was her sobbing. Throwing his phone in his pocket, he ran for his apartment door. He grabbed his keys from the hallway table only as an afterthought once he had opened the door.

It took only twenty minutes to drive from his tiny apartment to her house on the east side. During the drive, his thoughts turned to all that Remmy had endured over the last few years.

Shit! Shit! Shit! Remmy so does not need anything more happening. Oh God, oh shit... She was just getting over Haley. If anything happens to her father, it might just do her in.

Then something hit him. "Why is Taylor in the hospital?"

Jack pulled his truck into Remmy's driveway, turned off the ignition, and sat frozen. He remembered back over three years ago, when he had received a frantic call from Taylor in the middle of the night. He'd raced through the darkness that time also. What he found that night would haunt him his entire life.

Even years later, he could still smell the blood, see the destruction.

†

Three-and-a-half years before...

Jack raced from his truck up to the house that night. The screaming and smashing of items reached his ears long before he stepped foot onto the porch. Carefully, Jack opened the door to find Taylor standing on the other side of it. He was holding a dishtowel to his face.

Taylor turned to Jack; no words were needed to convey the unspoken.

Jack slowly stepped into the living room. He dreaded what he was going to find. Remmy turned toward him. Her eyes were no longer the beautiful copper color. To Jack, they looked red, as red as blood. In them, he saw a wild look, one he would never forget. She was no longer human; before him stood a wild beast with one thing on its mind - death and destruction.

He saw it in her wild eyes and had to stop her. She'd already destroyed everything in the room and Jack knew what would come next. Remmy would do harm to herself, more than she already had.

He looked from her face to her hands. Blood streamed down her arms onto her hands; dripping from her fingertips, it created pools of red on the hardwood floors.

Jack's arrival appeared to take some of the gale force from her tornado. He watched her face contort as the pain in her arms and left hand registered for the first time.

Their eyes met once more before hers lowered to the floor to follow the trail of blood to the dining room. Jack followed the same trail, which at the end held what used to be their dining room table, splintered into a million glass shards.

The fight drained from Remmy and she slumped to the floor. Luckily he caught her before she made impact. Putting his arm around her, Jack didn't know where the strength came from, but he picked her up and carried her to his truck, with a still bleeding Taylor following closely behind.

Remmy lay sleeping in the hospital bed, after the doctor had ordered the nurse to, as he put it, *knock her ass out for her own good!* Beside her bed, Jack sat in one chair, and Taylor in the other.

Jack had sat down after making the difficult call to Jacob. Unfortunately, there was no way Jacob thought he could get home. His next leave was two months away; however, he would try his damnedest to have it pushed up, so he could be there for his sister.

The nurse had just left after checking Remmy's blood pressure and dressings to assure none of the stitches were bleeding through. Remmy had spent several hours in surgery to repair the worst of the damage done to her arms and hand.

Turning to a bandaged Taylor, Jack finally asked what needed to be asked hours before. All he knew was that Haley had been killed.

"How did it happen?" Jack stared across the room, not sure if he truly wanted to know.

Taylor sighed and motioned for Jack to join him outside. They walked the length of the hallway to the solarium in silence, noting the hospital smell of bleach, sickness, and death.

Each took a seat in front of the windows. Taylor took a deep breath and told what had led up to the hell they found themselves in that night.

"That bastard in charge put Haley and the three others back in building four yesterday…"

Outraged, Jack shot up from the chair. "What?!"

Taylor held out his hand. "Jack…"

Jack sat back down, tempering his outrage upon seeing the tears forming in Taylor's eyes.

"Yes, he put them back there even though he knew there had been threats against them. He also knew they and many others had filed complaints with the state."

Taylor wiped the tears on his shirtsleeve. "He probably thought he would teach them a lesson. Haley said last week that they thought he might try something stupid like this. He was old school, didn't like freethinking in his ranks, just as much as he hated women working there. The investigator that came to give us the news told us he has been relieved of his position and a full investigation into the matter is being conducted. It seems our Haley called him in the wee hours yesterday morning, when she saw the schedule. Unfortunately, he arrived too late."

Taylor turned to look at Jack. "She wasn't just the woman my little one was in love with, Jack. She was my daughter as well. Haley was just as much a part of my future as she was of Remmy's. I thought for sure I was going to be a grandpapa soon." Taylor bowed his head and silence fell.

A thought occurred to Jack then. "Uh… Taylor, was she…?"

The older man had known he would ask. Taylor met and held Jack's eyes. In Taylor's eyes, Jack saw only anger and hurt. "Yes, she was, and Remmy must never find out."

Jack shook his head, the anger coursing through him. "Taylor, it's going to be in the reports and in the paper, as well as on the news. She's going to find out." His words held all the venom he felt.

"No! The investigator told me that they are keeping this under wraps. She will not find out! She cannot ever find out that her beloved was...was...oh God, Jack, what they did to her..." Taylor held his head in his hands and sobbed.

Jack knew the atrocities that had befallen Haley must have been unbelievable to break a man like Taylor. All his life, he had looked up to him as a father and as a man who would never fall under the weight of what life would deal him.

Jack remembered the promise he had made that day, not only to Taylor, but also to Haley's spirit, never to let Remmy find out what happened to Haley. He still abided by it over three years later. Remmy, the spouses of the other officers, and the state had reached an out-of-court settlement that totaled in the millions for each of them. He and Taylor both knew what the money really was - hush money. To his knowledge, Remmy never knew that Haley had been raped repeatedly and tortured, before her body finally gave out, before taking her last breath.

Jack took a deep breath and pushed all thoughts of the past where they belonged, in the past. Remmy would never learn any of the details if he had anything to say about it.

He stepped from the porch into the quiet house, closing the door and the outside world behind him. In the living room, he found her in the recliner, quietly crying with

Mr. Bubbles trying to comfort her. Sitting on the arm of the chair, he stroked her hair and hummed to her, waiting until she was ready.

This was what best friends did. They were there in the good times as well as the bad. They shared the tears as well as the smiles. They picked each other up when all seemed lost and carried each other until they could walk on their own again.

✝

After what seemed like hours, Remmy lifted her head from her arms and realized there was someone humming to her. She met and held his eyes, just as she had before. She was overcome with déjà-vu.

"Oh Rem..." His heart bled for his friend. "Your heart hurts now and it may hurt for some time. You may have lost your smile and inner light, but I know the Fates have their reasons. One day out of nowhere and for no reason, you will find it. It might be no more than a spark, but that will be all you need, that tiny spark. There is so much good and love in you that it will light up the whole town if you let it. You have the inner strength of ten men. What do you say to some sleep and then we'll go see Taylor, okay?"

Remmy laid her head on his shoulder. "Do you even believe half the shit you spew?" Her tears had stopped for now and an eerie calm descended upon her.

Jack held her tight within his arms and answered truthfully. "Yes, I do. Now come on, to bed with you. I'll take the couch."

Remmy hesitated.

"Remmy. Enough wallowing, come on. Off with you." He pulled her up and pushed her toward the hallway.

✝

After a few hours of fitful sleep, the two life-long friends exited the elevator and walked down the hospital hallway in silence. Approaching Taylor's door, they heard a familiar voice. The mere thought of that man bothering her father in his hospital bed sent anger bubbling through Remmy.

"How dare that slimy little bastard come here! He must think this is another prime opportunity to try to take the company from Daddy, just as he did two years ago when he was sick with pneumonia. Fucking little bastard, he'll never get Daddy's company. I'll make sure of it. One way or the other, I'll make sure of it." Remmy's hands shook so badly with anger that she put them in her jeans pockets in order not to strangle the unwanted guest.

Jack knew exactly who she meant - Ronald. He personally had never liked nor trusted him. When Haley was alive, she was the main course on his menu. Ronald just couldn't understand how Haley would pick Remmy over him. He had tried every moment of every day to steal her away, to make her see the error of her ways.

Jack smiled, though, as he remembered how Haley finally put Ronald in his place.

It had been just after Haley had asked Remmy to marry her. Haley had gone into the kitchen to retrieve another couple of beers for everyone and Ronald followed her.

Jack had pretended to have to use the bathroom and crept down the hallway. Silently, he slid next to the other door leading into the hallway from the kitchen. What he overheard coming from Ronald's mouth sickened him. He never realized how truly vile the man was until that moment.

Ronald's tirade ended with disgusting bluntness. "All you need, Haley, is to be fucked properly by a man. My cousin can never do it because she's only a woman."

Haley's growling at Ronald told Jack how enraged she was. Knowing how much Haley hated the little man, Jack knew she was fighting for control so she wouldn't tear Ronald to pieces.

Jack peeked through the crack between the door and frame. He watched as Haley reached over and nearly ripped his testicles off as she lifted him off the ground. At that split second, a look of fear washed over Ronald's face.

Jack clamped a hand over his mouth covering up his laughter. *Well, dude, I hope you liked your manhood while you had it.* He silently snickered to himself.

Jack listened as Haley took him down another peg. "Listen, little man, and listen really well. I will not tell you again. I want nothing to do with you or any man. My soon-to-be wife is more of a man than you ever will be."

Jack thought she must have squeezed tighter because tears were running down Ronald's face.

"As far as 'fucking me properly' goes…let's just say that the one she uses is bigger than your dick will ever be. And…" She pulled him up to her eye level.

"And…she does fuck me properly…every single night…in every possible way." Dropping him to the ground she pushed him to the back door. "Now get the hell out of here and take those visuals with you!"

After shoving Ronald through the door, Jack was startled when she pulled the hallway door open where he had been standing and listening. He had been so fixated on what she was doing that she had caught him off guard.

Jack looked up at her. "You knew I was there the whole time, huh?"

They both roared with laughter as they went back to the living room. Haley slapping him on the back, caused him to wince. "Sure did, Jack my friend, sure did. By the way, that never happened in there, correct?"

Jack shook his head.

Jack never said a word of what transpired in the kitchen to Remmy.

Remmy cleared her throat and brought Jack back from his memories. "Where did you go just now?"

Jack smiled. "Oh, just on an adventure, that's all. Now let's get this slime out of Taylor's presence."

Opening the door, she heard Ronald try to convince her father to hand over the company to him. He had not heard her come in. Remmy stepped up behind him and clamped a strong hand down on his shoulder. "Ronald, I'm only going to tell you this one last time. Daddy will hand over the company to you when Hades fucking freezes over! Now get out of here and leave my father alone!"

With Remmy on one side of him and Jack on the other, he was pulled from the chair and shoved through the doorway into the hall. They turned and closed the door behind him, shutting him out of their world.

Remmy turned to her father. "I'm sorry he found his way in here, Daddy. Are you okay?'

"Yes, I'm fine now. I hate to admit it. Maybe it is time to hand over more responsibility, but it won't be to Ronald. I may have made a promise to his mama to look after him and take care of him, but I won't throw away my life's work on him."

Picking up the coffee from the tray in front of Taylor, Remmy sniffed at the contents. "Yuck, they call this coffee? It looks and smells like dirty dishwater."

Taylor nodded. "Tastes like it too. That is the first thing I want when I get home. I want a good cup of coffee and none of that fruity kind you like young lady. I want real coffee."

"Daddy, I happen to like the coffee I make at home. I like my Jamaican Me Crazy." She shivered, thinking about the coffee her father drank. He liked it so strong you could put half a gallon of milk in it and it still would be black. "Besides, I don't think you should drink as much of it as you used to. And you sure as heck shouldn't drink it as strong."

Taylor scowled. "Then put me in the grave now. Sorry, honey, but I'm not giving up my coffee."

She went about fussing with the covers over his feet. "Okay, Daddy, we'll talk about it later. So, when can we spring you from this joint? It seems you'll get more rest at home than here. Especially with all the weirdos hangin' around here."

Jack stepped up to Taylor's bedside. "I happen to agree. Let's see if we can spring the jailbird."

Taylor laughed. This was what he needed. It was what would soothe his aching heart, not the medicines or the disgusting hospital food, but his family.

"I agree; I want to go home. The doc should be here any minute. Maybe one of you can convince him, since both of you are such *smooth talkers*. I just ask one thing, please don't manhandle the poor guy, I don't think his wife would like it too much." Taylor laughed.

Remmy shook her head at her father's attempted humor. "I'll try, Dad, but no guarantees."

†

In the hallway, Ronald's anger raged. Several nurses walked by him as they completed their morning rounds. They made sure to stay clear of him as he stood muttering to himself.

"That bitch! She'll get what's coming to her, just like that whore of hers did. How dare she think she can take what's mine! I hate doing sales, it's schlep work, just as much as I hate working with that little piss-ant of hers, Colin. When I have control of the company, I'll fire them all! They'll be sorry they didn't treat me with proper respect."

Another nurse walked by him. "Are you okay, sir?"

He glared at her, muttering. "How dare she talk to me, she's just like the rest of them, beneath me!"

The nurse met Ronald's eyes and saw nothing but unveiled hatred. Shuddering, she walked away as rapidly as she could.

He muttered under his breath again. "Damn whore, just like all the others."

He turned back toward the hospital room that he had been thrown out of. "Hear me well, you whore bitch, I'll bide my time well. I'll make plans, ones that won't falter. You'll fail when the company is yours. You're just a woman; you know nothing of a man's world. When you do stumble, I'll be waiting with open hands to snap your fucking neck."

†

The next morning one of the nurses who had overheard part of Ronald's mad ravings pulled Remmy aside as they were leaving to take Taylor home. She informed Remmy of what pieces she'd overhead.

31

Remmy took note of the name on her badge. "Don't worry, Rochelle. That little slimeball doesn't scare me. My cousin seems to try to make up for his shortcomings with anger and threats. Neither of which he has the balls to follow up with. Thank you for letting me know. It's nice to see that people do care about others." Remmy laughed all the way down the hall.

Remmy had wanted to push her father's wheelchair through the hallway and help him into Jack's truck but the orderly would not hear of it.

"It is my job, Ms. Garrick."

She watched the orderly a moment as he smiled and glanced over at Jack. "And I bet meeting new people all the time is fun as well..." She looked at his name tag. "...Patrick." *Ooh I think he might be smitten with my Jack from those looks he's giving him. He's shy, tall, and handsome, perfect for Jack I think.*

Remmy hung back a moment and watched Jack eyeing the orderly as Patrick helped Taylor from the wheelchair into the back of his SUV. When the younger man kept throwing shy glances in Jack's direction, Remmy knew her best friend was going to have to make the first step. She watched him wait until Patrick had Taylor in the truck, and the door closed, before Jack approached him.

Jack watched as Remmy walked around to the passenger side while he waited for the orderly to turn in his direction. Jack had maneuvered himself between the hospital door and the other man.

"Do you have a moment, Patrick?" he put his hand on the arm of the wheelchair, stopping its progress toward the doors.

Shy eyes met his.

"Yes, sir, what can I do for you?"

Jack cut right to the heart of it. "What you can do is have dinner with me on your next night off. And call me Jack, please"

A look of what Jack could only think of as fear washed over Patrick's face

"Tomorrow, Jack?"

Jack laughed. "Okay, tomorrow it is then. What time should I pick you up and where?" He thought to himself that Patrick looked like he was about to faint.

"Seven and here is fine."

"Good. I'll see you at seven, right here. Have a good rest of the day." Jack opened the driver's door and climbed in. He looked back and saw Taylor grinning.

"So when's your date then?" Taylor snickered a little when he asked.

At that, Taylor and Remmy both burst into laughter at Jack's expense.

"Ha, ha. Very funny, you two!" Jack wiggled his eyebrows. "Tomorrow night and it may be the beginning of something wonderful."

Remmy and Taylor both made gagging noises at the same time. "Keep it up, you two, and I'll pull over and dump you alongside the road." It was nice to see a little humor brighten his friends, even if it was at his own expense.

✝

They pulled into Taylor's driveway but remained in the truck. Jack quietly sat behind the wheel while Remmy argued with Taylor about what was best for him.

Remmy had turned around in her seat to face him. "Daddy, I'm serious. We're here only to pick up some of your clothes and your medications. I really feel it's for the best if you stay with me for a couple of weeks."

"Remmington, I still have my dignity. I ain't no invalid and I won't be treated as one. The doc saw fit to send me home... and home I'll be. All I need is a day or two of rest and I'll be up and running." Taylor opened the door.

"Daddy, I'm just trying to do what's best for you."

"I know, sweetie. I'm responsible not just for my clients but those who work for me, too. All of them are like family."

"But, dad, really you need..."

"Remmington Victoria, you listen once and for all. Just remember you're not too old for me to still whoop your ass."

Almost out of the truck, he continued. "I'm staying in my own home. We will handle the arrangements for your brother together. And..."

Taylor sat back down. he reached over the seat and laid his hand on her shoulder. She noticed how tired he suddenly looked.

"We'll discuss work at another time."

Remmy was out of the truck like a shot with Jack hot on her heels to help her father if needed. She couldn't let it drop. "Daddy, you can't go back to running the company yourself. The stress will kill you. We don't need to decide things today, but I really feel you need help. You need to hire an assistant."

Taylor turned to Jack, who had remained silent during the exchange of words. "Do you feel the same way, Jack? Am I a feeble old man?"

Her father's words stopped Jack in his tracks. She hoped he wouldn't say something that would tick both of them off.

Jack cleared his throat. "Well, here goes nothing. You're not old and feeble. Remmy, I agree with your father, he should stay where he is most comfortable, in his own home. Taylor, I agree with Remmy. You need to relinquish some of the control of the company. There, I said my piece."

Remmy and her father stood in the driveway looking at each other while Jack didn't take his eyes off the ground. Watching him shuffle his feet, Remmy wondered what Jack was contemplating. She didn't have long to wait.

"Besides, you live only a few moments away from your father. If need be, you could be here in a minute or two."

Remmy glared at Jack while she spoke to Taylor. "Fine, but just call me if you need anything. I'll check on you first thing in the morning and we'll go from there."

"Sweetie, I know you have your pride and stubbornness, you get that from me. I hate giving an inch as well, but sometimes you just have to." He sighed. "Okay... I'm going to hand over partial control of the company to you. You run the day-to-day operations and I'll remain as president. You'll need to hire someone now to help you for sure, as well as someone to replace most of your position. We can discuss all of this in the next couple of days, though. Right now, we have other things to take care of that are more important."

Remmy was immediately suspicious. Her father was backing her into a corner. Instead of remaining silent, she voiced her concerns as they walked the remainder of the way to the house. "Daddy, why did you give into the idea so easily? Is there something I don't know? And, why me?"

Worry and concern intensified. Remmy's face flushed and her heart pounded. Was there something wrong with her father? Could she truly hold the reins of the company he built up, without putting it under?

While in high school, Remmy had started working for her father. Her position started with light accounting, but soon grew. After a few years of experience, she moved onto handling the human resources and payroll, at which time she hired an assistant for herself to alleviate some of the overload. Unfortunately, the assistant was unable to handle such a high-volume workload and didn't last long.

The first of every year would find her and Taylor hashing out budgets for the upcoming year. Then the two would meet with their accountant for their taxes. Now she would be doing most of this on her own and that terrified her.

Remmy would also be overseeing all of the projects they had going on while her father watched like a hawk. He always wanted to make sure budgets were adhered to and the work they produced was quality. Taylor rationalized that if he put his name on it, it would be the best.

Could she do it or was she setting herself up for failure?

Remmy told herself she could do this. She had listened to her father live and breathe the company her whole life. It was now time to see if she absorbed it all.

"Remmy, first of all, I want you to take over part of it now because I'm thinking of retiring soon. So, my thought is why not now? Secondly, I'm as healthy as a bull, so don't think you're getting rid of me that fast."

Remmy unlocked his front door. "Okay, Dad, okay. Do you want a late dinner or do you just want to hit the hay for the night?"

After tapping his chin, Remmy's father looked at her.

"I think I shall retire for the evening, Ms. Vice-President & General Manager. I'm proud of you, sweetie, and all that you've accomplished."

Jack stood behind her and Taylor. "May I say something? Well crap, I'm going to say it even if you don't want to hear all the mushy stuff. Even after all these years, I'm still amazed at the closeness of the two of you. I gave up any thoughts of being close with my own father. Especially when he found out I, his only child, was gay. When he kicked me out I was only sixteen and had no place to go. You opened your home to me and I love you both."

Remmy looked from one man to the other; both were smiling. She couldn't help but laugh. Her father had turned the tables on her, once again forcing her to hire an assistant, someone to take over most of her old responsibilities. She'd been working twelve-hour days for so long that she wouldn't know what to do with herself if she had free time.

She'd promised him two years ago to hire someone again but the timing never seemed right or she could never find anyone she could tolerate. Taylor now left her no choice in the matter. She would have to find someone. Remmy didn't want her father worrying about her, so it was time to prove herself.

"Okay, Mr. President, you win. I'll look into hiring an assistant. Now, do you need anything before we leave?" She set his keys on the hallway table and took her own out of her pocket. Her father was a resilient man and would be fine.

Taylor pushed her and Jack toward the front door. "You two go, I'm sure neither of you have slept well for the last couple of days. So shoo, and let me get some rest too. Remmy, I will see you in the morning, and Jack…I want to hear all about your date day after tomorrow. Now… Good night to the both of you."

Remmy hugged her father and kissed him on the cheek. Jack stepped up and hugged him as well.

"Daddy, call either of us if you need anything, you hear."

She knew they would be okay. There were more sad times ahead, but they would get through them as they had before.

Taylor pointed to the door. "Go. Both of you. Now…"

Chapter Three

One Year Later

Taylor had told Remmy time and again that he refused to have anything to do with most lawyers. Over the decades in business, he had gone so far as to decline offers to renovate or build new offices for most of the lawyers in town. To him, they were "what you wipe off the bottom of your boot after putting the bull in the chute."

"Taylor, these are the last two pages. You need to sign here and again here." The lawyer turned toward Remmy.

Remmy liked him; he reminded her of Santa Claus. He had the same snow-white hair and full beard. Remmy chuckled; he even had the round belly that shook when he laughed.

"Ms. Garrick, the same please. If you could sign the bottom of both of these pages, then we will be done."

"Please, Sam, call me Remmy. You've known me all of my life, you're like an uncle." He and her father had been friends since they went to school together and Sam had been her father's lawyer for over thirty years. However, he had told her not to trust him completely. Remmy knew it was not Sam that her father didn't trust but the profession itself.

She and her father both did as instructed and signed their full legal names to both of the documents.

The lawyer gave the signed, legally binding documents to his assistant to make copies for both of them to take with them, along with a set of originals. He turned back to Remmy and her father.

"Congratulations, Taylor, you are now fully retired, and to you, Remmy, you now own Garrick Construction one hundred percent. If there is anything else I can help with, please let me know or feel free to call me at any time." He stood to shake their hands.

Remmy had reassured her father everything was fine, that all the papers were in order. To make sure, she had taken them to her personal lawyer earlier in the week to have her look them over.

"Nope, I think that's it, Sam. We updated my will last week and now all of this. I think that should do it." Taylor slowly stood from the conference room table.

The stroke two months before had slowed her father down, but not stopped him completely. It was then that he was right to hand the company over to her completely. Garrick Construction had continued to grow under her control over the last year, just as he told her it would.

Remmy stood as well. She was bone-tired. However, she would never admit it to her father. Her assistant had quit recently so she was back to twelve-hour days, seven days a week. It seemed her streak of assistants who were not able to handle the stress of doing a hundred things at once was continuing.

As much as Remmy loved what she did, she loathed putting up with her cousin Ronald. He was family, and in addition she felt obligated not to fire him because of the promise her father had made long ago. Each day, though, was a chore to get through if he was in the office instead of out trying to get new business as he was supposed to be doing.

✝

Taylor, aware of the conflict between the two, had tried talking to Ronald. Taylor told him the only reason he was still employed there was because he was family, and he had made Ronald's mother a promise, but he had better watch it because things could change in a heartbeat.

Change they had; Remmy now fully owned Garrick Construction. It was hers to do with as she pleased.

The conversation with Ronald had taken place a month before Taylor had suffered the minor stroke. He knew that turning the company over to Remmy would set the volatile man off completely. Taylor hoped she wouldn't tolerate his behavior for long, but he hoped she would at least leave him with what little manhood he did have when she was finished.

As he and Remmy exited the lobby of the old granite building onto the sidewalk, the heat wave hit them full in the face.

"Whew, damn Daddy, it's hot. This has got to be another record day. You can see the heat rolling off the pavement." Remmy motioned for him to sit on the bench. Even though the doctors all stated he was now in excellent health considering everything, his daughter still doted on him. Remmy wanted him around for a very long time.

"You sit while I bring the truck around." She ran over to a street vendor that was close by and purchased two bottles of water.

Loosening the cap on one, she handed it to him. "Here, drink some of this if you get too hot out here. Hopefully I'll be back around in a few minutes."

"Wait. I want to talk to you." Taylor looked at the bottle of water, then at her. "As I have said a million times, girl, I'm not an invalid. I can do things for myself."

Remmy smiled. "I know. I'm just trying to make things a little easier for you."

Taylor reached over and laid his bigger hand on top of hers. He noticed how she wearily sat down beside him, trying to hold herself erect. She didn't need to tell him how scared she'd been in regards to his health, he knew just by her doting over him for the past year. However, he felt she should be the one to bring it up, not him. Now Taylor wasn't so sure. Colin had told him recently that Ronald was getting harder to deal with every day.

He looked off into the distance and chuckled at the billboard with the scantily clad woman on it. "Damn, in my day they would never have allowed naked women on those boards. My, my... how times have changed." He smiled.

Remmy knew this was her father's way of leading into what he thought was going to be a difficult conversation. "I don't know, I kinda like them, Dad." She laughed, bumping shoulders with him.

The two had always had an open relationship, something others envied. No subject was taboo between Taylor and his daughter. Remmy smiled at her father. He believed in openness, honesty, and trust, and in turn, he had instilled those qualities in her at a very young age.

As a result, Remmy tolerated nothing less from those around her. Only in one instance had she ever tolerated anything else. She had held it within her for over four years now - the knowledge that she had been lied to, a secret that would never be known. Remmy would never tell Taylor that she knew what had happened to Haley in those last hours before she passed away, of the torture she had to endure.

Taylor laughed. "That's my girl. Just like your old father here, an eye for the pretty ladies."

She laughed some more, and saw the tiny wrinkles at the corners of his eyes dance, which always made her smile. "Nah, dad, she's not my type. I've never liked the satin and lace kind of girls."

She turned to look at Taylor. "Geez Dad, listen to us, will you? Sitting here discussing women. Most people would find this way too disturbing to even comprehend."

"I like to look at it this way, it tells me that you trust me enough to open up to me and likewise. That isn't what's on my mind, though, sweetie…" He squeezed her hand.

"I know, Dad, so what's going on?"

"You need to be careful with that cousin of yours. He's a sneaky little bastard. I don't trust him one little bit. It's your company now, so I can't tell you to fire his ass. I can only warn you."

She opened the bottle of water she held and drank down half of it in one gulp. Holding the ice-cold bottle to her forehead, she thought about what her father had said. She didn't trust Ronald either, but could she fire him? That she didn't know. "I know, Dad, I'm too nice a person. I hate firing people, especially when they are family."

"Girl, don't you take on my guilt of not being able to fire him. It was me that promised his mama, not you. Fire his sorry ass if you need to."

As she sat contemplating the demise of Ronald, a yellow Hummer pulled up in front of the building and a tall brunette butch exited the passenger side. Remmy tilted her head to get a look at the driver. She laughed at the stereotypical couple they made: tall leggy butch and small petite blonde.

Remmy felt Taylor poke her in the side with his elbow. He had caught her ogling. This woman oozed the qualities of the type of woman she was attracted to. Standing at six feet with short brown hair, her body wore the Armani suit well.

A smile cracked Remmy's features. "Damn, I have got to get me one of them."

With both of them grinning, Taylor let her know she'd been caught. "The brunette or the truck?"

Remmy's smile widened to the point of being lecherous. One word said it all. "Yeah..."

Gulping down the last of her water, she chanced another look at the woman who was just a few feet away. It was then she realized the woman had overhead them. Remmy watched as the other woman's eyes traveled up and down her body, her eyes settling on Remmy's breasts. Realizing what her father had said and her own response, she started choking on the water.

Remmy bent over as her father pounded on her back. She was horrified that she had been caught ogling the woman who, she then realized, had closed the distance between them in two strides.

The woman bent over so her lips were near Remmy's ear. "Want me to kiss it and make it all better?"

This only set off another coughing fit. Remmy held up her hand, speaking in between coughs. "Yes...I mean no, quite all right... thank you anyway..."

†

Roxanne, the blonde woman who had been in the truck with her, rounded the corner just as Jules was whispering in the coughing woman's ear. Jules knew she was in for an earful as her soon to be ex-partner walked over to her and stood next to her, glaring at her.

"Ah, I see you've impressed another one, Jules. What did you do, ask her out and send her into a fit of laughter?" There was nothing warm in her voice, only bitterness.

With a lower voice Roxanne continued. "This is how it always starts, doesn't it? First, you make them laugh and the next thing you're bedding them. I know I only caught you red-handed once but I'm sure there were times that I didn't."

Jules had only ever cheated once during their relationship and that was after she had known it was over between them. All the other times Roxanne had accused her of cheating were figments of her own warped mind. Roxanne was as cold as ice and had been for some time. Their first year together had been bliss; after that, it had been pure hell. The last time they'd made love had been over a year before.

When Roxanne refused to try to work things out, no one could have blamed her if she looked elsewhere for friendship and companionship. All of this had ended in visiting the lawyer to separate their remaining possessions.

Jules turned and glared. She wanted to tell Roxanne to fuck-off and die but instead, through clenched teeth, was a little nicer. "Drop dead, Roxanne, the woman was choking."

She turned back to Remmy, who sat with a shocked look on her face at the venom exchanged between the two women. "Are you okay?"

The no-longer-choking woman looked at Roxanne, then back at Jules.

"Yes, I'm fine. Thank you."

Jules realized this woman was looking down at her tattooed hands. It was then that it dawned on her that they were holding hands.

"It's Remmy."

Roxanne pulled her up and away from Remmy. "I'm sorry, Remmy, but Jules and I have an appointment. Let's get this over with. Then I'll never have to see your sorry pathetic ass again."

As the shorter woman pulled her away, Jules reached over and slid her business card into Remmy's hand.

Remmy looked at it quickly. *Wonder what the E stands for?*

It read: *E. Jules Masterson, Antiques Dealer, (585) 222-2222.*

Remmy and her father watched as the woman called Roxanne pulled Jules away. She could hear as plain as day the blonde woman cussing Jules out for not being able to keep it in her pants.

"Hopefully after she gets rid of the blonde bitch, she'll get her balls back."

Remmy turned so fast on the bench she almost got whiplash. "Dad!"

Taylor patted her thigh. "Tell me you weren't thinkin' the same thing. If ya do, you'll be lyin'."

Remmy hung her head. How could they be sitting here talking of such things when they had bigger issues to worry about?

"Remmington, I know that look on your face. Don't take on the world; no one expects it of you. You do what you must. Let no one, and I repeat no one, stand in your way. I know you don't want to deal with this now and that's okay, as long as you don't ignore it and let it get out of hand. Weigh all your options, and then do what is best. Don't feel you must do something you don't want to just because they are family. Don't shut the world out either. You need a life, sweetie. The past is just that, the past." He pointed to the ring still on her finger. "You are going to have to take that ring off at some point. Life goes on and you're still breathin'. I think you should take the bull by the horns and call that woman. There, I said my piece. I'll shut up now."

Remmy looked at the ring on her finger. It was the most precious thing in her life, other than her father. It represented a lost future she once had. Looking down once more at the card in her hand, Remmy smiled. Maybe she would give this woman a call. What could it hurt? Maybe this was what she needed. She read the card again as she ran her fingers over the raised bold script.

The woman was quite handsome; maybe a night out would be just the thing to bring her out of the funk she was in.

Her wandering mind was brought back when her Dad stood up. She looked up at him. "Where are you going?"

He pointed across the street. "I see a nice deli over there and I think we should go have some lunch. How about you? I know you could eat."

Later that night, Remmy called Jack to tell him she had met a mysterious woman. Jack urged her to call and ask her out on a date. Even if nothing came of it, she would begin to live again.

✝

She finally got the nerve two days later to make the call. She was laying with Mr. Bubbles curled up on her chest. All she had to do was hit the little green phone icon and the line would start ringing.

Watching her shaking fingers, Remmy hit the icon. Never before had she done the asking. It felt so foreign that she thought she was going to projectile vomit.

"Here goes nothing, Mr. Bubbles. Maybe she won't answer." He meowed in response and Remmy could've sworn he smiled.

"Jules Masterson speaking, may I help you?"

Losing her nerve, Remmy almost hung up.

"Hello is anyone there?"

"I, uh…well…"

"Remmy?"

Hearing her name startled her back into her own skin. "Yes, I'm sorry. I thought your voice mail was going to pick up. I, um…" Stuttering, Remmy's thoughts went off track once more.

"If you would like, I'll hang up so that you may call back. This time I won't answer."

Remmy felt like a fool. "I'm sorry. I feel like a sixteen-year-old." She giggled. Slapping herself in the head, she was even more mortified that she had giggled. "Oh, God…"

Jules laughed into the phone. "I take it you don't giggle normally? Tell you what, have dinner with me and I'll

48

make it up to you for my laughing at your discomfort." Jules was met with silence.

"Remmy... That was why you called, wasn't it? Or did I misread you?"

Covering her face with her arm, Remmy hoped to shield the embarrassment she was feeling. She was sure the woman could see through the phone right into her. "No, you didn't. Dinner would be nice." Remmy sighed. Jules had asked her; she was relieved. Remmy was sure her nerves would get the better of her and would have come across sounding like more of an idiot than she already felt.

"Okay, so how about tomorrow night? Are you free then? I would like to get to know you. Something tells me you're an interesting person to know."

"Yes, that would be nice." When Remmy got this nervous, she tended to shake her foot as if listening to music. Mr. Bubbles took that opportunity to pounce on her bare foot and sink his teeth into her wiggling big toe.

"FUCK!" The cat went flying as Remmy shot up from the couch, momentarily forgetting about the phone pressed to her ear.

"Remmy? What's going on? Are you okay?"

"Yes, I'll be fine. My demon cat decided my toe was a chew toy. I'll be fine, but the fur ball may not be when I catch him." This was not the first time her furry little child had attacked her feet. It had become a game between them. He would attack and run, and she would threaten, then Remmy would give him treats when she felt bad for yelling at him. "You're laughing at me again aren't you?"

"I'm trying really hard not to, but I'm picturing a cat pouncing then running away. I have a soft spot for all animals, which is probably why I'm a vegetarian. Are you sure you're okay?"

In the bathroom, Remmy had her foot on the toilet lid, wiping away the blood, in order to see the damage he'd inflicted. "Yeah, I'll be fine. I just need to clean off my toe and put a bandage on it. Damn little thing, I love him to pieces, until he does something like this, that is."

"Phew okay, call me if you need to, though. If you need me to take you for stitches or something. So it's a date. Text me your address and I'll pick you up tomorrow around six. Do you like Chinese?"

"Yes, I love it. I'll see you tomorrow then. Night."

"Yeah, night. Remember, if you need anything, call me. Bye."

Remmy hobbled out to the kitchen to find some aspirin. "I will, thanks. Bye."

Remmy couldn't believe it. She had a date the next night. "Okay, you freakin' little fur ball, where are you? You're going to pay big time for this one." She spotted his tail sticking out of the laundry basket, from under the clean clothes. "Ha! You can't hide from me…"

While nursing her wound with a cold beer, Remmy called Jack for his thoughts on her dating again. She knew he agreed with her father that it was indeed time she started to live again; she also knew he was liable to lecture her but she decided to call him anyway.

After downing half the beer, she dialed. A very irate best friend answered, "This had better be good, woman, you are interrupting my watching the Doctor and, oh, how I love this new Doctor."

Remmy had forgotten that his Saturday night was always spent watching his favorite British show. She herself had tried to watch it but could never understand the appeal of *Doctor Who* and the blue box. When the show had returned to the air after a long absence, Jack had thrown a "Who

Party" as he called it. Remmy called it a geek fest yet she enjoyed the evening, especially since it had been Haley's favorite show as well.

She chuckled. "Sorry, forgot your show was on. I can call back later. I just wanted to tell you I have a hot date. So...call me later okay? Bye." It was bad of Remmy to throw Jack a bone like that and then make him wait.

She quickly pulled the phone away from her ear as it was bombarded with screeching from the other end.

"Girl! Don't you dare hang up. You know I DVR it also, so I can watch again later. Now tell me all about this woman. Come on...details, details..."

Remmy laughed again. "Well, if you would let me get a word in, I might be able to. Let's see...she's the one I met two days ago. Her name is Jules. She's an antiques dealer. She is tall, brunette, and extremely gorgeous. Actually, she's freakin' hot. She has some wicked tattoos. I don't know, though, she's just out of a relationship that ended very badly. She also seems to be a bit of...well, from the conversation between her and the ex, Jules was caught cheating. I just don't know, though, you know what I mean. Do I take a chance? Of course, though, it's only one date."

"You never know, Remmy, maybe the ex was a bitch and she was just lonely. Why not take a chance and go to dinner with her? She sounds like an interesting person and a hard worker, especially if she restores antiques. Doing that kind of work takes dedication, hard labor, and love. Besides, you need to get out of the house and have a good time. Even if it turns out you have nothing in common and don't see each other again, at least you gave it a shot."

Remmy headed to the kitchen to retrieve another beer, listening to Jack prattle on about how she needed a life. She didn't disagree with him. It was just a tad humiliating having another point out your shortcomings at finding a girlfriend.

"Jack, I have a life. I own a great company, which employs good people. I have a wonderful father, a fantastic, loyal best friend. So what if there is no lover in my life right now? I'm happy."

When Remmy's own words soaked into her brain, she was sure they sounded as pathetic to Jack as they did to her. Remmy took a long swallow from her beer.

"Remmy, my friend, did that sound as lame to you as it did to me?"

She picked up the nearly empty bottle and wiped the sweat off the outside of it on her t-shirt. Stalling, Remmy polished off the remaining beer. "All right...all right. It was pathetic. I know I need a life, but maybe I don't want to just settle for whatever comes along."

Jack sighed. "Honey, she's gone and there will never be another like her. You need to stop comparing every woman you meet to Haley. Everyone is different. There is a woman out there that you might love as much as you did Haley. You just never know until you try. I say you should get out more, have a good time, and live a little. Okay? Call me tomorrow night after your date. Now, I am bidding you goodnight as I am going back to the hunk of man I was watching before I was so rudely interrupted."

Remmy laughed. "Okay, I'll talk to you tomorrow night. Oh, and don't forget to wipe up the puddle of drool from the floor when you're done watching your doctor. Night."

†

Dinner the next night was wonderful. They each learned much about the other. Jules told Remmy all about the antiques business and answered her questions about what made a piece valuable compared to a similar piece made several years later. She told Remmy that while she ate no meat, poultry, or fish, she did however eat dairy and eggs, and much to Remmy's surprise, tofu. Remmy told Jules that she could never understand eating such a disgusting substance. Their coffee tastes differed as well. Jules was a by the book unflavored, while Remmy was the opposite. They laughed about it, though, and carried on with dinner.

Jules walked Remmy to her door. She liked Jules and had been alone for a long time. Remmy couldn't believe it when she found herself inviting Jules in after their date. Yes, she was lonely, yet she felt she was betraying Haley. The loneliness won out and she felt Jules was someone who would become a good friend, if nothing else.

Remmy pointed Jules toward the living room. "Would you like coffee? I can put on a pot. Perhaps a beer, I have several different kinds in the fridge, ice cold and ready to drink."

Remmy watched Jules as she stood in the living room taking her jacket off while looking at the pictures on the shelf. Taking off the jacket left her in a black muscle shirt with her tattoos showing.

"I can feel you watching me, you know. I take it you like the tattoos covering my arms and neck?"

Remmy remained silent.

"Okay, you can look at them closer later, right now though a beer of any kind is fine."

From the doorway, Remmy watched her pick up the picture of her and Haley, studying it closely. Remmy stepped into the room, noticing where Jules was still standing. It was obvious she had been looking at the pictures. Now was not the time to tell her. They were just getting to know each other and Remmy didn't want to scare Jules off or worse, see pity in her eyes.

Jules took the beer from her and then sat next to her on the leather couch. When Jules put her right arm around her shoulders and gulped down half the bottle, Remmy chuckled. "Good beer huh?"

"Tell me about her."

Remmy's body went stiff. "What?" Old tears returned to her eyes.

"The woman in the pictures, tell me about her. I am guessing she was your wife. Tell me what happened."

The arm circling her shoulders was warm and inviting. Could she let her guard down with this woman? Turning her head, Remmy looked into her eyes. She saw only tenderness. The sparks were not there, not like when Haley would look at her. She saw no pity though, only caring. It drew Remmy in and she let it.

†

Remmy stood and went to the mantel. Picking up the picture from the last Christmas they spent together, she smiled. When she spoke, Remmy was no longer in the room with Jules, but back in time, a time before the pain - a happier time.

"Haley was a corrections officer. We were together for what seemed like a lifetime, yet at times felt like we had just found each other. We loved each other more than life itself. It was Christmas; she asked me to marry her. I'd never been happier in my life. All kinds of plans for a wedding were going through my mind over the next four weeks. I guess I never truly knew how bad the situation had gotten at the prison where she was." Remmy set the photo down and picked up another.

She looked down at the photo of her father, brother, Jack, Haley, and herself. The secrets spewed forth. Her voice was barely above a whisper. "They think I don't know all that happened. They tried to hide it from me. They don't have a clue and they never will." She gripped the frame tighter.

The presence behind Remmy gave her the strength to go on. She was unsure when Jules had moved from the sofa to stand behind her. "There were problems with the director. Haley said he had a God-complex and passionately hated women. Even the men who were old school didn't care for him much. Threats against her and several others were made but he did nothing about it. The officers contacted the state and filed complaints. One night she didn't come home. The bastard put them back in the place where the death threats had come from."

Remmy was suddenly cold as the room narrowed and she began shivering. She found she was standing in the snowdrift at the end of the driveway on that fateful night waiting on Haley's return. "How did I get out here?" Moments ago, she was warm and ensconced in the most inviting arms.

"God, how long have I been standing here waiting? It seems like hours. It's so cold out here. There must be over a foot of snow. I don't care though; I want to be out here waiting for her when she comes home. Oh, baby, you don't think I know how bad things have gotten. I know now though and we are going to talk about it as soon as you get home. I'm not going to let you change the subject this time."

Remmy stomped her feet, trying to bring warmth back into them.

She heard a distant voice. "Remmy?"

Reality slowly filtered back. "She didn't come home, though. She was one of the ones killed. They think I don't know…" Her hands held tighter to the frame as tears rolled down her cheeks.

"She was repeatedly raped and tortured before her heart finally gave out and stopped beating. They thought they could spare me the heartache of knowing. I knew, though. I knew she wouldn't go down without a fight. She took down several of the inmates with her. I haven't felt anything since." Remmy felt arms circle her waist as she set the picture back on the mantel.

Remmy turned in arms that held her. "I want to feel again. Please, help me to feel." Their lips met. She didn't care if there was no spark; she just needed to feel alive.

Jules poured everything into the kiss. The anger, the heartache, for Remmy's suffering flowed from her. Her lips moved down Remmy's neck to between her breasts. Her hands were already on Remmy's zipper, lowering it as she pressed her back against the fireplace.

Once again, their lips met. Her hand found its way under Remmy's panties and into the heat. The wetness she found startled her. Never had she experienced anyone being this excited this fast. She wanted to give Remmy what she needed.

Jules pushed into her and could feel the fire within Remmy explode. Two heartbeats later Remmy screamed as Jules slammed her fingers into her again. The action sent

Jules over the edge as well. Both slipped to the floor in a spent heap.

Burying her face in the other woman's T-shirt, Remmy was truly embarrassed. "Oh God... I am so sorry. I never meant to throw myself at you."

Jules put a finger under Remmy's chin and tilted her face up toward hers. "There's nothing to feel sorry for. It was wonderful and exactly what you needed. As delightful as it was, something was missing, wasn't it? There weren't any sparks, were there?"

Really embarrassed then, Remmy did what she always did to cover her embarrassment, she laughed. "Shit, I am embarrassed now for sure."

Jules laughed also. "Why? Was it not mutually satisfying? I think it is just what the doctor ordered for both of us. I can feel it, believe it or not; your heart feels lighter. You're a beautiful woman. You're intelligent and charming. I know we are going to be good friends, just as I know the perfect woman is going to come along. It's going to be a woman that you can't live without. She will have her faults yet she will be perfect. She will be the piece that is truly missing from here." She took Remmy's hand, put it over her heart, and held it there.

"Good God, you and my father both. What if this is all there ever is? I don't think I could ever truly fall in love again." The insecurities seeped back in, giving Remmy doubt.

"Oh, I have no doubt whatsoever that she's out there. It's just a matter of finding her, or her finding you. Have faith, I know it will happen." Jules held her tight, giving Remmy the support and the comfort she needed.

"You sound so sure, it makes me almost believe."
Remmy sighed, wishing she could really believe there was
someone out there for her.

"I do know. Believe it or not, no, it doesn't matter. I
want to be there for you. There is something in you that just
tells me that we've traveled this path before and that we were
the best of friends. However, that is all we ever were,
because you were meant to love another. Do not fear; she
will come. Whether you like it or not, she will. Until that
time and even beyond, I will always be by your side. There
will never be strings attached. I will be there for you, in
whatever way you need me. You can depend on me for your
strength and to kick you in the ass when needed." She
stroked Remmy's hair.

"Somehow I can feel this is a first for you, to give of
yourself and expect nothing in return. To be there for
someone as a friend and sometimes lover, not a partner. Does
it bother you?" Remmy sat up, to look the taller woman in
the eyes.

When Jules stood she pulled Remmy up with her.
"Now I think it's time for some sleep. I'll take the couch,
now get going." Jules swatted her on the butt.

Once again insecure, Remmy said, "Actually, would
you mind coming and lying next to me? I just don't want to
be alone. It's hard to explain. I feel wonderful, better than I
have in a long time, yet I just don't want to be alone in the
dark tonight." She hoped the security of a body lying next to
her would ward off the demons of the night.

Jules rubbed the back of Remmy's neck. "I
understand what you mean. Your soul feels lighter, as does
mine. I think tonight has been a change for both of us, just
for different reasons, yet both for the better. Yes, I would
love to hold you through the night. I'll be there to fight away

those demons that close in when you dream. I know it sounds too fucking corny, but something in you calls to me to protect you as I would a little sister." Jules received a smack in the stomach for her comment.

"Who you callin' little? You're just too freakin' tall, Jules." Remmy laughed causing Jules to raise an eyebrow as they made their way to her bedroom.

"Yeah, whatever you say. So do you like seafood? Maybe lobster or *shrimp*?" Jules found herself tackled and thrown to the bed.

"Shrimp, huh? I'll show you who's a shrimp. I think you've forgotten what I do for a living." Remmy landed on top of Jules and proceeded to tickle her senseless.

Peeling Jules' clothes off, Remmy found the woman was covered quite literally from neck to toes to fingertips, front and back, with tattoos. Studying them, she realized they were all interlocked and of Celtic design. Not one of them had color other than black or shades of grey. "Breathtaking. It must have taken years to have these done."

Jules let her inspect them. "Actually only a matter of days."

Tracing one that circled the woman's left nipple, Remmy shuddered. "Wow, that's incredible. What do they represent?"

"Sorry, all I can say is they are symbols from ancient times that were meant to keep the beast within contained. That's all I can tell you. Before you ask, yes, I'm very into mythology."

Remmy's eyes danced as she speculated what Jules meant. "Hmm, I think I saw a little of that just a few moments ago and it ended with a scream and a lot of wetness. I'd like to know…no, make that feel, what else that beast can do…what those teeth can bite and that tongue can lick."

Jules chuckled slightly, then a look washed over her face. The look turned Remmy on even more.

"She is never fully unleashed; these markings see to that. However, she does make her presence known from time to time…" Jules grabbed her by the hair, pulling Remmy up so when she bent her head, her teeth could grab Remmy's nipple. "If her prey begs for it. Are you…begging?"

Remmy next felt those same teeth bite so hard on her engorged clit that she was sure Jules had drawn blood. "Yes, please…oh god yes please, I'm begging." Jules continued to feast upon her center, making her scream in orgasm repeatedly. After what seemed like hours, Jules looked up at her and Remmy noticed Jules's eyes were glazed over. With each orgasm she experienced, she had become more excited. Jules was kneeling on the bed, between her legs, licking her center. Remmy began to come again.

"I'm coming…please oh my god please…"

Jules licked her clit. "Please what?"

"Release the beast, release her and bite me…I'm coming! Bite my clit now!" She heard the growl escape the woman feasting upon her and she felt her teeth sink into her clit.

Screaming so hard her voice left her, Remmy fell back upon the bed as Jules continued to bite and suck upon the blood-engorged clit. Remmy felt in a state of euphoria that she had never experienced before. Even though what Jules was doing was turning from pleasure to painful, she didn't care as another orgasm washed over her.

Chapter Four

The twisted mind worked overtime into the darkening night. "Women should know their place. It's a man's world and those bitches belong at home pregnant and serving the men. They especially don't belong in construction."

He would teach her and all like her. He would put her in her place. Women like her were the evilest of all. Not only did she hold a position that only a man should, but she was an evil dyke besides, luring women away from where they should be - with men.

"Yes, I'll teach her what her place within this world should be. I won't kill her; that would be too easy. I'll destroy her. Her fall from grace will be sheer torture. I'll make her see the error of her ways, even if I have to destroy everything around her to do it. Everything she encounters becomes soiled by her touch. She's a filthy woman. They're all dirty."

Obviously, she was ignoring the letters he had been sending and they were not scaring her into her place in society, so he stepped up his terrorization a notch. He was so sure she would have failed by now and handed over the company to a real man. He needed to make her pay for humiliating and degrading him.

The renovation of the video store was one of her three "pet projects." They were the first ones she had acquired, that she spent most of her time working on. He gained access to the store and the depraved short man and his friend went about annihilating all the work completed so far. They destroyed the newly installed walls that would hold the racks of DVDs, and then continued into the bathroom to destroy all of the new plumbing. The entire time, he was swinging the sledgehammer with a gleam in his eye.

"Yes, everything will be mine very soon. Men are the superiors; we will be obeyed at all costs. That dyke will learn her lesson." He continued on his rampage until the little store was in shambles. They moved rapidly as they destroyed the store. The faster he finished, the less likely he was to be discovered.

†

At ten to five in the morning, Remmy's cell phone sent a shrill ringing into the quiet morning. It startled her out of the best night's sleep she'd had in a long time. If it rang at this time of the morning, it was not good. The caller id told her it was Colin, which meant there was big trouble.

"Shit!"

Jules rolled over toward her. "What's wrong?"

Remmy's hand on Jules's chest quieted her as she answered the phone. "What's going on, Colin?"

Throwing the covers back and jumping from the bed spoke volumes of how bad it was. Remmy threw the phone against the wall. "Fuck! Fuck! Fuck!"

Jules stood beside her.

"Remmy, what's going on? It's not your father, is it?"

Remmy watched Jules as she picked up the pieces of her phone. Running her fingers through her hair, she tried to make sense of the conversation. "I'm sorry; I didn't mean to wake you up."

"Honey, come on, talk to me. Something is very wrong. What is it?"

Remmy let Jules pull her back down onto the bed. "We're remodeling a video store and Colin's the acting super for the project. He showed up to find the placed trashed." She hung her head, covering her face with her hands.

"Did he already call the police?" Remmy stayed silent.

"Not yet, that is why he was calling me." Everything good Remmy had felt earlier was now gone; in its place were anger and fear.

Jules knelt in front of her. "You've been having other problems like this, haven't you? You need to call the police right now."

Remmy studied the woman in front of her, realizing they were holding hands once more. It seemed to give her a sense of calm. "I've had threats. The kind a woman owning a construction company in a man's world would get. *Only dyke whores work in a man's world. Sell while you can bitch. All dykes need is to be fucked by a real man.* Those kinds of things were in the messages. It seems someone wants me out of business. I haven't done anything about it before this because that's all they were; nasty little notes. Now…"

"Ah, I see. Your father doesn't know, does he?"

She shook her head. "No. It would kill him for sure. I just can't figure out who would hate me this much."

"I can think of one. From everything you told me last night about your family, my guess is it's close to home. You said your cousin has been giving you problems."

Remmy looked mortified. "No! Family wouldn't do this kind of thing to one another. It has to be someone I've beat out of a contract lately. It has to be. I have to go and look at the store. You're right, though, it's time to call the police."

"Remmy, do me a favor, okay? Take a step back from everything and really think about it. It makes me really angry that this is happening to you. Do you want me to go with you? I will if you'd like me to."

"No, but thanks for the offer, though. Can I call you later, after I get everything taken care of?" Remmy didn't want to sound needy, but she wanted to spend more time with her. Jules hugged her.

"Oh darling, you can call me anytime for anything. Never forget that. I want us to be friends, which is something I've never really had before. Maybe it's time for me to finally grow up. Who would have ever thought of it...Jules Masterson, someone's friend, wow, it's a first."

Remmy held Jules as tight as she could. "I think that's what we both need, 'cause damn is my body screaming hallelujah this morning." She let go of Jules and stood back. "Now, I have to get dressed and get going. You go back to bed and get some more sleep. No arguments, just do it." She smiled as Jules looked at her with a shocked expression on her face that turned into an ear-to-ear grin. Jules kissed her hard.

"Someone's feeling their oats. If I'm not here when you get back, I'll call you later this afternoon. Maybe we can do dinner this evening."

She pushed a lock of unruly hair out of Jules's eyes. The hours they had spent having sex were wonderful, but there was still no spark, no feeling of *I want this woman in my bed and soul for eternity* like she had felt with Haley. "Coffee is in the bottom drawer in the fridge." Remmy saw the scrunched up look on her face.

"Don't worry, there is *regular* coffee in there also. Geez...why do all of you give me such crap over the kind of coffee I like?"

Jules laughed and swatted her rear-end.

"Sorry darlin', that pout doesn't look quite sincere."

"Fine, whatever, drink your bland coffee. Okay, later then." She pecked Jules on the lips and left.

†

Remmy had been unprepared for the sheer destruction she found at the video store. She and Colin stood on the threshold entrance to the store, surveying the damage.

"I think it's time we call the police, Remmy. Whoever this freak is, he means business. I'd like to know how he got in, though. The door was locked when I got here. I took two steps in and found the place trashed. I double-checked the door and the lock hasn't been tampered with, so I don't have a freakin' clue. I don't think we should go back in there until we call them."

Remmy sighed. Taking one last look at the devastated store, she prepared to make the call to Keith, the owner of the store and a close friend. "Let's not call Keith for the moment, no sense in him tweaking out quite yet. Thank the Gods he's a friend of ours, maybe he won't freak completely out when we tell him his store has been destroyed. I'll call the cops, and then later, you can call him."

"Chicken...you just don't want to hear him screeching over the phone at you, so you stick me with it. Woman, you have no balls," Colin said with a smile on his face.

"Yep, that and since you're the Project Manager for this company, you get to deal with all the lovely little shit-tasks like this one. Okay, let's get this over with. They will probably send someone from the trooper station down the road. Let's hope it's not the one who stopped you two weeks ago." Remmy playfully slapped him on the back of his head. He'd been pulled over for speeding and then found that his inspection had also expired on the truck. This earned him an ass chewing from Remmy, because it was a company vehicle, with her company's name on the side of it for all to see as the trooper pulled him over. She watched Colin cringe as she reminded him of the error.

"Yeah ,I took one hell of an ass reaming for that one. I'll take care of calling Keith. You can handle the cops."

Punching in nine-one-one, she smiled at him. "I thought you'd see it my way." A gravelly voice picked up on the other end.

Ten minutes later a state trooper vehicle pulled up beside their trucks. She listened on as Colin informed the policeman what he had found upon his arrival. Remmy then made the trooper aware of the letters she had received at their offices, and of the letter attached to the front door of their last project.

Remmy watched as the trooper made notes of all the details thrown at him, and she added that the incidents had occurred in three counties. "Ms. Garrick, since this has escalated from threatening letters to property destruction, and that this has happened over three counties, I am going to call in one of our investigators. In the meantime, if you will excuse me a moment, please stay out here; do not go into the store. When I return, I will obtain from you the exact wording that was used in the notes you received."

Remmy motioned for Colin to follow her. She sat on the bumper of her truck, contemplating how to break the news to her father. "I'm going to have to tell my dad now. Shit, he's going to be pissed I didn't tell him what's going on before this. How did the call with Keith go?"

Colin leaned back against the truck. "Actually, he took it quite well. He's more concerned about you than the store, as am I. I'm starting to think this is more personal against you than against the company."

It was the same thing Jules had said. Remmy nervously chuckled. "Huh, that's the same thing Jules said when you called me."

Colin whipped his head around and stared right into her face. "And who would Jules be? Did *we* have a date last night and into this morning?"

"Yes…not that it's any of your business how long it lasted. Nosey Nelly." Remmy teased him because he was so nosey, and since Colin was like a brother, she loved yanking his chain.

"Before you ask, the answer is no, no sparks." The previous evening replayed itself in Remmy's mind.

Colin patted her thigh. "She'll come along some day. It's good to see you're trying though. I've been worried about you for a while now. Haley was a good woman, but she would have wanted you to continue with your life and find someone."

"Jeez, it seems everyone has been taking a large interest in my private life lately. First it was Dad, then Jack, and now you. God, am I that pathetic?" She didn't see her life lacking in much, but apparently, others did.

He put his arm around her shoulders. "No, we just care about you that much. We want to see you happy again."

†

The trooper climbed into his vehicle for privacy to place the call. *Oh man, I'm going to let Kira deal with Keith. I don't care to listen to him screeching like a banshee. It was bad enough listening to him at my Christmas party when Kira told him she ate the last of the Rocky Road ice cream.* "Kira, it's Manny. I'm over at Keith's store. The place was trashed last night."

An irate female voice boomed through the phone into his ear, causing him to pull it away. "What the fuck! Probably some local kids, why you calling me? I don't have time to take care of some little pussy-boy who's pissed off at his parents, so he goes out and destroys something. I have four active cases going on right now, one of which is ready to blow wide open in the next twelve hours. Are you going to call Keith? I know we've all been friends since grade school, but I'm in no mood to deal with the hissy fits that he throws. I'm liable to finally tell him to man up and grow a pair of balls."

Laying his head back on the headrest, Manny gave her all the details he had. "Fine. I'll talk to him, but you owe me *BIG* time. I've got a bad feeling about this, Kira, that's why I wanted you here. Whoever is terrorizing this woman is escalating. This is more than just a couple of teenagers having a good time here. This place is truly destroyed. Do

68

you want to call in the processing team or do you want me to do it?"

Through the phone, he heard her truck door slam and the engine start. Manny knew she would take an interest once she heard all the facts and that a woman was the victim. Kira loathed seeing women as the victims because in most cases they could do nothing to defend themselves.

Kira sighed. "You call them and let them know I'm on my way. I'll be there in ten."

"Will do and I will get the rest of the details that were in the letters." Exiting his vehicle slowly, Manny dreaded what was coming.

Once he heard the remaining details from Remmy, he wasn't so sure he should have called Kira after all. It was a given that his life-long friend detested crimes involving women, but this one was special. This crime involved a lesbian, and since Kira was in the closet with the door permanently locked, he knew this one would be a strain for her.

"If you will excuse me, the investigator should be here momentarily." Wanting to finish his notes, Manny waited by his own vehicle for Kira and the technicians.

A siren caused Colin to turn in its direction. "Well, it sounds like more cavalry is about to arrive." He stood, brushing off the back of his jeans. Pulling into the parking lot of the strip mall was a huge SUV.

"God, that truck is mammoth, he must be compensating for something." Colin laughed at his own joke as a pair of black cowboy boots hit the pavement followed by very long legs. He could see the top of a head of jet-black hair appear over the top of the truck door.

"Crap, he must be like fucking seven feet tall. I'll bet he's a real bastard."

"Shit Colin! Just what I don't need, a male chauvinist state police investigator."

What Colin saw next almost caused him to swallow his tongue. He watched as the long legs transformed into the tallest, most gorgeous, butch of a woman he'd ever laid eyes upon. "Holy fuck..."

Remmy's gaze traveled up from the black boots that she had been looking at. Her jaw dropped; she was speechless. The woman standing by the SUV and looking at the front of store that held her demolished project was the most magnificent specimen she had ever laid eyes upon, other than her Haley. "Wow."

What Remmy's eyes beheld shocked her. The investigator had to be taller than any woman she'd ever met. That, however, was not what threw her. It was the black wavy hair, square jaw and the sheer presence of the woman. "So much like Haley, yet nothing like her at all."

"No, I know what you're thinking, Remmy; she is nothing like Haley. She's taller and has just a touch of femininity, whereas Haley...well, she was butch through and through."

Remmy looked at Colin whose mouth was hanging open as well. Remmy didn't know which was more shocking, the muscles that rippled under the skintight black T-shirt with a grinning Tweety Bird on it, or the legs that carried the exquisite woman.

Remmy watched the woman look at the storefront. The investigator took off her jacket, throwing it over the hood of the SUV. She pulled her hair up in a ponytail, put on a Tyvek suit, and walked into the store along with the two processing team techs who had just arrived.

The woman gave motioning directions to the techs, then stepped out of the doorway, turning toward her and Colin. Remmy's heart stopped. The eyes, they startled her. The woman's eyes were the color of the brightest Swiss blue topaz she had ever seen. Remmy felt an instant attraction to the woman. "No... nothing like Haley."

Remmy knew she had to stop comparing all the women she met to her lost lover, but it just happened. It happened without thought, the words always just came to her lips. However, the next words that passed her lips shocked her to her core. "No... Better."

†

The investigator didn't like the sound of this case. Anything involving women tended to get violent very fast. On her way to meet Manny, she had pulled up the name he had given her, a Ms. Remmington Garrick. She was surprised when there were no previous reports of trouble.

It made her curious as to why none of this was on record before this latest issue. What did the woman have to hide? The only thing she could find on the woman was a speeding ticket two years before. *So Ms. Garrick, what is a woman as young as you doing owning a construction company? Very interesting indeed.*

When she arrived, she focused on seeing the damage before talking with Manny. Kira was glad Manny caught this case. He was not only a co-worker, but also a friend. His partner, Paul, had been her best friend since she was five years old.

Kira walked around the building with one of the technicians. She spotted several cigarette butts ground into the pavement by the dumpster on the side of the building. "Charlie, bag those butts. There are too many of them. Someone stood here for a while, probably to make sure no one was around to see him. If you find any more of them, I'll be talking to Manny."

She spotted Manny leaning against the passenger's front door of his vehicle, waiting for her. Kira wanted to hear all the info he'd gathered before meeting the two who were sitting on a company truck bumper. Sitting her tall frame on the hood of his patrol car, Kira let her boots kick against the tire.

"Ah, come on, Kira, don't scratch my car. I had to pay out of my own pocket the last time for the scratches and the dent your fist put in it." Kira had lost her temper when a stalker had reached his victim before they had.

She grinned weakly. "I said I was sorry and I even offered to pay for it."

"Yeah, after Paul threatened you. Anyway, we digress here. I got as much info out of the two of them as I could. The male is the Project Manager for Garrick Construction; his name is Colin Browder. This is one of eight major projects they have going on right now. The female is actually the owner of the company, a Ms. Remmington Garrick." Manny slowly turned the page on his notebook, as if giving her time to digest those items.

Kira mulled it over. "There is more going on here. Tell me the rest."

She watched Manny's eyes as they scanned down the page of his notes. "It seems she has received several threatening letters at their offices, and just last week one was nailed to the door of another project site they were working at."

A thought occurred to Kira. "I know that look on your face. It's your 'oh shit she's gonna make my life hell' look. I may or may not, I'll let you know later. For now, though let's focus. Were the notes addressed to her personally or the company? Does she have a spouse?" She watched the tech crew sift through the ruins, bagging anything that looked remotely suspicious.

"Ah, they were not addressed to her personally, but the content left no doubt who they were directed at. She has a ring on her finger, so there is a possibility."

Kira raised her left eyebrow, pinning him to the vehicle with an icy glare. "What else?"

"They said things like *women should know their places, this is a man's world.* Shit like that."

"Manny, something else you're not telling me? You seem to be a little hesitant. Like maybe you think I possibly shouldn't be involved in this case. So spill it before I make you squeal like a girlie." Kira could make good on her threat and had several times in the past.

This made Manny visibly cringe. They knew each other so well they could read each other's thoughts.

While she waited, Kira cleaned underneath one of her short nails with the blade from the knife she'd pulled from her pocket. She looked like she didn't have a care in the world and was bored beyond words.

Nonchalantly, her friend took two steps backwards before telling her the rest. "Well…the letters also said things like, *all you dykes need is to be fucked by a real man, raping dykes is not a crime, it is a blessing, you dykes deserve death* and several others. Some really nasty stuff, Kira, someone really has her in their sights."

Kira shook her head, causing her ponytail to swish side to side. Any humor that was in her eyes was gone now. "Shit, a hate crime. This is just so what I don't need right now. Especially since I had to put off my vacation last month because of all the cases I had thrown at me. God, how I needed that vacation."

Kira thought about how several times a year, depending on her caseload, she would travel to Provincetown to relieve her hormones and hook-up with as many gorgeous women as possible. Now that she had to postpone her vacation, she was wound tight. Only five people, including her niece, whom she had raised, knew she was gay and she planned to keep it that way. The only reason Annabella knew was because she had promised the young girl, when she became her legal guardian, that they would never lie to each other.

Jumping off the hood of the car, Kira readied herself to talk to the two they'd been discussing. "Okay, let's get this show on the road. I got a feeling it's going to be a long day."

Kira did what she did best. She buried her wandering thoughts and libido where they belonged. Sent deep within her, they never stood a chance of seeing the light of day. Approaching the two in question, the *Frigid Bitch* as they called her was in place.

†

Colin watched the investigator approach them. He wondered what she and the officer had been discussing. One way or another, Colin would soon find out.

Beside Colin, Remmy stood up from sitting on the bumper and waited for the other shoe to drop. "Shit, they might want to shut down my projects if whoever's doing this is coming after me."

Colin leaned over. "Relax; let's hear what she has to say."

Remmy tried to focus on something other than the fact that this woman was devastatingly gorgeous. The effect caused her heart to beat harder and her jeans to become damp.

Kira extended her hand. "Ms. Garrick, Trooper Watts has advised me on all of the pertinent issues. You look like you haven't been sleeping well. Is something about this case causing you to lose sleep? Is there anything else you've thought of that we should know about?"

Remmy noticed that the investigator never introduced herself. She knew from previous conversations that Colin thought Ronald was behind all the trouble. Remmy shuffled her feet and looked away, not about to air family dirty laundry to strangers. "Nothing else comes to mind. Neither of us have a clue who would do something like this."

"Mr. Browder does she speak for both of you, or do you have anything to say?"

Remmy looked at Colin. She silently willed him not to cause her embarrassment by stating that he thought that it was Ronald who had been doing it.

"No ma'am. Nothing to add."

The investigator in Kira observed the ring in question. It was an interesting choice and spoke volumes to her. It looked to be a two-carat yellow diamond. "Are you and your spouse getting along? That's a very expensive ring."

Stepping back as if blindsided by a roundhouse kick from the inspector, Remmy spoke through clenched teeth. "My spouse is deceased."

Remmy's reaction told Kira there was a tale there to be told. It, however, had nothing to do with the case. Kira didn't take the time to worry about personal demons at that moment. She wanted to get all the details of the case first, and then Kira would see if the rest were relevant.

Kira's instinct told her Remmy was lying. It was just a matter of finding out about what. "Okay then, why don't you tell me what other projects you have going on. Then I want to go to those sites to look at them. I also want one of my techs to come by your office to pick up those letters. How soon will there be someone in the office?" Kira sounded detached and cold but that was her way.

"The receptionist will be there at eight; she can obtain the documents from the safe for them. We have several other projects going on. Five are remodels, a coffee shop and a craft shop. We are also building a gift shop from the ground up. I am not sure what type of information you are looking for, but I'm sure you won't find anything at any of them. So I see no need for you to go to them." Remmy's nervousness showed by how she was fiddling with the truck keys.

Bells went off in Kira's head. This woman was not only lying to her, but was on the defensive. This confirmed there was definitely more than met the eye.

"Actually, it sounds like a very good idea to me. I would like to start at the coffee shop. I hope that it's still open for business even though you're remodeling it. Actually, let's see the other two places first, and then we can sit and chat over a cup of coffee." She wanted time to dig into this woman's brain. Kira wanted to get the woman to relax, then she would pounce and obtain the rest of the information that Remmy was hiding.

They had known each other long enough that Kira expected Manny to follow where her train of thought was going, as well as what she was doing. Hopefully it wouldn't turn out to be an ex or family member; those situations always became very nasty in the end.

Colin cleared his throat and Remmy looked at him. "I hate to leave right now, but I need to if I am going to make it to Summerville in time for the punch. I already called all the contractors and told them this project is on hold for a couple of days."

Remmy waved him off. "Go, I can handle things here. I have the set of originals in my truck. Do you want to take them with you?"

Kira looked at Manny as she listened to Colin and Remmy discuss business matters. The confused look on his face told her he was just as lost on most of the terminology as she was.

Kira addressed Remmy. "Well, shall we be on our way then? I will follow you to each location. Watts, I'll speak with you later this afternoon."

Colin pulled out and headed west to the thruway as Remmy, with the investigator hot on her heels, headed east.

†

As they toured the first two stops, Remmy became curious about this woman. The sheer appearance of the woman was staggering. Remmy had to keep a check on herself so that she wasn't caught drooling. However, looks weren't everything. This woman seemed so ice cold and void of human emotions that Remmy wasn't even sure she was breathing.

Once they got to Blondie's Coffee, she suggested they get a table outside and sit a moment. She was exhausted and functioning on only the hour or so of sleep that she had gotten before Colin rudely awakened her.

Setting her coffee cup on the table, Remmy took a leap of faith. "How long have you been a cop?"

Kira's mind screamed. The inspector had really hoped this woman wouldn't come on to her. The woman sitting across from her was pretty; she had to admit that much. Kira didn't need this right now; besides, Remmy wasn't really her type.

Kira's defenses were low. If Remmy paid any attention to her, Kira feared she would do something she'd never done in her life. She would crumble at the feet of a woman in what she considered her own back yard. This was a situation that was far too dangerous.

She decided to focus on the case and try to get through the woman's defenses once more. "Okay, so now that we have relaxed for a moment, are you sure there is nothing else that you need to tell me regarding this case?" Slowly Kira sipped the extra bold coffee with its double shot of espresso. Coffee sometimes was the only thing that kept her upright. Today Kira was going to need all she could get.

Remmy picked up her coffee, putting it to her lips. Kira knew a stall tactic when she saw one. Her eyes drilled into Remmy's, searching for what she kept hidden. "Okay, answer me a simple question first then. What in the hell is that awful smelling coffee? Then tell me what I need to know." Kira liked to relax them, then she would go in for the kill.

Kira's eyes were such a radiant color of blue, Remmy would never forget them. They would haunt her dreams for years to come.

"Good God, does no one I know like flavored coffee? It is caramel. As for the other, there is nothing. We've told you everything. By the way, you haven't answered my question." Remmy tried not to hold back when she wanted to know something. She could be very bold sometimes, yet at others she was painfully shy.

"All of my life"

Remmy laughed. "Well, that was a little vague. Okay, let's try a different approach. How old are you, and by the way, you have yet to tell me your name, Ms. Investigator?"

Kira swore under her breath. There was no doubt the woman was interested in her. Kira surprised herself when she relented and gave a little information. "Kira Kirpatrick, thirty-one. Oh, and before you ask...yes, I am tall. I'm six-three."

She tossed her empty cup toward the trash can and easily made it in. "Yes, I also played basketball. I would have been a professional player instead of getting into this line of work if I hadn't blown out my knee in my senior year in college. I think we're done here for today. I'll contact you tomorrow or the next day, after I get all the reports back and can look through them."

In a split moment, Kira was at her truck and gone, stopping any further personal conversation that the other woman might have tried to have with her. Looking in the mirror, she had seen Remmy trying to catch up with her, but she started the engine and pulled away.

†

Kira's admission stunned Remmy, Kira could be relaxed enough one moment to give her personal details, and then, in a blink of an eye, she was all business again. When Kira had left Remmy had tried running to catch up with the tall woman, but those long legs were great for making a fast getaway.

It was then that Remmy decided to go home for more sleep before going into the office. She knew she was going to have to deal with her father about all that was going on at some point. On the way home, she called Jack to bring him up to date on the most recent events, including the aloof investigator. This sent him into fits of a different sort.

"Ah-ha, you got it bad for her, admit it. You want her, don't you? Is she really, really that hot or are you exaggerating? How old is she? Is she in a relationship? OMG.... you're interested in someone. I'm so happy. Are you going to ask her out? Where are you going to take her?" He twittered on, not letting Remmy get a word in.

"Jack, down boy, down. Yes, she is that hot. Oh. My. God. Is she hot! She is six-three and has so many muscles that her muscles have muscles. She has those classic features, you know. It was the eyes though, that really got me. They are the most fascinating shade of blue I've ever seen. I just wanted to crawl inside them. As far as a relationship goes, I don't have a clue, but if I was to guess...I would say no. She seems married to the job. One second she was kind of being nice, the next it was all business and she was cold as an iceberg." Opening the door to her house, Remmy went

80

straight to the kitchen for a bottle of juice. On the way to the bedroom, she ran the ice-cold bottle over her chest to cool herself off.

"However ice-cold she is, you want her. You so badly want to get into her pants, don't you? Girl, you got it so bad, you would spread your legs wide open for her in a heartbeat. I know you better than anyone. Something tells me you're already a goner on this woman. I'm so happy. You've needed to find someone and settle down."

✝

Remmy stood in the doorway, smiling at the sight before her. There, sprawled across the bed in all her naked glory, was Jules looking back at her, patting the bed beside her. "Jack, I have to go, I'll talk to you later. I have something I have to take care of right now."

Three seconds later, a completely naked Remmy crawled into bed. Two seconds later, she straddled Jules's thighs. Cupping her own breasts, Remmy looked down at the stunning woman. "I'm begging...please!"

Jules reached up, running her fingers through the wetness. "A little ready, are we? God you're so wet."

Within a heartbeat, Remmy found herself flipped over. Then Jules took her hard and fast.

Sometime later, after both were fully sated, Remmy told her about the morning's events. At first, she left out everything about Kira; however, Jules dragged it out of her and Remmy confessed how attractive she found the investigator. She became so turned on while talking about her that their lovemaking started all over again, with both falling into a peaceful sleep afterwards.

Chapter Five

He sat in the rusted death trap that once, about twenty years before, had been a fully functional Chevy Escort. He had paid one hundred dollars for it from the junk yard, and had it up and running in under a week. It was so nondescript that no one would give it a second glance. "If anyone spots me following the bitch, they'll just think I'm some loser who can't afford better."

He sipped his now-cold coffee, watching the two once more sit at the patio table talking. "They're probably drinking lattes or some other disgusting queer drink. The only real drink is good strong black coffee, not the shit these places come up with these days."

The disturbed man had observed them on three other occasions sitting at the same corner patio table talking, sharing laughter as well as coffee. He just knew the cop was a dyke, and the shorter woman was the bane of his existence.

"It's because of her my life is shit." His delusional mind took his hatred for her and turned it against all women.

"I tried scaring her with the letters, nothing. Then I sabotaged the video store. Still she continues as if nothing's happened. It's now time to put fear into her personally." What did he care if she received a few scratches?

He waited across the street until the two women climbed into their trucks and left the parking lot. He then proceeded to the coffee shop to relieve himself and buy more caffeine to keep him awake.

Between all the caffeine he drank and the energy pills he took, his mind was flying high and he slept only an hour or two a night. Plans of all kinds flew through his warped mind and if one failed, he always had hundreds of others as backups.

Ordering his coffee from the man behind the counter, he mentally went over the checklist of the tools he would need for his latest scheme. Now all he had to do was get into her office early in the morning before anyone else arrived.

†

Relaxed and calm for the first time in weeks, Kira sat at her desk in her home office. She preferred to work from home whenever she could, able to accomplish more in an hour there than during a whole day in the office. Connected into her work mainframe, she was able to search their databanks at three in the morning if needed. That way she didn't have to trudge into the office to do it.

She sifted through the piles on her desk, then on the floor, looking for the report she knew she had seen the day before. "Shit, my office has never been this much of a mess. It's driving me mad to be so disorganized. There's never enough time lately. Damn."

She finally found the report in a pile on the floor. "About freaking time! I've got to get this shit cleaned up. Maybe now that I have three of my five cases closed I'll get to it." Finishing the last of the reports for the Moraes case, Kira closed the binder.

Swallowing the last of her beer, Kira noticed the Garrick Construction binder sitting on the corner of the desk. Her investigation had come to a screeching halt on this one. Over the last five weeks Kira had pored over all the evidence on the case, what little there was of it. No matches came back on the DNA from the cigarettes. The only other evidence was that the lock on the front door had not been popped, but unlocked.

She asked Colin if the contractor from the day before could have accidentally left the door unlocked. He informed Kira it was possible. That fact left the case wide open, it could have been anyone.

Instinct told Kira that Remmy was lying about something. She was close to pulling the woman into the station to browbeat it out of her. *Damn woman, doesn't she realize I'm trying to protect her, trying to do my job?* The construction owner was as stubborn as Kira was, which meant the two of them would continue to butt heads until the case was solved.

Opening the binder, Kira studied the picture of the woman in question. She wished she could telepathically will Remmy to tell her what she needed to know. Kira thought that she finally, on the fourth time they met at the coffee shop, had gotten through to Remmy. *Yeah, as soon as I asked about any enemies, she clammed up tighter than an unpaid hooker's legs.* Kira laughed aloud at her own stupid joke.

Running her finger along Remmy's jaw line in the picture, Kira contemplated what her next move would be. *God, you're good-looking and distracting, Remmington Garrick. Why can't I get you to crack?* "What has made you so tight-lipped and afraid?"

Walking to the kitchen, she thought back to their conversations. *I have learned some interesting things about you, though. What does it matter? If we had met at a different time, maybe it would've been a possibility.* She pulled another cold beer from the top shelf of the fridge.

Kira couldn't believe how horny she was after each encounter with Remmy. She was glad she was able to get away for the last three days to Provincetown. It was not nearly long enough, but it was going to have to do for the time being. *I hope to hell things let up in the next several months so I can go back for longer. I sure as hell don't want to admit to anyone I find Remmy devastatingly beautiful and wonderfully intelligent.*

Picking up the binder, Kira threw it to the floor. "Fuck, listen to me. This woman has me spewing shit! I need to get this case done. I'll give it one more shot. If she doesn't break and tell me what she's hiding, then I'll haul her ass in. I can't do it tomorrow though because I don't want to ruin her birthday by dredging up this crap on her special day."

Looking at the mess in her home office, Kira sighed. "Shit, now I'm even holding conversations with myself."

Picking up the binder once more, Kira looked over the written notes from their last meeting. Kira, of course, didn't write everything in her reports; they'd discussed several things that had no place in any report. She wondered if Remmy would follow her advice from their last meeting. They had talked about how Remmy loved to write and how she'd once dreamed of being a writer. Instead of following her dreams, she had followed her father's into the construction business.

"I still can't believe I told Remmy *to follow her heart and let no one stand in her way*. She's so adorable when she talks about her writing. She gets so enthusiastic and animated." Kira smiled. Not wanting to ruin Remmy's weekend, she would wait until Monday to question her again.

†

Remmy's birthday dinner had been a nice steak at her favorite restaurant, surrounded by her friends and her father. All of them had returned to her house for birthday cake and the game. Missing from the party was Ronald; she had even, for one moment, thought to invite him but he surely wasn't missed.

The cake was already gone when Remmy looked around the living room. Her guests were hanging watching the Steelers' game, downing beer after beer. Jack and Patrick sat cuddled on the loveseat, Taylor in the lazy-boy chair, leaving her, Jules, and Colin on the couch.

"By the number of empties I'd say everyone has a good buzz going." Remmy received a shushing motion from everyone. The Steelers were ahead by twenty-one points in the third quarter and they didn't want to be disturbed. Remmy stood, gathering the empties as she went. "Everyone want fresh ones?"

Everyone nodded yes, not wanting to tear their eyes off the screen, except for her father, Taylor.

"Let me help ya, sweetie, you can't carry all those yourself." Taylor stood, following his daughter to the kitchen.

Jack had told Taylor about the state investigator that Remmy was having coffee with several times since the vandalism of the video shop. Now Taylor wanted to see if she would talk about it. It was about time she showed interest in someone. Taylor hoped it would be Jules, but Remmy had told him that they were only friends.

Taylor took the empties from her. He deposited them into the box by the back door that led onto the deck of the home that Haley had bought right after she met Remmy. Taylor tried never to interfere in his children's private lives but he was about to make an exception. He was concerned about his daughter's state of mind.

"Remmy, I hear you met someone that you took a shining to? Is it a state investigator, perhaps? It seems you left that part out of our conversations the last several weeks. So, tell me about this woman." Taylor popped the tops off the beers while Remmy pulled more snacks from the fridge.

"I'm going to slap those two boys freakin' silly! Who said something? Was it Jack or Colin?"

Taylor pointed the bottle he was holding at her. "They care 'bout ya, as do I." Remmy handed him the food to set on the counter.

"I know, Daddy, I know. What I don't know is…well, I don't know what to do. Do I ask her out? She seems like an ice-cold bitch one moment and almost human the next. Do I want to have anything to do with someone like that?"

Taylor watched her stall for time as she pulled two platters from the cabinet under the island, then close the door with her foot. He always felt his daughter wore her heart on her sleeve. Now was no different. "Maybe, sweetie, she has to be that way because of her job. Possibly that is how she deals with all the horrible things she must see. If you don't ask, you'll never know. So, you should ask."

Looking at his daughter's left hand, Taylor was stunned. The ring she'd never once taken off since Haley put it on her finger was now absent. It told him Remmy was finally making progress. Taylor knew his daughter was a tough cookie. It would take someone strong to break down the walls she'd built around herself. That person would have to be resilient enough to stand up to Remmy when she would undoubtedly compare them to Haley. He was aware his daughter did that with every woman she met. He hoped this one would stand tall, as well as be strong enough to hold on despite the opposition along the way. Taylor was positive Remmy would fight it every step.

Remmy cherished her father's views, knowing he was always right. Sometimes it just took her a little while to realize it. She went to work laying the cubed cheese and pepperoni beside crackers on the tray. Next, she spooned out the homemade salsa into a dish in the middle of the tray of homemade tortilla chips that she had made that afternoon.

"I don't know, Dad. What if she's not gay? What if I'm not her type? Worse yet, what if she laughs at me?"

Remmy was unsure of herself. With Haley, she had known immediately it was love and jumped in with both feet. This time she wasn't sure what it was. Was it the beginning of something wonderful or was it just horny lust? Lost in thought, Remmy picked up the two trays.

Her father kissed her on the cheek as she passed him.

"Honey, you've been alone too long. Ask her, please."

Pushing her way through the kitchen door into the other room, Remmy said, "Okay, Daddy, I will, but please let's just keep this between us. Now let's get this food into the wolves before they attack." Remmy had barely set the food on the coffee table when hands descended on it in a feeding frenzy. "Geez, someone at least leave me a morsel or two."

Remmy cheered along with the rest when the game ended in a shutout; the Steelers had won thirty-five to nil. "Well, guys, I don't think Jules is too happy on the outcome of the game. Either that or she's still pissed at you Jack for slamming the door in her face when she first got here. She can't help she's a Raiders' fan, it's just some kind of defect in her." This earned Remmy a swat on the thigh from Jules.

"Well, I can't help it if she's a nasty Raiders fan. Jules, this is a Steelers' house. So, *ppppffftt*, I'm not going to apologize."

"Thank you so much, Jack, for the raspberry. Don't you think it was bad enough to make me beg to come in? You made me say it loud enough for the neighbors to hear."

"Watch it, stretch, or next time I'll make you use the bullhorn."

Remmy smiled at them. She loved how they got along well enough that they could tease each other in such a manner.

After bidding the others goodnight, only Jules remained. Remmy smiled as she watched Jules put on her jacket

"Okay, Remmy, what are you up to? You look like the Cheshire Cat."

"It was a good day and a good game, spent with family. I also think maybe, possibly... Well, I think maybe I'll ask Kira out to dinner." Remmy's blood pressure rose as uncertainty crept into her mind. Jules pulled her into a warm hug.

"Good, I'm glad you're taking that first step. I'm leaving at five in the morning for the airport. Unfortunately, I can't postpone this trip to Houston or I would so I could be here with you for moral support. Call me, though, and let me know how it goes. She sounds like she might be an interesting person." Jules yawned. "Sorry, guess I'm tired. I need to get home and get some sleep. I'll talk to you tomorrow."

Jules kissed her on the lips and bid her goodnight. Remmy finished cleaning the living room and kitchen, muttering about *little piggies* the whole time. She crawled into bed, exhausted, planning on not going to the office until nine. That would be very late for Remmy since she was usually in by six at the latest.

†

Remmy felt wonderful and relaxed when she woke up the next morning. Only recently had she been able to sleep through the night without waking. Too often her nights were filled with nightmares of opening the front door to find Haley's bloody and beaten body upon her doorstep. It was only in the last several months that the nightmares had appeared less often. The previous night, not only had Remmy not awakened once, dripping with sweat, screaming Haley's name, but instead she had dreamed of the fun times they had together.

She was in a good mood and hummed the entire way to the office. Pulling into the parking lot, she found only Stephanie's car. Stephanie was the only person standing between her and insanity at that moment. Remmy had hired her three weeks previously.

Her previous receptionist left the morning the state police officer arrived to obtain the letters. She told Remmy she quit because of what was going on. Two weeks later, Remmy still hadn't found a replacement. Late one evening, her cell phone rang. It was Stephanie. She told Remmy she'd just got out of the Army and her cousin, Patrick, had told her Remmy still hadn't found anyone willing to work long hard hours for little pay.

Stephanie turned out to be more than a receptionist. She took over running the office as well. This freed up more of Remmy's time to devote to the projects she was working on. As a result, Remmy increased Stephanie's pay and gave her the title of Office Manager, completely doing away with the receptionist position altogether. Remmy still, however, hadn't hired an assistant for herself, as she had promised her father once again a year ago.

Remmy's accounting manager was on vacation, but she wondered where everyone else was. Mondays were always crazy, with everyone tripping over each other as they tried to get all of their paperwork completed from the previous week. Striding through the front glass door, with the company name in bold red lettering, she heard Stephanie on the phone with Colin.

"Morning to both of you."

She walked through her outer office, which would one day belong to her assistant, up to the door leading into her own office. Balancing her large coffee and laptop, she unlocked the door to her office and yelled back her frustration to the other woman.

"Steph, remind me later to go buy a new coffee pot for the office. This balancing act is a pain in the ass."

Remmy let out a whoop of joy as she was finally able to open the door. She heard a loud crack. The light fixture above the door gave way, crashing down upon her, hitting her on the left side of her head and arm. Screaming, she crumpled to the floor in an unconscious heap, her coffee coloring the beige carpet an ugly brown. The spot rapidly became a rust color as blood mixed in with the coffee.

†

Hearing the crash, Stephanie dropped her cell onto her desk and ran for Remmy's office, unsure of what she was going to find. She was shocked to find Remmy lying on the floor with debris on top of her. Carefully Stephanie moved the light. She saw blood on Remmy's head and gushing from her arm. She made sure Remmy was still breathing. Retrieving her phone, she told Colin what happened.

"Shit, I just blew through a red light. Call the fucking cops. I'm less than two minutes away. Hey, wait a second, do you have that state investigator's number?"

Stephanie remembered seeing the business card. "Yes, it's on Remmy's desk." Stephanie reached over and picked up the card.

"Good, call her and I'll call an ambulance. I'm right around the corner now, so I'll be there in a second. It was no accident, it was Ronald, I'm sure of it, and this time he's gone too far. He's going to pay. I've got to get Remmy to tell Kira about Ronald."

Stephanie dropped her phone on the floor when she heard Colin shouting as he came in the door.

"Steph, did you get a hold of the investigator? The ambulance should be here in a minute."

Stephanie looked up from the floor with fear in her eyes. She had grabbed clean rags from the box that one of their contractors had left behind on a job site. She was using one to try and stop the flow of blood.

"I did. She uh, she…well, she is not a happy camper right now. I think the word *fuck* was uttered every other word. She said she'd be here in ten minutes, but she'd call her office for backup. She said someone would be here in a few seconds. Oh… also, she said that her technicians would be right behind her. God, Colin, how did this happen? All she did was open the door."

"Don't worry, she'll be fine, she's a tough cookie. This will only make her pissed off more."

Stephanie heard the front door open and voices shouting, and she was able to finally breathe normally again.

†

Kira and her people arrived as the EMTs were wheeling Remmy to the ambulance. The injured woman had regained her wits and everyone around her was paying the price. Not wanting to go to the hospital, she was commanding the paramedics let her get back to work.

"Let me up off this fucking thing. I have things to do. Just put some gauze around my arm and head. It'll be fine. Now let me up!"

The stoic investigator stopped beside the gurney carrying the irate woman. "Listen to me and listen good: you are going to the hospital, no doubt about it. So, no more arguments, okay?"

Remmy laid her bandaged head back on the gurney. "Fine! Whatever. You're obviously 'the boss.' Colin, I need you to get over to the bookstore, you were supposed to be there first thing this morning and I don't want to jeopardize that job. Also, Colin...my father hears about none of this...get it?"

Kira patted Remmy on her uninjured arm. "I don't think you need to be thinking of any of that right now. I'm sure Colin is more than capable of handling anything." Kira turned to the female paramedic. "Get her out of here before she tries to argue again."

Kira looked Stephanie up and down, wondering who she was and why she was at Remmy's office. The woman was clad in jeans, a blue button-down shirt, and a little too butch for Kira's liking. She wondered why she cared about who Remmy spent time with, but her mouth got the better of her. "Who the hell are you?"

"I'm Stephanie, the office manager. Who the hell are you?"

Kira took notice of the woman's hostile tone and gave her a cocky grin. "I'm the fucking Pope."

Kira turned to Colin, motioning him inside. Once inside, she started in on him. "What the fuck is going on here, Colin? I know there is something Remmy hasn't told me." She waited for him to respond. When nothing came, Kira walked away, disgusted.

"Jesus H. Christ! Neither of you is going to talk until he's killed her and guess what..." She turned back, glaring at him. "...then it'll be too late!" Kira was furious.

Looking at the fallen light fixture, Kira realized how lucky Remmy had been. Instead of giving her just a concussion and a large gash in her arm, they might have easily been putting Remmy in a body bag. Why wouldn't this woman talk to her? Why wouldn't Colin talk either? Kira was determined now more than ever to get to the bottom of what Remmy was hiding.

"Charlie, I want everything in this room dusted and I mean everything." Out of the corner of her eye, Kira spotted something under the visitor chair. "Bag that butt. I want to know if it has the same DNA as the others we found at the video store."

Hearing a commotion, Kira stepped out of Remmy's office into the outer office area. She saw a man she didn't recognize, and asked him for identification. "Excuse me sir, may I see some ID, and please tell me what your business is here." The disgusted look on Colin's face didn't go unnoticed by Kira. She was positive it was these two men whom she'd heard arguing.

The man in question sneered at her. "I am Ronald, Remmington's cousin and next in charge here. Who the hell are you?"

Kira noticed that Ronald's declaration had the desired effect on Colin when his temper flared. "The fuck you are. You'll never be in charge here as long as Remmy and I live and breathe."

Kira now had an idea of what the two had been hiding. There was most definitely bad blood between the three. However, how far did it go? Something about the short man made the hairs on the back of her neck twitch. It was then that she saw the cigarette package in his shirt pocket. "Well, I think maybe you and I should have a little chat. Ronald it was, right?" He nodded. "Good, why don't you come outside with me?"

Colin stepped toward her. "Wait a damn minute…"

Pinning him with a glare, she shook her head no. Following Ronald outside, Kira mouthed *trust me* to Colin. Once outside, they found Manny waiting for them. Turning to Ronald, Kira pointed to his pocket. "May I?"

Kira in turn handed the cigarette to the state police officer who stood beside her. "Thanks. Give that to Charlie, please, I think he was looking for one earlier." Kira turned back to Ronald. "Now that I have your attention, why were you at the video store and why did I just find one of your cigarette butts in Ms. Garrick's office?"

Sputtering, Ronald's face and neck turned red. "How dare you, woman, accuse me of anything! I was nowhere near that video store and the one in Remmy's office could be from anytime. How dare you!"

Kira's hackles were rising. She didn't like this man. However, she wouldn't rise to his bait and slug him a good one, like she wanted to. "Well, since it's illegal to smoke in the building, how would the butt have gotten in there? Please answer me that."

As an afterthought, she added, "And by the way it's *Investigator Kirpatrick* to you."

Manny came back out and cleared his throat. "Please answer her, sir."

"Like I said, it could have been from anytime. I work late sometimes and have needed papers that have been in her office. I could have dropped it at any of those times. Since we are through here, I have an appointment with a client I have to get to in a few moments." Ronald turned to walk away.

"We're through when I say we're through. I'd like you to go with Officer Watts here and give him a detailed account of where you were the night the video store was broken into. I would also like your fingerprints just in case we come across a set in her office we can't identify." Kira wanted to pop this man's head like a pimple.

"Manny, call me within the hour with the information I requested. I am going to the hospital to have a chat with our victim." Pulling out her phone as she walked away, Kira knew the little weasel wasn't happy at all. She chuckled at that thought. *I don't like him and I don't trust him.*

Kira sent Manny a text with her plan of action and asked him to be discreet. She hoped Ronald, the dimwit, would feel the need for a cigarette while at the station, and asked Manny to discreetly bag it and send it to Charlie for testing. She wanted one with his DNA on it.

"Charlie, I'm heading over to see Ms. Garrick. Call me with anything you come up with, even if you think it isn't important. I have a feeling this is far from over with." Kira's gut told her something was very fishy with the cousin; however, proving it would be another thing. First thing Kira needed to find out was if Remmy had locked her office door. If she had, how did Ronald get in?

✝

Waiting was not one of Kira's strong suits. On more than one occasion, she'd gotten herself into sticky situations because she had such a twitchy disposition. Now, having to sit and wait to be able to see Remmy was eating at her. Finally, after patiently waiting two hours, she approached the nurse at the desk again. Kira knew the nurse from her trooper days, and unless something had changed, she was not about to let her push through the doors.

The nurse came around the desk, her walkie-talkie in hand. "Listen here, Kirpatrick, I'll tell you one last time, no."

Kira tried her most intimidating look.

The older woman chuckled, shaking her head *no* once more.

"Ah, come on, Maddie, I won't cause any trouble. I promise. Please?" Finally, Kira tried batting her eyes at the nurse.

"Listen here, *Ms.* Kira, I've seen all of your tricks over the years. Do I have to call Billy to come down here?"

Kira visibly flinched. She had had a run in with the orderly two years ago and didn't care to have a repeat of that. So far, in Kira's life, Billy had been the only one ever able to take her down. It still to this day irked her. "Ah, no... No need to call him. I'll go over there and wait."

"I knew that would stop that infernal pacing of yours."

Kira smiled.

Maddie laid her hand upon Kira's arm. "How is Annabella by the way?"

Looking down at the hand on her arm, Kira pulled away slightly. Then she smiled, thinking of her niece. "She's good. Her leg healed really well. The specialist was afraid she would have a bit of a limp, but she doesn't. It bothered her a bit after she had those damn fitness tests last month. Thanks for asking."

"Well, she's a good kid. Let's hope she doesn't have your temper, though, when she gets older." The nurse walked back behind the counter picking up the ringing phone.

†

"Ah yeah, let's hope not." Two years ago, Kira almost took out a doctor. In his stupidity, he'd told Kira she wasn't permitted to see Bella because she was not her mother.

Unfortunately, Maddie was in with a patient when the doctor approached Kira. Hearing someone screaming for help, the nurse had stepped into the hallway to see Kira holding the doctor two feet off the ground and against the wall. Seeing the situation, she called down the hall to Billy, who in turn tackled the irate woman. Maddie then launched a verbal assault at the doctor, calling into question his manly parts and parentage. Kira found out a few moments later this was not the first time there had been an issue with this doctor in particular.

Shaking her head, Kira muttered, "No, I don't care to see Billy again so soon."

✝

Manny approached Kira after watching her pace for another few moments. He had been waiting for her to cool off. Sitting down, she looked up at her friend and colleague. "Off duty?"

Manny sighed as he sat beside her. He'd just come off an eighteen-hour shift and was dead on his feet. "Yeah...dead tired. I was supposed to be home four hours ago. Paul is going to kill me. He'd planned a trip to the wineries for us today."

Pulling a cell phone from her belt, Kira hit one of the speed numbers. "I'll call him and explain."

Manny patted her thigh and hit *end call* on her phone. He and Paul were the only people Kira permitted to touch her with such familiarity; she'd been known to toss others to the ground for touching her. Laying his head against the wall, he closed his eyes. "Nah, I'll call him in a few minutes. I just need to rest my eyes for a moment. How is Remmy? Did they tell you anything yet?"

Kira followed suit, laying her head back as well. "No, they won't tell me a thing. Fucking doctors, I hate them all. Our lovely friendly neighborhood nurse, Maddie, did tell me earlier, though, they were doing tests and that they had to stitch up her arm and head. Find anything interesting at her office?"

"I know you wouldn't risk Paul's wrath for nothing, so it had to be something good."

"Well, it appears this was no accident. Whoever did this intended to harm her, not just scare her. That has me concerned. When Charlie was dusting the doorframe, he noticed a wire from the door leading up to the ceiling. From what we could tell, without pulling everything apart, it looks like the light was rigged to fall when she opened the door. The boys are going to pull it all apart and take a closer look. I'm thinking whoever did it planned on coming in and quickly disposing of the evidence. I can think of at least one who was in a hurry to get into the office."

"Yeah, so can I, there's something creepy about him." Kira rubbed her hands over her face, Manny could feel her frustration. "Don't tell me, you talked to everyone in the buildings surrounding hers and no one saw a fucking thing. Am I right?"

Sitting up straight in the chair, Manny felt the same frustration as Kira did. He was glad that in one week's time he would be a full-fledged investigator. That meant he could work directly with her and not be taking calls, then handing them off to her or one of the other investigators. He wanted to personally catch this one. Whoever this was, he was torturing this poor woman. They would catch him no matter how long it took. Manny just hoped it would be before he killed her.

"Not a freakin' thing. That's the problem with these kinds of locations. It's a commercial area. Yes, some of the businesses have cameras but they're trained on their own property, not the street or parking lots and sure as hell not someone else's property. You'd think they would help out their neighbors when they could." Manny didn't like it. They were back right where they started. There was very little to go on and the clock was ticking.

Kira sat bolt upright. "Does she have a camera on her property? Oh please tell me she did and it shows that slime bag cousin on it."

With Kira's pleading eyes aimed at him, Manny wished he had better news. "No, sorry. Nope, no cameras, no security system…nada. I would recommend after this that she put them in. As for the slime bag, I got his prints and found nothing to speak of, really. I could only find a couple of parking tickets and one speeding ticket on him. Charlie said he'll push through the butt from the office as fast as he can, but it will take time."

Manny watched as Kira started pacing once more, and knowing her as well as he did, understood this was a sign of her frustration.

"God, I hate fucking hospitals!"

Having another thought, Manny asked her something that had been nagging at him for several weeks. "Did she ever tell you the story behind her spouse?"

Kira stopped pacing for a moment. "Shit, no, and the ring disappeared off her finger."

She continued. "I'll talk to Henry today. I'm pulling you off the roads, 'cause I need your skills more. I want this case to be your main priority. I want to concentrate on the Daniels case. Just give me daily updates on what's going on."

"I'm speaking as your friend, Kira. Are you maybe too close to the case? Is it becoming too personal?" When Kira growled at him, he knew he had hit his mark.

"Enough! Good, here comes the doctor."

Manny kept quiet, he knew when not to press. *This topic is far from over, Kira, and we both know it.*

✝

Quietly, not wanting to wake Remmy if she was sleeping, Kira entered the room she'd been escorted to a moment before. Kira hesitated at the door. She needed to collect her thoughts and rein in her anger at whoever had done this. Seeing copper eyes looking back at her told her Remmy was awake. The frown meant, more than likely, Remmy was in a foul mood.

This was going to be one of the toughest things she ever had to do. Kira tried to detach herself from the reality that she liked this woman. She had to treat Remmy as she would any other victim.

Kira's voice was flat, void of emotion. "You're awake. I wasn't sure if you would be. Your doctor said it was only okay for me to be here if you were. I understand you're in pain and would rather I talk to you much later. However, we need to get this done while it's fresh in your mind."

Sitting up a little, Remmy slowly nodded. "Sorry, my head feels like it's splitting open, but my arm is numb. It kind of feels weird. Okay, so, all I know is, I unlocked the door and opened it. The next thing I know, I was hit with something."

Pulling the chair over to Remmy's bedside, Kira sat down. "It was the light fixture and it was rigged to fall on you. I want you to listen good to me." Leaning in closer, Kira looked at Remmy, noticing the color of her eyes as the sunlight danced off them.

Remmy leaned a little closer to her. "Is everything okay? You look very upset about something."

Shaking her head, Kira brought her good sense back on-line. This woman was infuriating. "Yes, something is wrong, very wrong. You see, the victim in the case I am investigating right now is hiding something, as is one of her employees. I am truly hoping now that *she* has *felt* the severity of the situation, she'll tell me what I need to know." Hoping she got her meaning across, Kira sat back in the chair, clasping her hands behind her head.

Remmy knew she had to tell the investigator of her suspicions. Whoever this was had now made it extremely personal. This lunatic had stepped into her personal territory and that pissed her off. The anger made her head pound even more.

Closing her eyes and using relaxation techniques Haley had taught her, Remmy was surprised when it alleviated the pounding slightly. Holding onto the thin blanket covering her as if it were a lifeline, she told the investigator of her theory.

"Okay. It very well might be nothing, but just in case it isn't, I'll tell you. My cousin Ronald is a not-so-nice man. He's been a thorn in my side since I was a child, only it's gotten worse over the last five years or so. There are some very personal reasons for not liking the man, which I really don't care to get into." Sensing the investigator was about to object, Remmy held her hand up to stop her.

"Please don't ask me at this time to go into those, they're of no consequence. At least I don't think so." Remmy fidgeted with the blanket some more.

"Without knowing everything, how can I determine what's important or not? How can I find who is doing this? You are the most..." Kira looked then at Remmy. She knew that look well, She'd seen it on many of the women she had to deal with in her line of work. It was a look of defeat and fear.

Remmy sighed. "Fine. He has never really gotten along with the rest of the family. There were especially bad feelings between him and Haley. It escalated when..."

Kira tried to comfort her. She patted Remmy's hand that lay on top of the blanket. "Take your time, I have nowhere to be." She watched as the look of defeat washed across Remmy's face again.

"There was an incident between the two and Haley threw him out of our house. It was the night that Haley asked me to marry her. She passed away shortly after that. Please don't ask me details. May I have a drink of that water?"

Kira's concern for the woman kicked in again, no matter how much she tried to push it away. Picking up the Styrofoam cup of ice water, Kira handed it to her. "Here, don't drink too fast though."

"Thank you. I thought, at first, maybe he just hated lesbians. Now, though, I feel he hates women in general. Even being in the same room with him wigs me out. He's tried several times over the last few years to wrestle the company away from my father. He really freaked out when Dad turned it completely over to me. I probably should have fired him long ago, but he's family. I just couldn't bring myself to do it. I'm not saying it is him, 'cause I have no proof, yet I don't trust him. So, that is my little bit of unsavory information that I haven't wanted to tell you." Remmy sipped more water then handed it back to Kira.

"Are they going to keep you overnight?" The doctor wouldn't tell her the extent of Remmy's injuries due to doctor-patient confidentiality.

"No, just for a few more hours. Colin called Jack and he will be here in a little while. I'll be back at work tomorrow. I'd planned to move my offices soon to a bigger place, so I think I'll start in the morning. I want someplace more secure. I also don't want my father to know about this unless absolutely necessary. Damn my arm is starting to throb."

Kira pointed to her arm. "I don't think you're going to be able to hide that scar from him. Besides, with everything that's been going on, I think it best if he's kept up to date." She felt for the young woman. Kira knew what it was like to have to hide things.

"Damn, I guess I won't be able to, will I? That is, unless of course, I cover it with another tattoo. I guess you are right. I'll talk to him in the next couple of days."

Kira noticed the wicked look on Remmy's face. "Interesting, you don't look like the type of person to have any tattoos. Well, anyway, I'll take this information and chew on it for a while. I have several items I'm looking into right now. In the meantime, I will let you get some rest." Kira needed to leave quickly before she showed any more interest in Remmy's personal life. Doing so wouldn't be a good thing.

"Okay it's now or never. Kira, uh...," she mumbled. "I was wondering if you would like to go out to dinner with me sometime this week."

Kira stood looking at Remmy as if she had grown a third eye in the middle of her forehead. "Dinner?" She was momentarily stunned.

"Yes, dinner, as in a date."

"I'm sorry. I can't for two reasons. First, I'm not gay and secondly, if I were, I would never date someone involved in a case I'm working on. If you'll excuse me, I really need to be going."

Kira felt a moment of guilt as she put her hand on the doorknob. This woman could never understand her reasons for how she lived. Remmy had probably never been in the closet a day in her life. She watched as Remmy's face went completely red.

Remmy laid back on the bed, turning her head away from Kira.

Opening the door, Kira felt the need to apologize once more. "I'm sorry if you've misunderstood—"

Remmy cut her off mid-sentence. "There is nothing for you to be sorry for. It was...I who assumed, not you. As you said, you have things you need to do, as do I. Good afternoon, Investigator Kirpatrick."

†

Alone a few minutes later with nothing but her thoughts for company, Remmy kicked herself for being a complete idiot. *I can't believe I just assumed she was gay. God, how stupid am I? Well obviously, I won't do that again.*

Remmy had no idea why she had stepped out on that limb to ask Kira out. It wasn't as if she would have time for dating anyway. There were way too many projects going on. That was what she needed to concentrate on, not on stupid frivolous things like going on dates. She dozed off while waiting for Jack's arrival.

†

Manny curled up next to his partner in bed. Their relationship was just as strong now as it had been the first day, when Kira had introduced them, ten years ago. They loved and supported Kira and Annabella. The two women were like a sister and niece to them and held both Kira and Annabella in the utmost respect.

That was until Kira did something to cause both to take her to task. "I can't believe it. Are you sure? Are you really sure?" Paul sat up.

"Paul..." Manny wasn't irritated just flustered. He knew his lover was having trouble wrapping his mind around the fact that their friend had finally fallen in love.

Paul kissed Manny on the cheek.

Manny smiled at his lover. "I know, I know. Wow, I'm in shock, too. From the sounds of it, it hasn't dawned on her yet what she's feeling. When she does though, she's going to have a meltdown. You know she'll fight it the whole way. She'll put honor and duty before herself every single moment."

"There are times when Kira infuriates me to the point that all I can do is spit and sputter. Then I have to walk away, gather my thoughts, and return to the fight. Oh God, this is going to be one of those times, isn't it? She's going to be a pig-headed mule about it."

Manny patted Paul on his stomach. "Yes, and that's what we're here for. We have to talk some sense into her once and for all. She deserves to be happy and I really like Remmy. She's a good woman and I think they would make a really wonderful couple. Now, it's just a matter of making her see the light of day."

"She should be calling me any day now, wanting to talk about something unrelated to either the case or Remmy. Then she'll casually mention them both."

Manny started to doze off, repositioning himself against Paul. "Yes, and that is when you will pounce…"

"That I will, and let's hope I can finally wake her up."

Chapter Six

The infuriated investigator's office was in shambles. When Kira lost her temper completely, the situation had to be dire. When she did, everyone waited until the tornado passed before contemplating an entrance. Crime binders lay haphazardly about the room with their contents strewn from one end of the office to the other. Remnants of what once were three nondescript coffee cups lay among the wreckage. Luckily, all the cups had been empty.

Penny, Kira and the commander's assistant, had learned long ago never to give either one of them expensive breakable items. She also learned to keep objects like letter openers and sharp pencils out of their offices because they made wonderful projectiles. This was a hard-learned lesson five years earlier when a newbie assistant coroner contaminated evidence in a murder case. The result had been a flesh wound to the newbie's left ear as a letter opener flew by and imbedded itself into the wall behind her.

When Charlie arrived a half-hour earlier, she knew the news wasn't good. He'd gone into Kira's office and closed the door behind him. Penny saw the frown on his face before entering and she was on the phone with Commander Henry Mitchell a second later. Kira and her superior had been waiting since the previous morning for Charlie's DNA news in the Garrick case.

Penny knew the news was not good. The crash a moment later, followed by Charlie fleeing from Kira's office, gave her the answer.

†

Both the people waiting knew better than to enter the office until Hurricane Kira had made landfall. Penny sat at her desk while the Commander sat in the visitor's chair with his long legs stretched out before him. Hearing the third coffee cup smash against the filing cabinet, Penny knew Kira was winding down.

The Commander laughed. "How many does that make?"

Penny chuckled. "Three and that was all she had." She laughed harder, amused at what she considered her two children. One sat in front of her, the other was currently throwing a temper tantrum.

It became silent in Kira's office. Sighing, Penny stood, already knowing what was behind the door. Coming around her desk, she nudged the Commander's feet out of the way. "I'd say by the sounds of it she's done. Want to take a chance?"

"Hell no, I know better than to go in too early. The stapler hitting me dead on in the chest a year ago was enough. Oh, and I noticed that the staplers are gone from our offices now as well. Why don't you go in first, Penny, and see if the coast is clear. I'll just wait out here."

Penny looked down at him in disbelief. "Chickenshit. Are you ever going to go in first?"

He looked up at her sheepishly. Penny stood with her hands on her hips, waiting for Henry's reply. "Well...well, I'm not stupid. Remember I know what it's like to open that door a little too early." He rubbed his chest where the stapler had hit.

Penny shook her head. "Yeah, like opening yours a little too soon. God! You two are just alike. Are you sure, you two aren't related? The two of you are like spoiled little brats and I am the nanny. Maybe I should call that show where they send out those nasty mean nannies." Her eyes twinkled. Penny loved teasing them, especially after one of them had been bad.

"Nope, sure not...it would, however, be an honor to call her family. She is the best trooper and investigator I've ever known and the best person. Alas, no, we are not related. Now go see if the coast is clear. I'll buy you lunch wherever you want."

"Yeah, yeah, you know what buttons to push. Food was always the answer with me."

"Yes, but I have yet to figure out how you stay pencil thin when you eat so much."

The blinds being closed in Kira's office, Penny would have to chance opening the door. Slowly, she opened the door a crack, peeking in. Behind the desk, which was now bare, sat Kira twirling around and around in her chair. Her head was resting on the back of the chair, staring at the ceiling. "Yes, it's safe, Penny, you can tell him as well."

Motioning the Commander in, Penny opened the door completely, pushing the rubble aside. As the two officers talked, Penny picked up the binders and papers, reassembling them as she went. After working directly for the Commander for sixteen years and Kira for seven, she was used to cleaning up after both of them.

Their tempers were legendary, yet no one cared. They never caused true harm to another individual, only their own property. In addition, only two cases in the last seven years had gone unsolved, and only six in the years before since the Commander had started as a state investigator. Kira was very good at what she did, just as Henry had been before his promotion to Commander and Kira's to lead investigator.

Henry shook his head. "Can Annabella really be fourteen this year? Wow, where have the years gone?"

"Sorry, I don't exactly follow your thinking?".

"Oh, sorry, just thinking about how old Annabella is going to be this year. Which led me to thinking about how you were so happy to get off the highways. I, of course, was damn happy about it, because you're the best we've ever had sit in that chair."

Penny, who was picking up the pieces of the Garrick binder, put in her two-cent's worth. "Damn little pipsqueak is taller than me already and she probably hasn't even hit her growth spurt yet."

An impish look gleamed in Kira's eyes as she shot back, "Well, hell, woman, even a midget is taller than you."

Penny straightened up from her task. "Listen here, young lady, do you want to clean this pigsty up yourself?"

The Commander chuckled. They were only bantering, so Henry let them continue on, as always.

†

Kira loved their little games, even though she usually lost. "Well, with your lower center of gravity, it's easier on you than the rest of us." Kira smiled, thinking her comeback was a good one.

Penny walked over with the papers that belonged in the Garrick binder and the binder itself, and pushed them across the desk to her. "Listen here, *high* and mighty... I heard a news report on the way in this morning. The Storm are looking for a new pole for their backboard. The Steelers also are looking for a new goal post. I think you'd be perfect for either one of those jobs. They're both tall and inanimate, brainless objects."

Kira stood now, leaning over her desk, closing in on the other woman. She towered over Penny by more than a foot. Kira looked her dead square in the eyes. "Listen here, you tiny little Lilliputian. I'm out of lollipops, so can you call your Guild friends and get some more for me?" Kira's smile extended ear to ear.

Penny smiled in return, standing with her hands flat on the desk, she met Kira's eyes. "*Montanha de um brutish lavadura de suinos.*"

Kira hated when Penny did this. Just when their insults where getting good, Penny would start in on her in Portuguese. Kira looked over at Henry. "Aw, come on, no fair. You know I can't understand her when she does that. What did she say?" She turned back to Penny. "Aw, come on, Penny, play fair."

Penny pointed to the binder and left the office, throwing a parting comment Kira's way. "*Si lesbiche* twit."

Following Penny out of the office, Henry roared with laughter.

Kira's frustration showed on her face as she blushed. She shouted to their retreating backs. "I don't speak fucking Italian either!"

Henry shouted back to her as he approached Penny's desk. "Try to Google it, why don't you?" He looked at Penny as she sat down behind her desk. "You are so bad. You know she's going to look that up. If I didn't know that the three of us were like family, I'd think you didn't like our Kira."

Penny looked up at him, her eyes twinkling. "Naw...I love her as if she were my own kid. Sometimes she gets me so frustrated, though. Earlier this morning, she asked me to make the usual hotel arrangements in Provincetown for her for the end of the next month. I just wish she would settle down with someone, instead of all these meaningless encounters."

Less than a handful of people knew Kira was a lesbian. Those who did protected her secret with their lives. Kira's own small family had been the only ones to know. Now, however, they were all gone except her niece, Annabella. If Kira hadn't let it slip years before that she had been whale watching off the coast at Provincetown the same time as Henry's gay son, neither would have known. Not that it mattered, because Henry and Penny loved her just the same. As he had said, they had been a big happy family before finding out and they remained one afterwards.

"Ah shit!" He turned around and went back into Kira's office.

Kira was busy on her computer, trying to find a translator on the internet. "This is futile, seeing as I can't even spell the words." Kira didn't turn around. "Just remembered what you came in for?"

Henry sat in the chair, put his feet on the desk, and waited for Kira to tell him what news Charlie had given her. Taking pity on her, Henry told Kira exactly what Penny had said to her.

"Since I am in such a giving mood today, I'll translate for you. The first one was a *mountain of a brutish swill pig* and the second one was *you lesbian twit.*" He watched Kira's eyes light up.

"Ooh, that woman is good."

Henry swore he saw a light bulb clicking on.

"Hey, wait a second, what did I do now? Why is she calling me a twit?"

Steepling his fingers under his chin Henry let Kira in on why. "I understand she made some hotel arrangements for you this morning. She's worried about you, as am I. I've told you many times no one here cares one way or the other. Don't give me that look. You know it doesn't bother me one bit, especially since my own son is gay."

Kira rolled her eyes. "Henry, I'm fine and things are going great as always with Bella. The only issue I have is this case. I really don't want to discuss my personal life, or lack thereof, with you at the moment."

Henry sighed loudly, his frustration showing. "That's not what I mean and you know it. So, where do we stand with the Garrick case? I thought you were going to concentrate on the Daniels case, of course that isn't going to happen...is it? You can't let this one go, right? Instead you gave Watts the Daniels case."

Kira's anger at the situation hissed out of every pore of her body. Henry felt it even though he was several feet away. "You're right. I can't let this case go until I solve it. No-fucking-where is where we stand. I was so sure it was that little slime bag cousin of hers." Pounding her fist on her desk, Kira's anger visibly grew.

Trying to rein Kira in and keep her focused, Henry put his feet on the floor and leaned forward. "Kira, focus..."

Kira ran her hand through her hair. "I know, I know. This is just pissing me off. No one has seen a thing. No one knows anything. All we have are the butts and guess fucking what? They don't match the bastard's DNA." Kira pushed the binder to him.

Opening the folder to the DNA evidence, Henry couldn't believe it. "Shit, I would've said it was him too. Damn! So that gives us two suspects. One unknown and him, cause I'm not quite wanting to rule him out completely. There is something about Ronald the weasel that just doesn't sit right with me. So, what's your next step?"

"Since the person or persons doing this more than likely had keys, I think I know where to try next. They have a couple of contractors that do quite a bit of work for them and sometimes need to get into the warehouse at odd times. Colin told me those men have keys to the loading dock area. How fucking hard could it be to find their way to the offices? Yeah, I know it sounded sarcastic, but my hackles are up over this case." Kira paused.

"Damn it, Henry, what am I missing here? The thought of someone slinking through those offices at night, then waiting in the dark to strike out at Remmy has me worried."

Henry felt for her, this case was affecting Kira as none other ever had. The Commander found it very curious as to why. Even though Kira was the lead investigator on the case, he still worked the case with her, as he did with all of his people. Today Henry was especially glad that he did, because he felt this case might be getting to her.

"I agree with you. You need to look at the contractors. I have to go, but touch base with me as soon as you do."

Henry stood to leave, a thought occurring to him. "Hey, don't you have that parent-teacher thing for the squirt in a half hour?"

Kira jumped from the chair. "Ah, shit! I forgot all about it. Thanks, Henry, it would have been my ass if I missed the third one in a row. Her teacher called me to tell me after last time that if I missed one more, it was I who was going to be in detention for a week. I'll talk to you tomorrow, and hopefully by then I'll know something more."

✝

Running to her truck, Kira hoped she'd be on time. She seriously didn't want to incur the wrath of Bella's teacher again. The pissed-off teacher made Kira feel as if she herself were back in school and had just been caught smoking in the girls' room during lunch. Besides, Bella would have her head also. If one thing in the world was for certain, her niece took after her in the temper department. Annabella Marie Kirpatrick was a spitfire and smarter than anyone Kira knew, which, of course, Bella pointed out to her Aunt Kira at every opportunity.

Starting the ignition, Kira said, "Yeah, let's hope that her temper never gets as bad as mine though."

✝

Kira dropped Bella off at a friend's house and then went to her meeting. Bella, as usual, was all straight As. Her niece was also the best student they had had in the last ten years. After spending the hour-long meeting at Bella's school, Kira picked up a much needed caffeine from Starbucks.

As she drove home, she thought about Annabella, her brother Geoff's only child. When he and his wife were killed nine years ago, Kira had been given custody of the five-year-old kid. Geoff's wife had no family since she had grown up in an orphanage. After the sudden death of their father, Kira and Geoff's own mother had moved back to Ireland four years before the accident. Bella had not been the cutest baby when she was born; however, now she was as beautiful as her Aunt Kira.

Kira had just turned eighteen and Geoff was a new dad at twenty-four when their mother left the US. She wanted nothing to do with her two children; they reminded her too much of her dead husband. After Kira's mother left them high and dry, they never spoke of her again, as if she had never existed.

God! I hope I don't make the same mistakes she did. Fuck, Geoff, if that drunk who ran into you hadn't died, I'd be in jail now. I'd have killed the bastard for what he did. Behind her, a horn blared. She looked up and realized the light had turned green.

She waved and pulled away. *Shit, Geoff, I knew nothing about raising kids. I still don't. I wing it every day. I help her as best I can with her homework and shit like that, but I'm not as smart as you were. And damn, brother, has she got your brains.*

Kira took another long swallow from her coffee. Lost in thought once more, she changed direction and drove to the trooper station on autopilot. She thought about her conversation earlier with Henry. Being Bella's guardian, Kira couldn't afford for anyone to find out she was gay. She was terrified that one of the caseworkers who checked on her twice a year from the state would deem her unfit to raise the kid. She had devoted her personal life to raising her niece.

Society might have come a long way, but there was still a long road to travel before it was rid of all the bigotry. Even in the most progressive towns, there were still zealots who would gladly stone to death a gay person if they could get away with it.

Until recently, P-town had satisfied her cravings. She would return fresh and ready to work. This last time, though, she had returned feeling no different. In the end, she turned every woman away. She looked at them and saw only Remmy.

Pulling into the station parking lot, she threw her truck into park and pounded her fists on the steering wheel. "Fuck, fuck, fuck! They're right. I can't keep going on like this, but I have no choice. I have to for Bella, even though I find Remmy so…well, so devastatingly beautiful. She has wonderful curves in all the right places. So what if she's not all feminine and frilly. To me she oozes femininity." Resting her forehead on her hands, she let the weariness creep into her bones.

"By the gods, I do like her. I like her quite a bit actually. Geoff, I wish to hell you were here. You aren't, though, are you? It's just Bella and me. I'm all she has and nothing is going to take me away from her. So, I need to buckle my nerve and get on with it, don't I? Damn it!" She exited the truck, making a mental note to call Paul and Manny and invite them out to dinner. She owed them for looking after Bella while she was gone.

†

Kira and Colin spent the following three days meeting with each of the contractors with keys, one at a time. They couldn't meet at Colin's office since Garrick

Construction was in the process of moving their offices. Instead, they met with them at Blondie's where Kira was now treated as a regular. She had stopped by at least five times a week since having coffee with Remmy there at the beginning of her investigation. All four of the contractors had rock solid alibis. During each of the incidents, they were on job sites in different parts of the state. Not one of them made the hairs on the back of Kira's neck stand on end as Ronald had. She just knew he had something to do with every malicious incident. It was just a matter of proving it.

Kira found herself right back at the beginning, with no solid evidence or suspects. She had even gone as far as meeting with the other construction companies that Remmy was in competition with. None struck Kira as the stalking type. In fact, they came across to her as very protective. Every single one of them swore to Kira they would find out what they could. Some even threatened to do bodily harm to the person who had hurt Remmy. It stunned Kira to hear burly construction men defend a woman within their ranks, and a lesbian at that. It seemed Remmy held their utmost respect.

It didn't shock Kira that not one of them had a good thing to say about Ronald. One of them went so far as to tell her to look into his doing something vicious like that to Remmy.

✝

The building was one of two Remmy had found over the last several years that she'd taken a liking to. She couldn't believe her luck when it became available just when she needed something good to happen. She called her lawyer, who in turn called the brokerage that was handling the sale of the building.

The brokerage even had a buyer within two weeks for Remmy's smaller building. It had been three weeks since the light had fallen on her, and everything was finally settling into place for her. Upon signing the papers, she called Jules to remodel and hired someone to update the alarm system. Since the building was only on a single level, it was much easier and cheaper to secure. Cost, though, was not a concern to Remmy when it came to the security. She wanted the best; it would be the only way that she would feel completely safe again.

The front of the building faced the road, and had an art deco style façade, with the warehouse extending behind it. The front doors leading into the building had copper inserts in each door that resembled the queen chess piece, each one holding a large sword pointing downwards. On either side of the ornate doors were four large windows. When entering the lobby, where the receptionist would normally sit, Jules knocked out the wall and made it open into the hallway where offices were located on each side.

Sitting in the newly opened area was a mission style oak desk, several bookcases, and Remmy's new assistant. A main hallway led right through the building to the warehouse portion. Off the hallway were offices for her employees, two large conference rooms, a set of restrooms, and a kitchen. Remmy's office was the first on the right side and the largest. The windows looked out upon a patch of forest, which also grew on her property. The warehouse portion was in the same style, covered in the time-washed grey stone.

Remmy liked the fact that the loading docks were in the rear and out of sight from the parking lot where the clients would park.

After having no assistant for so long, Remmy hired Colin's cousin Mackenzie. On the first day, she asked to be called Mack, not the frilly name she had been born with.

Sitting at her desk, looking out at the trees, Remmy wondered if she would see any birds or other wildlife. She felt content for the first time in quite a while. The company had so many projects going that all her people were working six days a week and ten-hour days. No one complained, though; they liked being busy as well as the bonuses they knew they would get at the end of the year.

Remmy absolutely loved what Jules had done with the building. She heard Jules in the hallway thanking the security contractor as he was leaving. Remmy smiled.

Jules knocked on the open door to Remmy's office. She entered without waiting for acknowledgement. "Well, you are all set. It's been a long four months, but we're finally here. I think it was all worth the extra wait. How does everyone like their offices?"

Swiveling in her leather chair toward the door, Remmy had a smile upon her face. "Do you know what we need?"

Jules smiled, the answer slipping through her lips. "Yeah, sex."

Remmy laughed, twirling her pen between her fingers. "Well, that's a gimme. However, what I was thinking of was *a party*. I want to throw a party to celebrate a fresh start. What do you think?"

Jules sat in the chair across from Remmy's desk. "It sounds good. Are you going to invite Kira?"

The pen stopped movement. "I don't know. She seemed to make it pretty clear she wasn't interested. Maybe I should, though, that way she can see the new security system."

"I still say that Kira is lying when she says she's not gay. I know your gaydar works just fine. So, what I want to know is why Kira is lying. Hell yeah, invite her. Maybe Ronald will do something stupid and she'll have to shoot him."

Remmy's head snapped up. "Jules! You're so bad. I will invite her, though."

Jules saw the faraway look in Remmy's eyes. "You really like her, don't you? I was really hoping you would've moved on by now."

Remmy started a mental list of the people she wanted to invite when Jules's question sank in. "Shit Jules! I wish I could just turn it off and not care about her. She is, well...I don't know how to explain it other than...I feel safe with her around. She makes me laugh. I feel at home when I am with her, even if it's just for coffee. I haven't felt that way since..." The words caught in Remmy's throat.

Jules finished Remmy's sentence for her. "Since Haley was alive. You can't compare the two, Remmy. Kira is a completely different person. You have to truly look at them as individuals. I'm sure Haley had flaws, as I'm sure Kira does. The same goes for their good points. Please don't compare them. If you have feelings for her, they have to be for her alone, not because she is like Haley."

Annoyance flashed across Remmy's face. "I know that. Why does everyone feel the need to keep telling me I compare everyone to Haley?" Remmy rubbed her face with the palms of her hands. "Shit! I'm sorry, Jules. I do, don't I? I don't mean to, it just happens. I do like her though...a lot."

Jules came around the desk to give Remmy a hug. "You work on the invitation list and I'll take care of the food. We'll lay out the food up where Mack is. I'm glad you're going to invite Kira. I know you're lonely; maybe the two of you can be friends and see where that goes."

Remmy swatted her on the stomach. "Always playing matchmaker. Well, this time it won't work. Remember, she's not gay. It would be nice to have her as a friend at least."

Jules's phone chiming a reminder of an appointment made both of them jump. "Shit, I'm going to be late. My appointment is across town at the Flushing Building. Call me when you get the list together and I'll call the caterers. Thanks again for letting me redo the interior of the building. I had been thinking of expanding into interior decorating, especially with all the antiques I find."

✝

A little over two weeks later, the new Garrick Construction Building was alive with clients and vendors. The food was delicious and the drinks cold, and both were disappearing rapidly. Knowing that the type of people Remmy did business with could eat and drink heavily, Jules had ordered the caterers to bring twice as much as they normally would have for this size of a party.

Since retiring, Taylor had time to meet some of his old buddies for beers at the local pub or just shoot the shit for hours watching sports. The party was a prime opportunity for him to catch up with the other contractors. Two of his old buddies had properties that needed work so he sent them over to Remmy and Colin. Taylor even sent one of them to Jules when he asked Taylor if he knew a good decorator. She had an appointment with him the following Monday, even though he told her he was going to hire her on Taylor's word alone.

Jack approached Jules, gushing over the work she had done. She laughed as he went on and on. "Calm down, human torch, geez. Do I need to spray you down with a hose?"

Jack bowed his head, blushing. "God, I swore I would never act like that. Sorry. You just do such fantastic work." Jack's smile turned to a frown. "Ah, shit."

Jules turned to see what had upset him. In through the front doors walked one of the most stunning women she'd seen in quite some time. Then it hit her. Jules had seen this woman before. It was two years ago in Provincetown. The woman had been with a blonde at the time, neither seemed able to keep their hands off each other.

Noticing Jack's hackles were still raised, Jules elbowed him. "Okay, I'll bite, who is she?"

Already having an inkling, Jack confirmed her fear. "That would be Kira. You know. The one who says she's not gay."

Jules could hear venom in Jack's voice. Watching the woman cross the lobby as if she owned the place, she just had to ask him. "So I take it you don't think she's straight?"

Jack ground his teeth. "Hell no!"

She patted him on his back. "Well, friend, I can assure you she's not."

Jack spun around on her. "Why, have you slept with her?"

Jules laughed. "Ah, no, but I can tell you she likes blondes. I saw her two years ago in P-town and I can guarantee you she's a dyke."

Jack's body stiffened. "That bitch! She lied to Remmy."

"Yes, and I intend to find out why she lied. Don't worry. I don't plan on saying anything to Remmy." Jules walked toward the aloof woman who stood off to the left side of the lobby holding a glass of wine.

Jules walked right into Kira's personal space. "Hi, I'm Jules, a *very good friend* of Remmy's. You are?"

Taken aback by the abrupt woman, Kira's defenses kicked into place. "Inspector Kirpatrick." She wanted to escape from this woman, who she now recognized from somewhere but couldn't place her. Kira extended her hand, which Jules took, squeezing it hard.

Kira studied the woman. "So, you're a friend of Remmy's, you say." She didn't like the way she'd said *very good friend*. "Just how good?"

Jules smiled. "*Very good*. Don't I know you from somewhere, perhaps Provincetown? You've been there, correct? With a blonde maybe?"

Kira felt cornered; the walls were closing in on her. Did this woman truly recognize her or was she playing some kind of game? Kira also questioned her own jealousy of this woman. Why should she be jealous? Remmy was free to date whomever she wanted. All Kira knew for sure at that moment was that she needed to get away from Jules. "Excuse me, I see someone I wish to speak with."

As Kira rushed off she heard Jules mutter behind her. "Well, I'll be damned, the tough dyke cop is in the closet. Very interesting...yes, very interesting indeed."

Kira didn't have time to worry about what Jules thought about her. Seeing Taylor and Jack across the room, Kira practically ran over to them. "Taylor, Jack...it's good to see the two of you. The new building looks good."

Taylor extended his hand to her. "Everything okay? You seemed a bit flustered as you walked over here. Colin and I had been waiting here in the lobby in case someone showed and started trouble. He just left a few moments ago to check the parking lot, and Jack was kind enough to keep me company."

Kira saw Colin come through the doors, motioning to Taylor. "Excuse me, Kira, but Colin needs my help with something. I would love to talk to you more. Please catch up with me later. Jack, you behave."

Jack looked indignant. "Hey, I always behave. It's Remmy who causes the trouble and blames it on me!" His smile and laughter told Kira that his irritation was a put on.

After Taylor left, Kira looked around at the glasses of wine and bottles of beer people held. "Ah, Jack, did Remmy make arrangements for these people to get home if they drink too much?"

Jack looked up at her as if she'd grown a third eye. "Yes, it was right on the invitation. Colin hired the valet attendants from the country club to drive people home if they wish and Remmy has rooms reserved at the hotel across the street if people wish to stay there. Do you ever stop being in cop mode and just live like a normal person? I bet a date with you is just a bundle of fun. Not!"

Kira ignored his sarcasm as well as his questioning her personal life. It warmed Kira to think that Remmy would go that far. It told her that the woman was more caring than the average person who would have left everyone to their own devices to get home.

She tried valiantly to ignore the woman across the room who was watching her. Jules had hit home with her questions. Kira felt as if the woman were trying to crawl inside her head. "Glad to hear that. What do you know about that Jules woman? How long has Remmy known her? Did she know her before these things started happening to her?"

Jack shook his head. "First of all, they are good friends. Secondly, she has nothing to do with that." Jack pinned her with an angry glare. "It sounds to me that you're a little jealous. That maybe someone else is infringing on your turf."

Kira's heart sped up. She felt a bead of sweat run down the back of her neck. "I'm not sure who you are referring to, but I know it's not me. Remmy can see whomever she wants. It has nothing to do with me."

Kira looked up from her glass of wine to see the object of their conversation strolling down the hallway toward them. Remmy was a vision of beauty to Kira and her mouth went dry. Downing the remainder of her wine, Kira's inner voice spoke aloud without meaning to. "Wow, she's beautiful."

Knowing she hadn't meant to say the words aloud, Jack looked stunned. "Kira..."

Kira looked back at him with eyes glazed over as if she were about to cry. "It could never..." Turning her back to the approaching woman, Kira needed time to compose herself.

A parade of emotions crossed Jack's face As Remmy approached him and Kira. "Excuse me, I need to go find Taylor." He walked away.

Remmy cleared her throat. "I'm glad you could make it. Would you like a tour?"

Finally getting herself together, she turned. Once again, Kira's breath caught in her throat. "Yes, I...I'm honored to have been invited. I would love the tour." Kira refocused herself. "I'd like to get the feeling for where everything is and also a look at your security system."

Remmy sighed. "Tell me, do you ever stop working?" Holding up her hand, she added, "No, don't answer that. Why don't we start in the warehouse and work our way back here?"

Kira followed behind her. Once they were alone, she answered Remmy. "No, I never stop working, especially when I have a case that's at a standstill."

Remmy leaned back against a tall stack of two-by-fours, resting her elbows on them "Are you busy tomorrow night? I have this dinner thing I have to go to and well, I...ah...would you like to go with me?"

Kira had let her mind wander, noticing the cameras in the corners of the warehouse. She was snapped back when what Remmy had asked sank in. "Remmy, uh...I'm sorry but I can't, for a number of reasons. The biggest one being I'm not...well, as I said before, I'm not gay. Besides wouldn't you be taking Jules, seeing as she's your girlfriend?"

Remmy laughed. "Ah, no...Jules is not my girlfriend. We're only friends and that is all there will ever be. I kind of have my eyes on someone else." Remmy's face turned beet red.

Kira's heart beat out of her chest. Had she heard her right? Was it she that Remmy had her sights on? Why would this woman not take no for an answer? "Ah, well, I just thought the two of you made a good couple is all. I'm sorry if I spoke out of turn."

They walked into the larger of the two conference rooms. Kira ran her fingers along its length. "This is a very nice table."

Kira was embarrassed and hoped Remmy would drop the issue. Taking in the craftsmanship of the décor, it struck home that she would never be able to afford something this nice. On her salary, Kira would be lucky if she could afford the plant in the corner of the room, let alone the ornate furniture and paintings. Kira sighed. That was another reason…she could never afford to care for Remmy in this manner.

"Okay, how about friends? We could catch a movie or have coffee once in a while. Nothing special, just talking and friendship is all."

Pointing around the room they now stood in, Remmy sighed. "This is the kitchen; I wanted people to feel as if they were at home here."

Kira liked the kitchen, noticing it had all the amenities of home. She had to put a stop to this right now though. She couldn't chance Remmy saying the wrong thing in front of the wrong person. "Remmy, I'm truly sorry, but I don't have time to devote to friendship with anyone. Besides I have way too many cases right now, yours still being one of them. So as I said, I'm sorry, but I don't have the resources to devote the time and energy for friendship."

"I'm sorry, I seem to embarrass myself a lot lately. Thank you for being honest with me. Honesty means everything to me. I'm just glad you didn't pawn me off to someone else."

They walked into Remmy's office. Kira stood in the doorway, taking in the office in awe. She ignored Remmy's ramblings, hoping she would let it drop.

Remmy turned around in the middle of the office. "Last but not least, my office. Do you like it?"

Kira looked around, noticing the camera in the corner. None of the other offices had one, only hers. "It's exquisite. I'm glad you have a camera in here. Your security looks good. I do need to get going though. I'll call you when I have something more."

"Well, you seem to be in a hurry to leave, hopefully you'll solve this soon. That way my case will be closed for you and I'll be out of your hair. I'm sure you can find your way back out."

Sensing Remmy's embarrassment, Kira left as fast as she could. "Yes, thank you. Have a good evening."

Tears threatened to fall as Remmy turned to the windows. "You too, Kira, you too..."

†

Colin had found Ronald's truck in the parking lot. Taylor felt the hood, finding it cool. "Colin, have you seen him in there?"

Colin shook his head. "There are so many people wandering around, he could've snuck in at any time."

The hairs on the back of Taylor's neck stood up. "I know Remmy told him not to come. I don't like this one bit, him being here and sneakin' around."

†

A dark figure stirred in the shadows of the trees outside the windows of the office of the owner of Garrick Construction. When he saw figures entering the office, the evil eyes looked through binoculars to see who they were. He watched as the two women stood in *her* office, talking.

From the expression of the woman who now looked out upon the trees, he could tell their conversation wasn't going well. To him it seemed she was about to cry. This startled him. "What? Why is she crying? Dykes don't cry. They have nothing to cry about. They deserve what they get. That bitch is going to get hers. She'll never see it coming."

He continued his ranting as the taller woman left the office. A few moments later, he noticed the same woman

131

rapidly leave the building. "I could follow her and run her off the road, but it's not that dyke I want to teach a lesson to. It seems to me you have two girlfriends. I'm shocked that you're such a whore. I thought you were a one-woman little dyke."

His binoculars once again trained on his primary object standing within her office, he swore vengeance. "You really should be wary of the coffee you drink, bitch, you never know when it will slow you down enough for you to lose your edge. Once you let down your guard…the minute you do, I'll be there, ready to pounce on you. When I do, all of this will be mine. I'll make sure of it."

Chapter Seven

Remmy really didn't want to go. Vacationing was something other people did. She had no idea how she'd let herself be talked into this situation and tried valiantly to get out of it. In the week following the party, the company had quoted twenty new jobs, eighteen of them already accepted by the clients. She was going to visit the remaining two later in the day herself since she had cut Ronald out of most of the ongoing business. She used him as an errand boy and nothing more, monitoring every step he made within the company.

She wanted to fire her cousin and was trying to come up with the best way possible to do it. For the time being, though, ignoring him seemed to be working. He occasionally would storm into her office and throw a temper-tantrum because he was out of the loop on most things.

Remmy sat on her back deck, sipping coffee and talking to the rising sun. "I have to admit things are going great. The company's growing and we have more business than we can handle. All the people working for me pull their weight and know their trades. Damn, maybe Jack and Dad are right. I can leave for a week or two without the company falling apart. Mack and Stephanie can handle any issues that would arise, so that's not a concern."

What did bother Remmy was the previous evening. Jules had stopped by after meeting with a client. She had readily agreed with the other two that Remmy needed some time off, that she did indeed look exhausted.

Shit, I do have to admit I'm bone-weary lately and not feeling up to par. She did not like others seeing her under the weather, so she told Jules she had several proposals to finish for clients she was seeing the next day. Remmy hoped she would take the message that she wanted to be alone. Jules did understand, wishing her good night only after making her promise to take the next two weeks off.

She poured the last of the coffee from the carafe and sat it back on the patio table. She ran her fingers over the pewter emblem attached to the carafe, thinking how she loved it now as much as she had when Haley gave it to her for Christmas.

"Oh, baby…" Remmy knew what Haley had gone through in order to walk into the store and buy it for her. A devoted Red Sox fan buying anything Yankees was a sin in Haley's mind, especially when the owner of the store was her best friend and a Sox fan as well. Haley finally admitted she'd felt dirty and soiled buying it, but she had bucked up and done it anyway.

It was one of the items that Remmy treasured most in her life. Thinking of Haley always brought a smile to her face. Knowing what her lover had gone through, the razzing Haley had taken for weeks from her friend, made Remmy's heart swell with love for her lost lover.

Slowly, she sipped the hot coffee, watching the steam from the cup float into the chilly morning air.

Remmy spoke aloud to the dead woman who would forever own a piece of her soul. "God, Haley, I miss you. I know in my mind I have to move on. I've tried but it's just not working out. The woman I'm interested in...well, she's not gay."

Remmy loved mornings like this when there was a chill in the air and she sat enjoying a good cup of coffee. It was a good time to think and contemplate things in her life. She couldn't come up with a good enough reason not to go with Jack. Besides, he'd already made the reservations. Who knew, maybe he was right. A miracle might occur and she would meet someone new to take her mind off Kira.

Laying her head back on the chair, Remmy closed her eyes for a moment. "Besides, I'm tired all the time lately. I need to recharge my batteries. Oh, God, Haley, this is so hard. I wish you could somehow tell me what to do, tell me that everything is going to work out." Remmy let her mind drift.

Her cell phone took the moment of silence as an opportunity to ring, startling Remmy from her daydreaming. Looking at the caller ID, she laughed, silently thanking Haley. She opened the phone. "Hello, Kira. What can I do for you? Do you have any news?"

"I'm sorry, but no, no additional news. I was just speaking with Colin and he said you were going on vacation. I just wanted to uh...to uh confirm when you would be coming back."

"I'll be gone for a little over a week." She noticed that Kira seemed a little tentative when asking her how long she would be gone.

"That's good. You need some time away. So, where are you going?"

Remmy found Kira's line of questioning bizarre. It delved into the personal area, which was totally unlike her. "I'm not sure. Jack made all the arrangements; he told me to just be ready in the morning for the airport."

"Okay, well, have a good time and I'll touch base with you when you get back."

"I will, have a good day." Just as she was disconnecting, it rang again; it was Jack. "No I haven't changed my mind. I'll go with you, and yes, I'm all packed. I just have to go meet with Colin this morning. Then I need to finish up some stuff in the office."

"I…um…I'm shocked. I'm glad though that you didn't change your mind. I had even prepared a speech to try to change your mind. Oh well. Our flight out is at seven in the morning."

Finishing off the last of her coffee, Remmy set the cup back down. "Jules is taking us to the airport, so I'll see you in the morning."

✝

Colin was more than stunned when Remmy called him three days earlier to tell him she was thinking of taking a vacation. He tried to remember the last time Remmy had taken any time off and couldn't, because it had been that long. He had no problem covering for her and was more than willing to plunk his behind in the office for a spell.

They currently had so many jobs going that he was running from one end of the state to the other almost on a daily basis. When Remmy came back from being injured, he'd planned to talk to her. He'd wanted to hire another project manager to absorb his overflow, but had not had the chance as of yet. There was no way he could devote the appropriate amount of time to each one.

He met Remmy at a jewelry shop they were to start rebuilding within the next week the morning before she was to leave on vacation. He watched as her truck pulled up and she climbed out. He grew concerned when she closed the door then leaned against it.

He rushed to her, concerned she was ill. "Remmy, what's wrong?"

She straightened up. "Nothing's wrong, just a little dizzy. Why does something always have to be wrong? I've been busy thinking of all the things I need to get done. My mind is on business."

Her mood swings in the last couple of weeks were starting to concern him. He hoped this vacation would help her rid herself of what bothered her. He looked at her, clearly not buying her story, but let it drop. "Okay, if you say so. Did you call Lee already?"

†

Remmy and Colin walked into the remnants of what used to be a shop filled with beautiful pieces of handmade jewelry. It had been reduced to rubble several weeks before by fire. Lee Tompkins and her wife, RJ Hood, were old friends of Haley's. Remmy had lost touch with them when Haley passed away.

Lee owned the store, which contained her work and that of her friend, Korie. RJ was a photographer for a local television station. Remmy had loved Lee's jewelry. When she heard the news story about the fire, her heart sank for the two women. Taking a chance, she called Lee and offered her services to rebuild the store at cost.

Pulling open the charred door, Remmy sucked in her breath at the remains of what had once been a thriving business. "Yeah, I talked to Lee yesterday, when I got the key from her. She knows you'll be taking the lead on this one. God, this sucks!" Remmy felt a hand on her left shoulder, bringing her back from the destruction.

"Yeah, it does, but hey, I get a new look out of it. RJ and I were talking about remodeling next year. Now I guess we get the full deal, just a little early." Lee hugged Remmy, kissing her on the cheek.

Turning to Colin, Lee studied the man. "I still can't believe you got her to take a vacation. I'm glad, very glad indeed. When was the last time you took one?"

Remmy blushed. "It's been a while."

Colin laughed. "I think it was like six years ago when you last took a day off. I remember you and Haley going to P-town in June six years ago."

Remmy stiffened at the mention of Haley's name and Lee slapped Colin on the bicep. She did her best to change the subject. "So, you like my rubble? I think it's kind of on the gothic side. I, however, don't do gothic. When are you going to get started?"

Stepping back out into the daylight, Remmy motioned to her truck. "Let's spread out the plans and take a look at everything. Colin's crew will be here at six Monday morning to start cleaning out the debris. The waste company will drop off the dumpster tonight on their last run of the day."

Remmy spread out the prints on the hood of her truck. Over the next two hours, they went over every detail from start to hand over that would occur in five weeks. Lee left to meet her father for lunch and Colin wanted one last look inside. Throwing the rolled up prints into her truck, Remmy watched RJ pull up beside her and get out of her car. Coming around her Mustang, RJ held out her hands to Remmy and pulled her into a hug. Remmy let the woman hug her tightly. Seeing RJ always caused Remmy to smile. "RJ B. Hood, am I ever going to find out what the B stands for?" It had become a joke between them years ago when they first met. Remmy knew Haley had known, but had taken it to the grave with her.

"Nope, sorry. Remember, it's a family secret. Now, for more important things, thanks for coming to our rescue. Lee took this damn hard, but knowing she can rebuild it made a world of difference. In the good news department, Kira did look into the fire, just to double check, and she confirmed it was an accident. We tried to tell her Lee's stalker had been dealt with a couple of years ago, but she insisted."

Smiling, Remmy knew what she meant. Haley had made a phone call and the stalker was never heard from again. They had soon afterwards found out that the person Haley called worked for Lee's father.

"How's Lee's father doing these days? Is his shop still rocking like it was?" *How the hell does she know Kira?* In a rush, she added, "How do you know Kira?"

"And then some. He has bike orders backed up for at least a fourteen-month wait." RJ smirked when Remmy asked about Kira. "She saved my life when I got burned, and I can tell she's made quite impression on you as well."

"Yeah, you could say that." Remmy's heart skipped a beat, thinking of watching the state trooper at work. *I'll bet she was sexy as hell.*

"So, I hear you're going on vacation. Good for you."

"I know…I know, I need to get on with my life." Remmy's body shook slightly; she attributed it to being so tired.

RJ put her arm around Remmy's waist. "Yes, you do. Take it from me; don't wallow in your grief. She wouldn't want you to. Haley would've been kicking your ass if she found you feeling sorry for yourself. I still have the boot print on my ass after all these years." RJ laughed as she squeezed Remmy.

"Yeah, I know. That is why I'm trying. I want her to be proud of me. Okay, enough of this mushy crap. I need to get going. Tell Brett, Dylan, and Jac I said hello. We'll all get together when I get back to catch up. It's been far too long and we shouldn't let it happen again." Even kissing the butch woman on the cheek didn't cause Remmy to flinch when her lips touched the scarred flesh.

"Will do."

Remmy couldn't remember the scar ever bothering her. It was part of who RJ was; it helped to make up her personality. It had taken Remmy three months to get the story out of Haley as to what happened to her friend to cause such scarring on her face, shoulder, and arm.

RJ had been filming a major pile-up on the thruway in a snowstorm when the gas tanker that had jackknifed exploded. The photographer being the daredevil she was, had gotten too close and suffered the consequences with severe burns to the right side of her upper body. Luckily, the state trooper at the scene had acted quickly and thrown her into a snow bank to stop the flames and burning.

The stoic photographer had regaled them for days with the story of the heroic trooper. Haley told her to shut her trap and ask the trooper out on a date. Blushing, RJ admitted that she had asked the Amazon trooper, with the most devastating blue eyes she'd ever seen, and the woman had turned her down, stating she wasn't gay. They all laughed at her then because RJ always claimed there was no woman, straight or gay, who could say no to her charms.

Remmy smiled, remembering the teasing RJ had received as a result, and now, after all this time, she knew who the trooper had been. It touched her that it had been Kira. "Who knows, maybe I'll find the perfect woman to spend the next twenty years with." She climbed into her truck and started the engine.

"Are you sure you're okay? You seem to be a bit shaky. Hey, you never know. She might just be around the next corner. Have a good time and please *do* try to get into trouble." Laughing, RJ closed Remmy's door, sending her on her way.

✝

Remmy fumed as they exited the small twin-engine plane. It was bad enough that she had let them talk her into taking time off and that she was feeling a little off her game. Once they were on the chartered plane, Jack told her where they were going and that it was Women's Week. The place was going to be overrun with a couple thousand lesbians. A great number of them would be looking to hook up, and most vying to meet their favorite authors at the readings and signings.

Taking her bag from the attendant, she stomped off in search of a taxi, not caring if Jack was following or not. "Yeah, and I fell for it hook, line, and sinker." She yelled over her shoulder to Jack.

Motioning for a taxi, she wasn't surprised when a tall handsome butch got out of the driver's door. Muttering under her breath, Remmy handed the woman her bag. *Color me fucking surprised.*

She turned to find Jack behind her, looking everywhere but at her. Going to P-town didn't upset her; it was that the place would be packed wall-to-wall with women looking for only one thing. She had spent the entire flight screaming at the man for *forgetting* to tell her that one little detail.

After giving the driver the name of the hotel, Jack climbed in beside her. "I said I was sorry. You want me to slit my wrists to prove it?"

He sounded so pitiful she almost forgot her anger. Then she saw several very good-looking butches sitting at a café table watching all the femmes walking by and her anger flared once more. "I can't fucking believe you, Jack. You suckered me into coming here, knowing..." She took a calming breath. "Knowing there would be so many women here."

Remmy saw the cab driver eye them suspiciously in the rear-view mirror. When the driver laughed, instinct told her the woman was laughing at them. Remmy was sure they sounded like an old married couple.

Looking in the mirror again Remmy saw the woman smile a broad grin. Speaking to the driver. Remmy laughed as well. "I'm sure you have a friend like him too."

The woman behind the wheel laughed more and shook her head. "Yes."

"Come on, Remmy, you needed a break from work. There's no better place than where there are lots and lots of sexy butch women, just dying to fawn over your every whim." He pushed his shoulder against her, trying to get her to relax.

She grinned. He was right. "So, tell me then. Why are you here?"

"Why, to keep an eye on you of course, to make sure you have fun. To see if you possibly meet the butch of your fantasies." He wiggled his eyebrows.

"Yeah, right. You'd take any chance you could to look at the young men. Am I wrong? So tell me, what does Patrick have to say about you coming here alone?" Jack would behave, but Remmy loved to tease him anyhow.

"Ah, come on, I'm going to be good. Patrick knows I love him. It doesn't hurt to have a little eye candy though, does it?" He opened the door as they pulled up in front of the hotel.

After depositing their bags on the sidewalk, the driver handed Remmy a business card as she took her payment. Remmy looked at the card, then at the woman, who smiled in return. As the driver turned to walk away, she mouthed *call me* to Remmy.

Jack stood with his mouth hanging open as the woman hit on Remmy. "See…"

Remmy cut him off. "Shut up! Let's get our rooms. Then go in search of dinner. I'm starving. Maybe tomorrow we can visit a bookstore or two to see who all is here."

"Cool, maybe you can make a few contacts and get a few of those short stories you write published. That would be like way cool, you being an author." Jack put his hand over his mouth, but the giggles escaped anyhow.

Remmy turned to study him a moment. "Please do not giggle. If you do, I will be forced to slap you." She contemplated his words, though. "Yeah, I guess it would be kind of cool, huh."

Approaching the check-in desk, Jack quietly agreed. "It would be way cool. Imagine the women you'd attract then."

Remmy's only acknowledgement that she had heard Jack was the glare he received. The look was all that was needed. The subject was dropped as they checked in.

✝

The next day was a whirlwind. Jack had inquired at the front desk if they had a list of all the activities going on that week, which of course they did.

Remmy thanked him for the kind gesture by paying for breakfast. The meal turned out to be the most relaxing thing they did all day. She wanted to make sure she hit every shop that had something going on at it.

In the process, she did indeed make several contacts, one being a well-known publisher and author who told Remmy to email her manuscripts to her and she would gladly look at them.

Remmy ended up buying so many items that Jack volunteered to find the post office. He would ship them home while she went in search of a nice bar to get a couple of drinks at later that evening. It had been so long since Remmy had been in Provincetown, that she was sure most of the places she and Haley had visited were either gone or changed.

Much to her surprise, one of the bars she knew was still open and exactly as she remembered. It had become one of the most popular in town, because they had fabulous food and they never skimped on their drinks.

Jack shared Remmy's love for sitting at the bar and being able to survey the whole establishment from one spot.

He had been in this one many times over the years, several times with Remmy and Haley. The best feature in the bar was the mirror. You could sit on your stool, look in the mirror, and no one realized you were watching them.

They walked in a little after seven that evening and had their choice of several empty tables or seats at the bar. They chose the latter, taking the two empty spots on the corner of the L-shaped bar. It wasn't very crowded yet, making it still possible to hear one another. Eyeing the bottle of Patron on the top shelf, Remmy knew exactly what she was ordering for them.

Remmy didn't have to motion for the bartender; she'd been watching the two since they arrived. She paid close attention to Remmy, almost ignoring Jack. When she spoke, she came close to purring, just as Mr. Bubbles did when his tummy was rubbed. "What's your pleasure?"

Remmy looked her over; the woman was not really her type. She was too short, but most of all too lanky, lacking in the brawn and muscle Remmy loved on women. "Two Patrons and Molson's please."

After handing over the money, the two life-long friends picked up the shot glasses and toasted.

"To a lifetime of friendship..." Remmy said.

Jack's eyes twinkled. "To you getting laid...cheers."

Remmy laughed. "Yes, to that too, then." She held up two fingers to the bartender. Two more shots were placed in front of her. She then repeated the same motion two more times, each time giving the girl a ten-dollar tip, which she readily accepted and stayed at their disposal. After the four shots and three beers each, neither could remember why Remmy had been so mad the day before.

Jack normally didn't drink tequila. It went right to his head, making him even more open-lipped to speak his mind.

"I really, really think you should just find some hot butch and let her fuck your brains out." Jack slammed the shot glass on the bar. "There, that's what I think. Damn, woman, you got me drunk." He laughed as Remmy shook her head, which made Jack almost fall off the stool as he tried to keep up with her head moving from side to side.

Remmy, on the other hand, only had a nice buzz going, not totally ripped as Jack apparently was becoming. Tequila had always been her choice of alcohol, with beer coming in second. "You know what, Jack, it's good to be able to just sit here drinking with my best friend without a care in the world. Let's just enjoy it for a little longer before the real world comes crashing back in. What do you say, huh?"

When Jack didn't answer her back, she turned to find him staring into the mirror with a horrified look on his face. The beer she had been lifting to her lips dropped from her hand, causing the bartender to grab for it before it hit the bar top.

Neither could believe what their eyes beheld. Remmy felt her chest grow heavy and she had trouble breathing. Her hands clasping the edge of the bar to keep from falling off the stool, Remmy couldn't tear her gaze away from the two women in the mirror.

Jack started to stand. "I'm going over there and give that fucking bitch a piece of my mind!"

Remmy was pushing him back in his seat as the bartender questioned them.

"Everything all right here? Is someone bothering you?" The bartender eyed them suspiciously.

Remmy smiled at the smaller woman behind the bar. "Everything's good. We're not really ready for another round. Could you give us a few minutes?"

Even so, the bartender opened a fresh beer and placed it in front of Remmy.

Lowering her gaze to the beer that now sat in front of her, Remmy threw her a ten. "Thanks."

Draining half the beer in one gulp, Remmy almost choked on it when she looked back in the mirror at the sight before their eyes. "Well, now at least I know. I guess there was no way I could compete with that. If I knew she was into blondes, I guess I could have dyed my hair." She pointed her bottle to the blonde's reflection in the mirror.

Remmy could tell Jack was furious. "Remmy, you are so much better than either of them. The bimbo doesn't hold a candle you. As for the bitch with her, I knew she was lying. I just knew it!" He made as if to stand again.

Once again, Remmy stopped him. "Jack, don't make a scene. Please, for me, just let it go. Obviously, she likes someone who is beautiful, blonde, fluffy, and quite young."

"Remmy, you are all of those...well, except the blonde, and I *do not* think you would look good as a blonde. Or fluffy...you have more brains in your little toe than that bubble does in her whole body. Let me go talk to Mz. Bitch-Butch and get the dirt." His eyes begged her.

"No, I don't want you to do any such thing. I am going to go for a walk then back to my room." She stood from the stool.

"I'll go with you then." He downed the last of his beer, his eyes never leaving the couple's reflection.

Remmy hugged him and patted him on the shoulder. "Thanks, my friend, but no. I want to be alone right now. Maybe tomorrow, tonight I just want to be alone."

As the bouncer opened the door for her to leave, Remmy looked at the couple sitting at the table in the corner. They made the picture-perfect couple. Kira and the beautiful

147

woman she had her arm wrapped around seemed not to notice the attention they had drawn. Remmy did nothing to stop the tears from flowing as she walked back to the hotel, deciding to leave for home that evening.

She called the number on the card the taxi driver had given her and requested she drive her to the nearest car rental business. Once there, Remmy rented a car and asked directions on how to get to the airport in Boston.

✝

Remmy was not through the door more than a minute when Jack jumped from the bar stool and strode across the floor toward the table where Kira and the blonde sat having their personal little party. The pair never noticed him until he placed his hands on their table, leaning over so his face was level with Kira's.

Kira's body stiffened upon seeing the man.

"Hello Trooper or Detective or Agent or whatever the fuck you call yourself. I, however, call you scum. How dare you lie to Remmy! Not gay? Yeah right! I knew you were a dyke the second I saw your pathetic face. I didn't believe you for a second. Remmy, on the other hand, did. You should have just told her she wasn't your type. That you liked the blonde slut kind."

Jack was on a roll then. Even seeing the deadly look in Kira's eyes and the stiffening of her body didn't stop him. "I thought you had more balls than to do something like this. You have no idea what it has taken for her to start living again after losing Haley. You might as well as have taken a knife just now and cut her heart out."

Kira jumped from the table, knocking the blonde from her chair. "Is she here? Where is she?" She had a panicked look upon her face.

Jack straightened, standing toe-to-toe with her. "No, she's gone. Remmy didn't want to come here. She thought we were all trying to make her forget about Haley, but we're only trying to help her move on with her life. Now, you've set her back who knows how far."

Kira moved to go around him. "I have to find her. I have to explain."

Jack put a hand on her chest, stopping her dead. "No, you're the last person Remmy wants to see. You're not wanted, especially after lying to her. Lying is one thing she tolerates from no one. I still can't believe you would do something like this to her. I truly hoped you were a good person, not a liar and a snake."

"Jack, let's talk outside." Kira motioned to the door. The other woman started to follow them, but Kira waved her off.

He followed Kira to the sidewalk, the good drunk he had going long since evaporated. "So tell me, oh mighty one, what do you have to say that would make this any better?"

Kira sighed, running her fingers through her hair. "Well, this night has gone straight to hell, hasn't it?"

"Yeah, you thought you were gonna get laid tonight, now the shit's hit the fan."

"You don't understand, Jack. No one at home can know I'm gay. I can't take the chance. It doesn't matter that I could picture a future with Remmy. That I could...love..." She faltered.

Clearing her throat, she continued. "It doesn't matter. It can't matter. I might lose Bella if the wrong person found out. They could take away my custody of her by saying I was unfit to raise her and I'm all she has. I won't take that chance. I would die before I lost her." Kira was begging him.

Jack shook his head in disgust. "Bullshit! That's a cop out. This is the twenty-first century. They won't take her away from you, especially if you're the only family she has. You just don't have the balls to try. God, I really thought you were better than this. Good-bye, Kira, have a nice life." Jack walked back to the hotel, muttering the whole way. He still wanted to slap Kira silly for her foolishness.

He knocked on Remmy's door but heard no response. Thinking she must still be out cooling off, he retired to his room next door. He sat on the bed and found a note on the floor addressed to him. "What? What? Why the hell would she have left? How the hell would she have left?" He then remembered the cab driver. "Ah, that's how."

He dialed Remmy's cell number. "Come on, pick up, pick up." Finally, on the third ring, it went to voice mail. "Remmy, call me, please, I'm worried about you."

†

As Remmy drove, she heard her phone ring the pirate movie theme which meant Jack was calling. She wanted to talk to no one at that moment, so she let it go to voice mail. Driving through the night alone. Unfortunately it gave her plenty of time to think. And. of course, hold conversations with herself, which she found lately she was doing quite a bit.

"Why did she lie? I don't understand it. Haley would never have hidden who she was. You were proud of yourself and of us and made sure everyone knew it. God, Haley, I always took for granted you were going to be here, that nothing would ever happen to you. Why does she hide who she is? It doesn't matter. It probably wouldn't have worked out anyway." Driving on, she listed as many reasons why as she could.

✝

When Remmy called asking Taylor to pick her up at the airport the next morning, he didn't question her at the time. Seeing her in person, looking like something the cat threw up, he could no longer bite his tongue. He waited until they were on the road before questioning her. Taylor already knew what happened to send her running home. After receiving her call, he in turn called Jack, who willingly spilled his guts on what had taken place.

"Sweetie, you know I ain't one for stickin' my nose in, but I think I will on this one. What's going on? Why did you come back early, did something happen?"

She sighed. "Just not feeling well, Daddy, and thought I would come home."

"Maybe you just want to see a certain someone. You know…in order to see how the case is going." He pried, wanting to see if she would tell him what happened. He respected her privacy but was worried about her heart.

Sighing, she closed her eyes, leaning her tired head against the door window. "Daddy, don't try to play matchmaker. Kira isn't my type, and it's a big mistake to even think so for a second. It seems scruples have taken a holiday."

He patted her thigh. "Honey, we have always been close, you've always told me everything. I know you're lyin' to me, but I'm going to drop it for now."

"Daddy…"

He cut her off. "No, honey, don't bother denyin' it. Now get some sleep on the way home."

After depositing his daughter at her home and returning to his own, Taylor called the subject of their conversation on her cell phone. He was furious with both women, at Kira for lying and not taking a chance, and at Remmy for running and not giving Kira a chance to explain and then fight for her. Kira told him to stop by her house the next afternoon and that she'd like to talk with him as well.

While sipping the hot coffee the next afternoon, Taylor listened as Kira explained how she had come to have custody of Annabella and why no one must know her secret. She tried to keep the worry from showing but she failed.

"After they left the bar, I decided to drive home last night. Taylor, I feel physically sick because of what happened. I ran because I didn't want to run into either of them. I had no idea Remmy had already left."

Setting the cup on the kitchen table, he contemplated all she had told him, some of which he already knew from the conversation with Jack. "Tell me, Kira, which bothers you the most: someone finding out you're gay or Remmy learning you lied to her? I have half a mind to spank the both of you."

Neither of them heard the front door open and close or the young girl come into the kitchen. "Ooh, can I watch?" Kissing her aunt on the cheek, Bella turned to the older man. "What did Aunt Kira do now? Hi, I'm Bella."

Taylor liked the young girl immediately. She was a younger version of Kira. Right down to the perfect blue eyes. "Wow, if I didn't know she was your niece, I would have thought she was your daughter. It's nice to meet you, young lady, I'm Taylor Garrick, Remmy's father."

"I remember hearing the name mentioned when Uncle Manny and Uncle Paul had stopped by a couple of weeks ago. I also remember the look in your eyes when they mentioned Remmy's name. Ah. I see, now it's all falling into place. Can I get either of you more coffee? Okay, then, I'm going to my bedroom to do my homework."

✝

A short time later, as Taylor was leaving, Kira promised him she would call Remmy and try to talk to her. Exchanging her coffee for a beer, she picked up her cell phone and walked out to the patio. When Remmy didn't pick up, Kira left her a voice message. "Remmy, I need to talk to you, please. I need to explain. I guess…uh…I guess I'll try you later."

Drinking her beer while watching the sunset, she wondered what exactly she would say to Remmy when she was able to speak with her. An hour later, her cell phone rang. However, it was Jack, not Remmy, calling. She answered, curious as to why he was calling her.

"Hello, Jack, what can I do for you?" When had her life become so complicated, that everyone wanted to run it for her?

"Kira, I want you to talk to Remmy. Tell her what you told me. Make her understand. I'm really worried because she won't return my calls."

Closing her eyes, Kira rested her head on the patio chair. "What is it with everyone? It seems lately everyone is trying to run my life. Jack, I don't see where it would do any good. I tried to call but she didn't pick up nor has she returned my call."

"Then stop by the office. Use any excuse to see her. Please, Kira, go talk to Remmy. She'll just curl back into herself if she's allowed to." She could hear Jack's desperation.

"Okay, if I don't hear from her, I'll go see her tomorrow afternoon. She is lucky to have such a good friend as you. You don't know men named Paul or Manny, do you? They seem to have the same pushiness as you do." Kira laughed. She hung up and went in search of Bella to make sure she had her homework finished.

✝

When Kira didn't hear back from Remmy by mid-day the following day, she drove to Remmy's office to see if she was there so she could talk to her. Upon her arrival at Mack's desk, Kira heard shouting coming through Remmy's open office door.

Mack stood to greet Kira. "Hello, may I help you?"

Kira held out her hand in greeting.

Mack took the offered hand, never breaking eye contact. Kira found herself on the receiving end of a *fuck-off and die* glare the entire time they shook hands.

Kira didn't like this woman. Not knowing why her hackles were up or why the other woman disliked her, she continued. "Investigator Kira Kirpatrick, I am here to see Ms. Garrick."

"I'll see if she's in." Mack sneered at the investigator. Not only was Remmy in, but her raised voice could be heard. Picking up the phone, Mack sat back down behind her desk.

Kira wanted to scream at her, but she held back. "Fine…" Then it dawned on her what she felt. It was jealousy, pure and simple. It was apparent to her this woman was very protective of Remmy, and she'd observed at the party how Mack looked at her. Mack had looked like she wanted to have Remmy as a midnight snack. Kira paced while waiting to see if she would be allowed into the office.

✝

Remmy's morning upon arriving at work had been one moment of hell after another. Colin called her at six that morning to inform her that the cabinets had never showed up the previous day for the gift shop project. They only had three more days to finish the job before the grand opening was to take place. With this setback, Remmy wasn't sure they were going to finish on time.

To make matters worse, Ronald was waiting for her to arrive at the office that morning. He wanted to know why he wasn't informed she had left on vacation and why he wasn't in charge while she was gone. He then asked why she was back so early.

Telling him it was none of his business why she was back early as well as that she would never leave him in charge only fueled his anger. The two spent the next hour screaming at each other and quite possibly would still have been at it if Jack had not called her on her direct office line and interrupted the fight.

Jack told Remmy he had talked the previous day with Kira. Her anger shot through the roof, causing everyone within earshot at the time, except Mack, to physically leave the building for a long lunch.

He had listened to her scream at him for over thirty minutes. When she finally wound down, his chance came and he jumped right in. "Damn it, Remmy, you need to talk to her. You need to understand a few things before you judge her. Maybe the two of you can be friends. I think she could use one and it wouldn't hurt you either. You never know where friendship can lead in the future."

"Jack, how could you call her? You had no right. I already know where she stands, so I'm sure nothing I say will change that fact." Her intercom buzzed. "God, now what? I have to go, Jack, all hell is breaking loose here. I'll talk to you later about this."

Pushing the talk button, she never expected to hear the next words. "Remmy, there is a Ms. Kirpatrick here to see you." She cringed, knowing that not being addressed by her appropriate title, Kira would think Mack was dissing her and she'd be correct in thinking just that.

If Remmy could've seen through the wall, she would have laughed at the sight.

Kira stopped pacing upon hearing Mack call Remmy's office. She then stood in front of the other woman, glaring down at her as Mack returned the angry look with a scowl of her own. If others had been watching, they would have described it as two dogs marking their territories.

Releasing the talk button, Remmy sat in her chair, feeling all the air go out of her chest. Her headache now bordered on a migraine. Sitting back, she spun around and gazed out the windows at the trees. She was even more exhausted than when she'd left several days before for vacation. The dizziness and shaking had even returned that morning. "Maybe I should go to the doctor. Maybe I have a bug or something."

Turning back around to her desk, she made the decision; she didn't want to see Kira. She would see her on her own terms all in due time. As she reached to pick up the phone, a new wave of dizziness with nausea mixed in hit her. "Shit…not now."

Remmy picked up the phone, dialing Mack's extension, not wanting to talk over the intercom. "Please tell her I am on my way out and that I do not have time right now, unless it is an emergency related to the case. Please have her make an appointment if it's not."

†

Kira knew she could've demanded to see Remmy, but didn't want to sound as if she were desperate to see her. It would have looked bad, especially since she had nothing new to report in regards to the ongoing investigation. Instead she had been forced to make *an appointment* to see Remmy in two days.

Starting her truck, Kira called Paul in hopes of getting sympathy from him. Instead, she received the same verbal assault she'd received from both Taylor and Jack. Resigning herself to the idea that she might have to grovel to the woman when she saw her in two days' time, she headed home.

Kira was supposed to still be on vacation, so if she showed her face in her office, Penny would give her an earful. *When did my life spiral out of my control?* Smiling, she answered her own question. "When I met a spitfire named Remmington, that is when."

†

Remmy watched from the lobby as Kira pulled out of their parking lot onto the main road. She carried a set of blueprints in one hand and her laptop in the other. She intended to review the list of unfinished work, called a punch, for a coffee shop.

Without looking back, Remmy laid out the rest of her day for her assistant. "I have to go to the punch for the Java Junkie."

She saw Mack's eyes sparkle when she heard the name. "Oh, I love that coffee shop. I'm glad he's opening up one on this side of town. It's nice living next to one, but it will be nice to have one on this side of town."

"He said he might be opening a third and would let us know in six months, so put it on your calendar to touch base with him at that time. After the punch, I have to head over to Lee's place. I have the updated plans if Colin calls. I'll talk to you later." Remmy headed out to her appointments. Halfway to the coffee shop, another wave of dizziness swept over her, causing her to pull over. She really didn't feel well enough to conduct business and called Colin.

When she informed Colin she was going home, he became concerned. She was never sick enough to miss a business appointment. "Remmy, I think you should head straight for the doctor."

"Colin, if I don't feel better by the morning, I will. I just need you to come and get the revised plans for Lee's place, then go to the punch over at Java Junkie's. I called him and told him you'd be there later and he's fine with that. I'll leave the front door unlocked for you." She gripped the steering wheel tighter, feeling her strength draining from her.

"Okay, see you in a bit. I do want you to consider at least calling your doctor."

†

Pulling into her driveway, Remmy turned off the engine but didn't move. Hoping the panic she felt would abate, she rested her head on the steering wheel. Never before had she felt so tired. It actually was a chore for her to open the truck door and walk up the few steps to the house. The weather matched her mood, dark and gloomy. The black clouds that had set in several hours earlier turned day into night.

Unlocking and opening the front door, the first thing she noticed was that Mr. Bubbles didn't greet her. Only once had he not greeted her upon opening the door. That time was because he'd gotten himself stuck in the closet when the door closed on him. "Mr. Bubbles, here kitty, kitty... Okay, where are you, you little puff ball? I don't feel up to searching for you."

In the hallway, she felt a strong breeze coming down the hall. Realizing it could only be coming from the patio doors, she decided to cut through the dining room. She knew she didn't leave the patio door open that morning. Walking through the doorway, movement caught her eye. She brought her arm up in defense just as she saw a bat swinging toward her.

As the bat made contact with her body, from the kitchen she heard another voice. It was a voice she had known all her life. "Can't be..."

Her self-defense instincts kicked in, causing her to duck the next swing. Not knowing who this man attacking her was, she addressed the man in the kitchen, knowing full well that she was now in a fight for her life.

"You fucking bastard, get in here and have the balls to fight me yourself! Ronald, you're a fucking pussy!" More pissed off than afraid, she went on the attack. However, with her diminished strength, she didn't last long.

In the end, he was too big and too strong, easily beating her to the point of unconsciousness. Lingering on the edge of darkness, Remmy watched as a figure crouched over her. "Bastard…"

Chapter Eight

She hung on the edge of darkness and pain, listening to him regale her with his exploits. He had been the one, with help of the man who had just beat her senseless, who destroyed the video store. He was the one who had been sending her the *lovely* notes and the one who had rigged the light to fall.

Remmy's arm was broken, as well as several ribs. She tried to assess any other damage but was having trouble focusing, knowing she probably had a concussion as well. Colin would be there soon. Knowing she had to hang on a little longer, she tried to keep him talking. She had landed several blows to the other man, but they never slowed his assault for one second.

When the man broke his bat upon missing Remmy and hitting the doorway, he used his fists instead. By the time he was done, she lay in a crumpled bloody heap on the dining room floor. The final blow smashed her face into the edge of the table, causing her left eye to swell shut.

She coughed and tasted blood. "Why...make me understand...please, Ronald." She tried to inch her body slightly toward the table, but gave up from the pain.

Ronald's laughter was evil. That was the only way it could be described...pure evil.

"You pitiful dyke. Garrick Construction was meant to be mine, never yours. You never even realized I broke in a couple of weeks ago and put a little something in with your coffee grounds. You know, the precious coffee that no one else can stand. I added a little drug called Percocet. I know you've heard of it, it's what you took after your whore's death because of your injuries. I made sure to keep the amount I put in the coffee grounds down so as not to kill you. I knew it would make you vulnerable and ripe for the picking. No one would think twice finding it in your blood stream. They would just assume you are a junkie, addicted to the shit."

Ronald kicked her in the chest breaking another rib. "How could you humiliate me? This is a man's world. Women belong in the home, serving their husbands, on their hands and knees. You and your kind are an abomination. When we were growing up, you always said you wanted nothing to do with the company. So you can see how surprised I was when that bastard you call a father gave it to you."

Neither words, nor the venom in his voice, shocked Remmy. She'd expected no less of him. Through her life, she always found him to be an angry, loathsome man. Now she found him pitiful and pathetic as well.

The drugs in her system did nothing to dull the pain. It was so bad that possibly only death would take it away. She coughed against the Oriental rug, watching as it turned crimson. "Ronald, please...we're family...it doesn't have to be this way." She no longer had the strength to lift her head from the floor.

He crouched down next to her. The look upon his face distorted his features, to what she thought Satan himself must look like. Reaching out to grab a fistful of hair, he pulled her head up so their faces were closer.

His eyes blazed with pure hatred for all women, not just for her. "Your whore deserved what she got before she died. Did anyone ever tell you what the bad little boys did to her?"

Remmy's breath come in shorter gasps.

"Ah, so you do know. She deserved it. She was a pervert who needed to be taught a lesson and so do you. I am sure my friend here will be more than willing to teach you the same."

The man who had beaten her to within an inch of her life made kissing noises. She was in even more trouble than she first realized. Remembering Colin was on his way there, she sent a silent prayer that he would be in time.

She prayed that this was not how her life was to end.

Ronald saw the fear in her eyes and thought he'd won. "The company should have been mine when Jacob was killed in Iraq. Sign these papers right now, turning it over to me, and I'll take my friend and leave." He thrust papers in her face.

He pushed a pen between her fingers and held her hand over the paper for her. He watched as her hand started moving. Instead of signing, she wrote the words *fuck you* in big bold letters and dropped the pen.

Her actions sent Ronald over the edge. "You fucking bitch! Fine! I'll get the company when you die instead." He kicked her again in the chest then turned to the other man. "She's all yours."

He picked up the pen and stuffed it along with the papers in his briefcase. "Have fun with her and make sure to leave no traces behind when you depart." He left through the patio door and walked to the next street over, where his car was parked so as not to be seen near Remmy's house.

The other man lifted Remmy from the floor by the collar of her polo shirt and pulled her against his body. She had no strength left to cry out and simply let the tears fall when he bit into her neck and ripped her shirt open. "We're going to have a good time, my little pretty."

†

Traffic was lighter than usual and Colin arrived at Remmy's faster than he expected. He pulled into her driveway and decided to call the doctor if Remmy had not already done so. Putting his truck into park, he noticed the front door was standing wide open. He grew concerned and rapidly made his way toward it. Remmy would never just leave any exterior door or window open because of Mr. Bubbles.

Stepping through the doorway, Colin heard material ripping and a man's voice. Something was seriously wrong. "Remmy, where are you?"

Starting for the dining room, where he thought the sound came from, Colin called out again. "Remmy?"

Colin heard a loud crashing noise, followed by running footsteps heading toward the kitchen. Throwing open the door to the dining room, he saw a man racing through the kitchen and out the patio door. Tripping over something, he looked down to find a broken bat covered in blood.

Not far from the bat, he discovered a prone, unconscious figure lying in a crumpled heap. Dropping to his knees, he rolled the body over. Shocked speechless at finding Remmy bloodied and beaten, he let his survival instincts takeover. He carefully picked her up and ran to his truck as fast as he could without jostling her too badly. Throwing his truck into reverse, he snapped out of the shock, pulling his phone from his pocket.

Pushing Taylor's speed dial, he choked on the words as Remmy's father answered. "Taylor...Remmy's been hurt. Call Jack and meet me at the hospital."

†

Arriving only seconds after Colin, Taylor, and Jack watched as the emergency room attendants gently removed Remmy from the truck, laid her on a gurney, then rush her through the sliding glass doors.

Snapping on gloves, the doctor looked at all three men, and then at the gurney. "I know all four of you. I treated Remmy's wounds the last time she was brought in. What the hell happened this time?"

Taylor turned to Colin.

Tears welled up in Colin's eyes. "She didn't feel well so she went home. She told me to stop by and pick up some new plans. I got to the house and the front door was open. She'd never leave it open. I knew something was wrong."

He felt guilty for letting Remmy go home alone, knowing how sick she was. "When I went in, I saw a man running through the kitchen. Remmy was lying on the floor. I didn't want to wait for an ambulance, so I picked her up and brought her here."

The doctor stepped up to the gurney. "Please call 911 and return to her house. I'm sure they'll have questions for you."

The doctor turned to Taylor. "You're legally her next of kin, correct?"

Taylor stepped forward, his eyes never leaving his daughter. "He bit her chest and neck. Bastard. Yes, there are only the two of us."

The doctor picked up scissors from the tray the nurse had rolled over. "Please go with the nurse and fill out all of the paperwork. I need to examine her and you shouldn't be in here for that."

Jack looked at the doctor in disgust. He remembered him from before. They all had thought he had no manners then and from the looks of it, he still hadn't gained any.

Jack took Taylor's arm and led him out of the room, leaving the doctor to do his job. Maddie came to sit beside him in the waiting room. "I know it looks like a lot of forms but it's really not that many. Most are the same ones you filled out before. She's in good hands, Taylor. He might not have the best bedside manner, but he's the best in everything else. I'll go pull up her file from before."

Colin put his phone away as he walked across the room to where they sat. "I need to go to the house to meet the police. I'll be back as soon as I can."

Jack looked up at him. "I'll stay here with Taylor. Make sure they know about the other shit too. I'll call Jules to let her know what is going on."

As Colin left, he called back to Jack. "I will, don't worry. I'll make sure they call Inspector Kirpatrick as well."

Taylor was silent as he filled out the paperwork. It angered him that they hadn't found who was harming his daughter. Once he was done, Jack told him to stay put as he returned the forms to Maddie.

†

Colin arrived at the house just as the police cars flew up the street. He explained to them what he had witnessed and gave them the description as best he could of the man he saw fleeing from the house. He informed them as well of the ongoing investigation being conducted by the state police.

He watched as the officers entered the house, realizing now it was just a waiting game. *Which I can tell is going to turn into a pissing game between these losers and Kira.* He wished all their lives could just get back to normal.

Whatever the hell normal may be...

Too much had happened over the last few years for any of them to return to normal lives. He snorted, sarcastically laughing, "Maybe we can get a group discount rate on therapy after this bastard is caught."

One of the officers exited the house and approached his truck. "Sir, I have a few more questions for you. The first one being the phone number for the *person* handling the case you were telling us about." Sarcasm oozed from the officer.

Colin sighed. It was starting already. He pulled up the numbers he had been given for Kira and Manny. "Inspectors Kira Kirpatrick and Manny Watts..." Colin didn't get to finish, hearing the office groan.

"Oh fucking great...Kirpatrick. The Captain isn't going to like this. I gotta call them though. Excuse me a moment." The officer walked back to the house, leaving a puzzled Colin wondering what all that was about.

†

The attending doctor called Maddie back into the exam room where Remmy was lying, still unconscious. As she entered, the assisting nurse had just finished cutting away Remmy's blood-covered jeans. She then began to wipe away some of the blood on her face and chest. The doctor pulled Remmy's cell phones from the shredded pants, handing them to Maddie.

"Please, give these to her father and let him know I will be out in a few minutes. Meanwhile, I'm going to need all the usual tests. Her arm is broken and most likely her ribs as well. I also want a cat scan and an MRI done as fast as possible. I'm afraid of one of the ribs will puncture a lung if we're not careful and I want to rule out a skull fracture. It looks like she took quite a bad beating."

As Maddie handed the phones to Taylor, one of them started to ring, scaring him in the process. Almost dropping it, he stared at it. "I don't know anything about these gadgets." He thrust it at Jack.

"Excuse me, Taylor, it's Kira. I'll take this." Jack walked across the waiting room. He wanted to save Taylor any further pain by having to recount the small bits that he already knew.

"Kira, it's Jack. Remmy has been hurt really badly. Looks like someone tortured her and left her for dead. Taylor and I are here at the hospital and Colin went back to the house to meet with the police." Jack heard something crash on the other end of the phone, followed by lots of cursing.

The line went eerily quiet for a moment. "I'm on my way there."

168

Jack prepared himself to be screamed at rather loudly. "No. I think you should go to her house. Kira, I want you to find this bastard. Find him and kill him...do you understand?" "I don't know." More silence followed. "Fine...call Colin and tell him I'm on my way."

☦

Driving to Remmy's house was sheer torture. Kira pounded her fist on her steering wheel and vowed to find the bastard. She knew she had to rein in her emotions and get back to business. *God, what is it about her that causes me to lose focus?*

She pulled into Remmy's driveway and saw the police cruisers waiting for her. She steeled her nerves and called to the cop deep within her. She knew what she had to do. She would find who did this, close the case, and never see Remmy again.

She saw Colin and waved for him to stay put as she walked by him.

As Kira showed her badge and was allowed into the crime scene, across town a father sat listening to all the tests his daughter's battered body was going to be subjected to. Anger warred with fear as one name kept popping back into both their minds. Somehow, someway, Ronald was involved.

☦

Knowing what Ronald was capable of, a horrific thought occurred to Taylor. "Excuse me, Doctor, but she's been sick for a while and she never gets sick. She's been really tired, sick to her stomach, migraine headaches..."

Jack chimed in. "She's also had dizziness and the shakes. Oh God...you don't think he would..."

The doctor, following their line of thinking, frowned. If she had been drugged, they would need to find out fast what it was in case she needed surgery. "Excuse me, Mr. Garrick. I need to get a tox screen run immediately on your daughter. If we need to do surgery, this could cause serious problems."

†

Manny arrived at the chaos-filled house only moments after Kira. He had raced to Remmy's after receiving her call. He'd never known Kira to sound panicked. After showing his shiny new inspector's badge, he was escorted into the house, then into the dining room, where Kira stood motionless staring down at the floor. In front of her, a rookie officer stood erect at attention.

Never turning, she addressed the others. "No one steps in this house. I want Charlie over here. Now! Manny, take some quick pictures of this bat."

Pulling on gloves after Manny photographed it, she picked up the bat handle, leaving the other half laying where it was. Kira carefully inspected it.

Her eyes lit up when she rotated the bat toward her. "Manny, special bag this, it has a print on it. Let's hope this bastard was stupid and that we just got lucky. Also bag those butts from the floor." Kira had a hinky feeling they would match one of the others they had previously found.

The local detective, upon seeing his nemesis' truck parked in front of the house, rushed back up the steps and down the hall with his partner in tow. He didn't like her and, furthermore, didn't want her taking over their case. The short

170

rotund older man walked up behind Kira as she handed the bat handle to her co-worker. "Excuse me, but why are you messing with my evidence?"

Kira turned to the two detectives and the tall, quiet, younger man immediately recognized her. The moment he'd seen the truck, he just knew his partner was going to shoot his mouth off. He hung back, waiting for the sparks to fly. The taller string bean of a detective cringed at the amount of trouble Kira could cause them because of his partner's mouth.

The older detective's face held a smug look. "Kirpatrick, what are you doing here? Slumming it?"

Kira sneered at them. She'd dealt with them before. The short fat one was Detective Buttburn and the tall younger one was Detective Nettles. They were bungling idiots and she had told them so at the time. She felt sorry for the younger one. He'd been trained by the older man and never stood a chance.

"This is related to one of my cases, so *my* team will process the scene. You got a problem with that?" Kira pulled herself up to her full height, towering over the shorter man. The taller one she wasn't worried about; he'd learned his lesson the last time they met. She knew the portly detective loathed her. Just as she knew his favorite place to be at all times was at the local bar swigging back a beer

"Fine, let me call the Captain and let him know you're here and taking the lead on this one." He had a sneer on his face.

Kira knew he wouldn't bother to fight with her or he'd lose, just like every other time they tangled. In addition to that, he was a lazy, bigoted man who was coasting until his retirement in one year's time.

One of the first two officers on the scene called them to the deck at the back of the house. It was then that Kira realized the patio doors were standing wide open. Feeling the rookie still standing beside her, her curiosity rose. "Did either of you open those?"

He shook his head. "No, sir, we didn't touch a thing."

Kira shook her head at the rookie when he called her *sir*. She smiled briefly, then it was gone. Kira loved scaring the rookies. It seemed someone had already warned him about her, which caused her to smile once more. Kira basked in the fact that her reputation had preceded her once again.

Turning to the rookie, she instructed him what to do. "Go tell him I'll be right there and not to step onto the deck. I have a feeling that's how our guy got in and out."

She surveyed the room's destruction inch by inch, without moving a muscle. A vase of flowers lay destroyed, with glass strewn on the rug. Her gaze froze on a spot where she thought Remmy must have been laying, bleeding. Her eyes lingered on the blood splattered on the rug. For a moment, her heart stopped and she couldn't breathe. Muttering, she turned to leave via the front door to look at the rear deck. "Fucking bastard."

✝

An hour later, Kira sat with Colin on the front bumper of his truck. "The bastard got sloppy, Colin. He left several things, including a bloody boot print on the back deck. There were also cigarette butts on the dining room floor and on the deck. We can process the evidence faster than the locals; besides, this falls under my jurisdiction because it's part of my ongoing case."

Colin wiped the tears with his sleeve. "She doesn't smoke and neither do any of the rest of us, except Ronald, and he hasn't been in her house in several years. Whoever dropped those is the one who did this. Find him Kira. Find the bastard who did this."

Kira silently vowed to herself to personally find him and make him pay for what he'd done. Hearing the meowing coming from her truck parked next to his, Kira smiled. "Don't worry; I don't mind taking the furball with me. I'm glad that whoever did this just locked him in the bathroom and didn't harm him."

Colin looked over at Mr. Bubbles, who looked out the cab window at them. "Are you sure? I hate to ask that of you as well, but I have allergies."

"Colin, I never make an offer I don't intend to keep. Besides, I don't want to be accused of trying to kill you when you can't breathe because of your allergies. We can't leave him here."

Standing, Kira straightened her jeans over her black cowboy boots. "I'll take Mr. Bubbles to my place, after stopping at the pet store. I so do not want any accidents on my floors. Then I am going to the hospital. I'll meet you there after you go home and change out of those clothes. I already told the rookie he was going with you to bag them."

Colin nodded as he closed his truck door and started the engine.

As Kira closed her own door, Mr. Bubbles snuggled close to her, curling up on the center console.

Kira reached over, stroking his shiny black fur. "Well, Mr. Bubbles, be prepared to be completely spoiled rotten. Bella is going to love you to death. You're going to go back to your momma fat and happy if my niece has anything to do with it."

†

Maddie escorted Taylor and Jack back into the room where they had previously been. Several moments later, the door opened, followed by an orderly pushing a gurney. Patrick locked the wheels with his foot, preventing it from moving. He turned, hugged Jack, and shook hands with Taylor.

He had been shocked when he received the page to return a patient to the emergency room and found Remmy lying upon the table. Now as Jack filled him in on what had happened, he tightened his arm around Jack's waist in quiet support. His pager buzzed. Silencing it, he read the display. "Crap. I have to go."

He hugged Jack once more and turned to Taylor to offer some comfort. "I'm sorry. I'm off duty in an hour. I'll be back after I'm done. Dr. Katz is a good doctor, even though he's rough around the edges. If I can be back sooner, I will." Patrick nodded to the doctor as they passed in the doorway.

Remmy lay naked on the gurney, covered only by a sheet and thin blanket. "Taylor, I know she'll be cold when she wakes up. I'm just going to get several of those blankets on the shelf in the corner and put them over her."

"Thank you, Jack." Taylor moved a strand of hair away from her face. "This would annoy her if she saw it."

The display of affection for the woman warmed the doctor's heart. Remmy would need all of this and more in the days to come. It disgusted him that anyone would do this to another human being. Anger flared within him at the thought of anyone harming either of his own daughters this way.

Taylor's face was too pale and had a desolate look.

"Taylor, why don't you sit down?"

He wanted to argue with the doctor, but Dr. Katz pointed to the chair.

Dr. Katz didn't feel it necessary to mince words about Remmy's injuries. "First of all, she hasn't regained consciousness, which is common with these types of injuries. She has three broken ribs, one of which has punctured a lung so we had to put in a chest tube to keep the lung inflated. She has a fractured vertebrae and her arm is broken in three places. She also has a severe concussion, causing the brain to swell slightly. Luckily, there's no skull fracture."

He turned the page in the binder. "She's damn lucky there's no skull fracture. My opinion is she protected her head with her arm, which is why her arm is so bad. We do have to do immediate surgery to repair the broken eye socket, arm, and lung. Don't worry, though, there's no damage that we could determine as of yet to her eye. We also will have to put screws in her arm. As for her toxicology, someone has drugged her. This would account for all the symptoms and why she couldn't fight back. She would've been extremely weak."

"Doc, I got to ask..." A look of dread washed over Taylor's face. "Was my daughter...was she raped?" He clenched his fists.

The doctor didn't need to look at the paperwork. It had been the first thing he looked for when the nurse had removed Remmy's clothes. "No, she wasn't. She was very lucky that Mr. Browder arrived when he did. We found bite marks on her neck and several on her left breast. While her injuries are severe, she will make a full recovery, but it will take some time. Taylor, we need to get her into surgery."

Taylor nodded. "Do whatever you need to do to make my daughter better." He stood and kissed his daughter on the cheek. Just then the door opened and a six-foot-three storm cloud blew in, with Colin hot on her heels.

†

Kira pulled up outside the emergency room, parked her truck, and dared anyone to say a thing to her. Colin, arriving a few seconds before her, had already parked and was right behind her as she stormed toward the doors into the hospital. A guard approached only to back off when Kira pulled her badge from her pocket, attached it to the front of her belt, and told him to get out of her way.

Striding through the waiting room, Maddie called out to them which room Remmy was in. It was where they took the worst of the patients brought into the emergency room. A thought occurred to Kira, sending her blood boiling even higher. She turned back to Maddie. "Was a rape kit done?"

"Only her shirt was torn open. It wasn't needed. Colin got there in time."

Kira thanked her and continued to Remmy's room, with Colin behind her. She opened the door and stopped dead in her tracks. The sight froze her to her very core. Nothing had prepared her for this – not the battered women she'd saved from their kidnappers nor the ones she had scraped off the ground to send to the morgue. Not in Kira's wildest nightmares had she been ready for this.

Colin motioned for Jack to step into the hall for a few moments, leaving Taylor and Kira in the room with Remmy.

Walking to Remmy's bedside, Kira felt as if her feet were weighted with cement. She felt the room closing in on her, trying to suck the very life from her. Never once did her eyes leave the woman's body. Taylor stood beside her and rested his hand on her shoulder. He felt her body tense, then slump as if giving up.

"Taylor, how bad is it?" Kira let Taylor hold her.

"It's just you and me Kira, I won't let you fall. I am going to say my piece once and for all. I know you have feelings for my daughter. Just as I know you will adamantly deny them. Something tells me though that you both will eventually find your way; it is just a matter of time."

"Taylor...I can't. I just can't."

"I know now is not the time. Okay, doc says he has to take her into surgery as soon as possible. He has to fix her eye, put screws in her arm. He already put some tube thing in her chest. He said she'd be okay though. That's all that matters to me."

Gently touching the bruising on Remmy's face, Kira skimmed her fingers through the unconscious woman's hair. A light rap on the door caused her to snatch her hand back as if she'd suddenly been burned. Out of the corner of her eye, she saw an orderly slip into the room. He spoke quietly with Taylor, who then turned to her.

"Kira, this is Patrick, Jack's partner. He's here to take Remmy to surgery. Patrick, this is Investigator Kira Kirpatrick. We're going to the cafeteria for coffee and food. Please let Dr. Katz know where we'll be."

Kira held the door open for Taylor, then helped Patrick wheel Remmy from the room. She helped in order to have just one more moment with her.

Standing in the hall watching him wheel Remmy away, the four people felt like lost souls.

Kira turned, addressing the other three, with rage in her eyes. "I'll find who did this. Have no doubt about that. I *will* find him and when I do..."

Taylor put his hand on her arm. "You'll charge him with everything in the book and you will do it by the book so it sticks."

It was clear what he meant. She was not to lose her cool and whale on the loser. Kira was unsure if she could keep that bargain.

"Jack, Colin, go on ahead to the cafeteria, we'll be right behind you." Taylor turned back to Kira. "You'll do nothing to get yourself in trouble. Remmy would be mighty pissed off if she found out you lost your badge because of her."

Kira shook her head. "I can't promise."

"You will promise. I guarantee you don't want the wrath of my daughter brought down upon you. Woo girl, I'll tell you, Haley brought that upon herself once and that was all it took. My daughter has quite the temper and stubborn streak." Taylor stopped when he mentioned Haley's name.

She tilted her head in contemplation. "Kind of like her father, huh?" She wanted to ask, but was a little afraid to go the extra step.

"Ask." Only that one word was needed.

She stopped walking and studied something on the floor. "What was she like, Haley?"

"Tough as nails. She was a prison guard, but never brought it into the home with her. They were each other's rocks. Haley worshipped the ground Remmy walked on. My daughter in turn idolized her. I only know of the one fight they ever had and it was over a baseball game."

Kira gave him a puzzled look.

"In our house, we take our Yankees very seriously. Let's just say she sat on the opposite bench." Taylor chuckled. "I was just remembering the glass of ice that had been dumped down Haley's shirt to cool her off."

Kira laughed. "Ah, a Red Sox fan, huh?" Taylor nodded. "Wow, I'm amazed she was even allowed into the house in that case. It didn't seem to hurt their relationship that much, though."

"No, there are more important things in life than that." Kira had a sheepish look on her face that told him one thing. "So, tell me Kira, what team do you root for?"

She looked down the hall to where she knew the cafeteria was. "I think we better catch up with the two of them." She started off down the hall, not wanting to admit the truth.

"Kira..." When Taylor said her name, he lengthened the *r* to sound like a stuck record.

Kira knew she might as well admit it; he'd find out eventually. Knowing her luck, Bella would blurt it out when she found out Taylor and Remmy were also Yankees fans. Something hit her then. Why would she think something like that? It was not as if they would all be hanging out watching games together after she was done with this case.

Trying to shake the cobwebs from her mind and stop the throbbing in her head, she rubbed her temples when they stopped outside the cafeteria. Taylor looked at her expecting an answer. "Okay...fine. I'm a Mets fan." Kira was afraid to look at him again. When she did, she wasn't surprised at the look she got.

He looked horror stricken. "Damn, woman, are you trying to kill me? That's as bad as a damn dirty Sox fan. Ooh, Remmy's gonna give you what for when she finds out." He laughed. "Sorry just laughing at the thought of the brow beating you are in for when Remmy finds out."

"Please…I take enough abuse from Bella. It seems no matter how much I tried to make her into a Mets fan, she still turned into a damned Yankee." Kira pushed through the door into the cafeteria, the smell of food reminding her she hadn't eaten all day. Her stomach growled.

"It would seem someone is hungry also. So let's get us something to eat and discuss this dilemma in more detail."

Taylor slapped her on the back and she knew she was in for it.

They purchased their food, found the other two, and they all discussed the merits of being a Yankees fan and the pitfalls of being a Mets fan. Kira soon realized it was a conversation she would never win with any of them. It was then that it sunk in that this is what it felt like to be in a family. Her heart did a step-stutter and she joined in on the fun even more.

†

Stepping off the plane in Raleigh, North Carolina, the man's demented mind convinced him the police could never prove he had anything to do with what had happened to the woman. He had not been the one to beat her to within an inch of death. He had not been the one who raped her and then when all was said and done, left her dead body on her ugly oriental rug.

As far as anyone was concerned, he'd been on his way to North Carolina when the attack had taken place. When she died, the will would read that all was left to him as next of kin. Remmy had never realized one of the papers she signed two days before was a new will naming him as her sole beneficiary.

Forging the new will had been a piece of cake for Ronald. He had known who her lawyer was and went to have a fake will for himself made up so that he could scope out the set-up of the office. He knew he had lucked out when he figured out that the lawyer's assistant was fresh out of high school. She never noticed his theft of letterhead and Remmy's original will. Ronald had gone to the office on the pretense of needing to change something on his own when he obtained the articles. He knew the lawyer wasn't there and the naïve young girl had been in the office by herself.

Ronald talked her into opening the cabinet that contained their paperwork and when he distracted her, he slipped Remmy's will out of the drawer. He then had his friend forge the new one which Ronald then slipped into a pile of papers that he had Remmy sign when she got back from vacation. She'd been so pissed off at him that she blindly signed all of the papers in order just to get him out of her office.

Later, he replaced the will in her home safe which was located in the bedroom closet. When Ronald had broken in several weeks earlier, he had tested the combination and found Remmy had never changed it from years before when Haley had kept her guns in the safe. When the original from the lawyer's office came up missing, he'd file a protest that the assistant was incompetent and had lost the document.

Ronald's friend would never dare turn on him. He owed Ronald his life from the time he had saved him over a decade before. The man had been wanted by the police for murder, and Ronald had provided him with the alibi, and they were best friends since.

Now it was just a waiting game to Ronald. He knew the call would come soon that his dear sweet cousin Remmy had been brutally murdered, and that he was needed back home to help with the arrangements. Ronald basked in all that he had done. He'd won and all would soon be his.

He had no idea that all his plans had become skewed.

Chapter Nine

Hours after she had been taken to surgery, Remmy was wheeled into recovery. Those waiting each controlled their emotions and impatience in their own way. Colin paced outside the entrance to the emergency room, contemplating all the different ways he could kill the man who did this to his friend.

A cigarette dangled from his lips as he called Mack to tell her what was going on. He had stopped smoking a year before, however, with all that was going on, he needed the old crutch to help him deal with the stress. He knew Remmy would be pissed, but he would worry about that latter.

Inside the hospital in a private waiting room, a storm was brewing beneath the surface.

Kira noticed Taylor hadn't moved from the window that he stood in front of for over an hour. He looked out at the skyline as the sun started its descent. Quietly he spoke to her. "I've tried to fathom who upon this planet could hate my daughter enough to do this. I just can't wrap my mind around what is happening."

"Wish I knew." Kira was going over the evidence in her head. In addition, she was trying to ignore the presence of Jules, who had arrived straight from the airport thirty minutes before.

It was not any one thing in particular that Kira didn't like about Jules. She disliked everything, right down to the way Jules sat watching her. She hadn't taken her eyes off Kira since she arrived, just as Kira had done the same to Jules.

†

Patrick had come back after his shift and now sat on a sofa in the corner with Jack's head upon his lap. As he sat caressing his sleeping lover's back, Patrick studied the others.

He watched as Taylor quietly kept watch over the city skyline and Kira paced back and forth.

Patrick whispered to Jack. "I know you're awake. Can you feel the tension building in the room? I'm hoping the two don't come to blows. I know Jules didn't like the inspector, but I can't figure out what Kira's issue is with Jules."

Kira turned and paced back toward Patrick's end of the room. The man chuckled as he secretly observed Kira scowl at Jules. He suddenly knew why she was acting like a caged tiger that wanted to sink its teeth into someone. She was jealous of Jules. Patrick knew that to be a fact, just as he knew Kira herself had suddenly figured out why. She stopped dead in her tracks, looked at Jules again, and then at him.

Only one word escaped Kira's lips. "Shit..."

✝

Kira, while pacing for the last half hour, tried to figure out what bothered her most about the other woman. She knew Patrick had been watching her since they had taken Remmy into surgery. She was just as sure that Jules had never taken her eyes off Kira since her arrival.

She disliked Jules for several reasons, the biggest one was that she was positive Jules had slept with Remmy. That alone made her hate the woman. Why should she care, though? It was not like she was looking for a relationship with Remmy.

Then it dawned on her. She really was truly jealous. That was when she stopped, looked at the two people watching her, and realization hit home. She liked Remmy. Actually, she more than liked her. She could visualize the two of them dating. She could see Remmy walking down the aisle in a beautiful white gown. She could see the two of them having children.

It was not any one single vision that scared Kira; they all scared her to death. Any one of those ideas falling into the wrong hands meant she could lose all that held her life together.

She looked over at Taylor and silently voiced her thought. *Well, damn!*

Jack had awakened a few moments before but remained motionless, watching the scene play out before him. When Kira turned back to Taylor, Jack sat up and whispered to Patrick, "Are we about to see a pissing contest?"

This caused Patrick to chuckle again. "No, I don't think so. Kira would never allow it."

Jack stood, stretching his stiff muscles. He stood on Taylor's right side as Kira stood guard on the worried father's left. All three remained in silent contemplation for what seemed an eternity.

Kira bowed her head. She had to leave and regroup her thoughts. She was doing no one any good like this. She couldn't concentrate with the other woman watching every move she made. Just as she couldn't put the pieces together while standing there counting the number of ways to break every bone in the other woman's body.

Kira had to find a way to rid herself of these feelings. "I need to go, Taylor, I'm sorry. Annabella is at a friend's house. I have to pick her up, take her home, and get some dinner in her before it gets any later. I'll try to be back first thing in the morning. I need to take Remmy's statement as soon as she wakes, so as not to lose any details."

Jack cleared his throat. "What if she can't remember anything?"

Kira frowned. "Then we will deal with that then." She turned toward the door. "If there is any change during the night, please call me. Also, if you need anything, Taylor, before I return, please call me."

She had one last thought. "Have any of you heard from Ronald?"

Jack shook his head no. "Nope, and if he knows what's best he won't show his face here either. Check with Colin, he might know where he is."

"Okay, I'll do that. Like I said, Taylor, please call me if you need me."

Taylor only nodded, unable to find the words to express his gratitude for all she'd done for them. Kira had vowed to find this bastard. He was sure she would do just that. He did worry what she would do once she caught him. He worried she'd do something stupid to ruin her career. Taylor felt if Kira could admit her feelings, she might be able to release some of the pent up anger and the emotions stampeding through her.

✝

Never before had Kira blown up at her niece. They disagreed on many things but she never actually lost her temper. As they drove home in silence, she regretted her actions ten-fold. On the way to pick up Bella, she had called Charlie to see how the processing of evidence was going.

Charlie informed her he had no bat to take fingerprints from. She asked about the cigarette butts, only to be informed that he knew nothing about those.

She had placed a call to Manny, who informed her that her least favorite detective was the one who was in charge of taking them to Charlie. Her gut told her he had tampered with the evidence transfer and was doing everything he could to make her look bad.

It was the same scheme he'd tried to pull before. He made the evidence disappear and then, when Kira was at a standstill in the case, he mysteriously found her missing evidence, calling it his own find. She had caught him that time; she would again.

This latest news, adding to her already muddled thoughts, made her extremely cranky by the time she arrived to pick up Bella. She went over the edge when she walked in to find Bella and her friend playing on the x-box. They were supposed to be studying for their finals.

What followed was the battle of two strong-willed, stubborn women. Both refused to be the first one to cave and apologize. When something happened to make Kira lose her temper, it was always a sure sign that there was something very wrong. However, if she was pushed, Kira would clam up completely.

Bella waited in silence, hoping it wouldn't take too long for the silent older woman to open up. Kira always did; sometimes it just took longer.

That was the rule between them since day one. They always told each other if something was bothering them, and they always spoke the truth. Bella especially knew something was amiss when they arrived home. Opening the door, she was greeted by the cutest black cat she'd ever seen.

Kira kicked off her boots inside the front door as Bella fawned over the cat. She felt all the guilt hitting home as her niece knelt and picked up the furball, kissing him on the forehead. Crossing her arms and leaning against the wall, she sighed. She knew she might as well get on with it.

Reaching over, ruffling Bella's hair, Kira let the crack in the silence open slightly. "I'm sorry, sweetie, for being a bitch. It's been a bad day, but that was no reason to take it out on you. As long as you think you're ready for your tests tomorrow, that's good enough for me."

Kira had to cook dinner and needed a beer, but not necessarily in that order. As she headed to the kitchen, the inevitable questions started.

Bella stood, carrying the cat with her, and followed Kira to the kitchen. "What's his name and whose is he?" Bella cuddled the cat as he purred in her ear.

Kira wished she had her camera out to get a picture of the two together. "His name is Mr. Bubbles. A friend..." Kira stuttered.

Did she really consider Remmy a friend? She warred within herself. Did she dare? Maybe if she just said *someone,* Bella would drop it. Kira needed time to think, to gather herself and align her priorities back to where they should be.

"A friend was hurt today." Why had she said that? *Fuck...* she muttered under her breath.

Bella knew the only friends Kira had were Manny and Paul, and their cat looked nothing like Mr. Bubbles. Did her Aunt have a girlfriend? She wouldn't voice it, however, knowing how far in the closet Kira was.

Bella took the safe route, looking up at her aunt with a sad expression. "Did Manny get hurt?"

Kira shook her head. Bella's hand, that had been petting Mr. Bubbles, ceased movement. "Has something happened to Paul then?"

Bella watched as her aunt pulled items from the fridge to make a salad. "Bella, drop it okay? Now, do you want a chef salad or just a plain one?"

"Aunt Kira..." Now Bella was positive something was seriously wrong.

Kira didn't look up, but continued cutting the red bell pepper for their salads, clenching her teeth. "Annabella, drop it, okay? As I said, it was a really bad day."

†

After the dinner dishes were washed and put away, Kira let Bella watch some television. She grabbed another beer and retired to the spare bedroom that served as her office. She needed to talk to Paul. She trusted him completely, even if she sometimes ignored his advice, and only later needed to admit he was right.

Paul had been in her life for as long as she could remember. They were there for each other to share the ups and the downs. When Kira's brother Geoff died, it took all the strength he and his partner Manny had to hold her together. Her life turned upside down overnight, and she had found herself alone in the world and responsible for raising a child.

Paul had held her through the weeks after the funeral when Kira sobbed herself to sleep. The men became instant uncles to the small child, and the four formed a new family which became stronger than any they were born into.

Any major decision Kira made she ran by Paul first, even after all these years. Just as any time she found herself stumped on what to do about something, Kira called him as well. This was one of those times. Kira trusted him completely. Paul would never break her confidence, not even a word to Manny unless she said it was okay. Kira found sometimes if she talked things through with him, clues would pop out of nowhere. She took a long drink from her beer, sat back, put her feet on her desk, and rested her head on the back of the chair, comforted by the feeling of the leather.

When Paul answered, he already had an idea why she was calling. Manny had told him about the case. They were both sure Kira had feelings for Remmy. Now came the true test...could he make her see the light of day and finally come out of the closet? It wouldn't be easy, but they would get through it together as Kira inched her way along whichever path she chose.

"Hey girl, you want me to get Manny on the phone, too? He's in the den playing video games, but I can get him."

"No! You can give him the highlights later."

"Okay, let me get comfortable, it sounds like this is going to be a doozy. What's going on? You sound upset about something."

"I lost my temper with Bella tonight."

"I hear guilt in your voice. And now you feel like shit, right? Well, did she deserve it? What did she do?"

"I arrived to pick her up tonight at her friend's house, where they were supposed to be studying for their finals tomorrow, only to find the two of them playing video games. I lost my temper, never giving her a chance to explain. I mean, I know she's always scored perfectly on her tests and is at the top of her class and all that but..." Kira sighed.

"Kira...I'm going out on a limb here. It's not Bella you're upset with, but yourself for losing it. Am I right?"

"Okay, so I'm pissed at myself and not her, what else, Freud?"

Manny quietly came in, handed him a beer, and left. "I would say there is more here. What else is upsetting you? The case you're working on, perhaps?"

"Yeah, you could say that. I'm at a complete fucking standstill in this case."

"Run through what you have and what you don't have."

"What I have is a destroyed video store. From that came only the cigarette butts, which may or may not be tied to the case. I have no witnesses, nada. Next, I have the victim receiving nasty letter threats. No fingerprints on those either. Then there was the light fixture falling on the victim. I got another butt from that scene. However, the DNA on the two don't match, but the second DNA is the victim's cousin. So…now, I have two suspects, one known and one unknown. Now the latest is that Remmy's…" She seemed to lose focus for a moment and her heart skipped a beat, thinking back to what would have happened if Colin hadn't arrived in time.

"Kira…you okay? Could it be that what's upsetting you most was not being able to find the bastard before this to prevent Remmy getting hurt."

"Sorry…uh, Remmy was brutally hurt, almost killed because I can't catch the bastard. I just know her cousin had something to do with it. I just can't prove it. If that sick asshole had raped her…there would be no place for him to hide on this planet. As it is, I'll hunt him for the rest of my life if I have to." Kira drained the last drop from her bottle, slamming it down on her desk.

"Oh God, Paul, you should've seen her."

"Sweetie, I want you to think about what I'm about to say. Think about it with your heart, not that stubborn brain of yours. Do you have feelings for this woman? If you do, then maybe you're too close to this case. You might need to take a step back and ask for help with it. Think about it, don't blow up, just think." Silence greeted him for ten long seconds.

"Yes." More silence.

"Yes, what? You have feelings or that you're too close to this case?"

"Fuck, yes, all right…I have feelings for Remmy. Shit, Paul, I could actually visualize myself married to her, living in a beautiful home, perhaps raising a kid or two of our own. But I can't and you know that! Those feelings are nothing more than a fantasy. A fantasy that…oh God, Paul it hurts so much."

"You need to admit to yourself out loud how strongly you feel about her."

"I…I love her. It doesn't matter though; I can't act on my feelings. I will not do anything to lose Bella! Besides, that Jules woman keeps showing up everywhere. I know she says they are only friends, but I know they've slept together."

"Ah, and that makes you jealous. Thinking that someone else has tasted what you want. Possibly, what you crave?"

"Crave her? She's all I think about. She invades my dreams as well as my nightmares, whether I'm awake or asleep. Every night I dream I'm making love to her. Christ, Paul, I woke up yesterday morning mid-orgasm crying out her name. Besides, there are other ways to lose Bella. I could lose her faith and trust in me. Knowing I'm a lesbian is one thing, but seeing it, if I were to date Remmy, is another thing." The thought of Bella hating her made Kira's tears flow once more.

"I would die if I lost her. I won't do anything to jeopardize that. If that means I have to remain alone until she's married with children of her own, or I have to remain alone the rest of my life, then so be it. I'll do what I have to for her. I would die for her."

"Kira, I want you to listen to me and listen good, okay? Bella loves you. She'd never hate you no matter what. She accepts you for who you are. All of us want you to be

193

happy, including her. It would hurt her to think you're unhappy because of her. Please talk to her. Then maybe you should think what it would be like to have Remmy to share your life."

Manny had long since given up on his video games, and Paul was grateful that he was sitting beside him in quiet support.

"I've done all the thinking I'm going to do. As for being happy, I am happy, as happy as I ever can be. Bella is all I need in my life. What would make me overjoyed is to get this case closed. I can then get her out of my life."

Paul pinched the bridge of his nose, trying to curb the migraine he felt starting. She obviously hadn't heard a word he'd said. "Kira, no one is going to take Bella away from you. You have nothing to worry about. Please think about what I've said, okay?"

"My friend, my fear of losing Bella is what keeps me from doing something stupid, in matters of the heart and on the streets. She is all I have, and that is the way it'll stay. Now go talk to your husband, I'm sure he's dying to know what we talked about. I need to get the little one down for the night."

Even as Kira spoke the words, her heart tightened at the thought of not seeing Remmy again. Closing her eyes, she let the tears fall as she rested her weary head on the chair, unaware of the bare feet that had quietly crept up outside her office door, or that Bella was listening to the brutally honest conversation taking place while Kira bared her soul.

As Kira returned the phone to its cradle, the door flew open. Standing in the doorway was a mightily pissed-off teenager with tears streaming down her face.

Kira's mind flipped. Had Bella heard the whole conversation? "Ah, Bella, sweetie, how long have you been there?"

Standing with hands on her hips, Bella looked identical to Kira at that age. "Long enough to want to slap my aunt, the one I love so much, silly."

Kira's palms rarely sweat. Now however, they were dripping. "Uh, how much of the conversation did you hear?" She really didn't want to know, especially not when Kira thought about some of the things she'd said.

"I heard all of it, every last word of it. I love you, Aunt Kira. Nothing will change that. Uncle Paul is right; you piss me off when you put me before your happiness. I'm not going anywhere, well, not until I go to college that is. Then you can have the house all to yourself. We've always been close. He's right; no one is going to take me away from you. However, it is possible that you could drive me nuts! All that matters to me is that you're happy and right now you are not happy, which is making me unhappy. Do you understand? Ooh, you frustrate me so much."

Kira's eyes glazed over, which meant she wasn't giving Bella her full attention. "Ah, so...you heard the *whole* conversation? Shit, I knew I shouldn't have had him on speaker." Kira was truly embarrassed, knowing that Bella had heard her talking about waking up mid-orgasm. Sure, they talked about sex, but never about *her* love life.

Bella rubbed her temple, then ran her fingers through her hair. It was the same stress maneuver that Kira herself did many times a day. Her niece was growing into a young adult, one who reminded Kira of herself in every single way.

"Yes, Aunt Kira, the *whole* conversation, including the part about you getting off while dreaming about Remmy."

Kira flew up from the chair, wanting to run from the room. Embarrassed beyond words, Kira tried to control her temper. "Annabella Marie Kirpatrick...you...I..." She couldn't even get the words out.

"Aunt Kira, that woke you up, didn't it? Good. Now that I have your attention, please listen to me. I love you no matter what. I want you to be happy. If that means having a life with Remmy, then please go after her, even if that other woman gets in your way. I know you came back early from vacation because something happened. I'm going to assume it had something to do with Remmy. I am also going to assume you made an ass of yourself. Go to her. Ask for forgiveness, for whatever the hell it was that you did." She put her arms around her aunt and hugged her tight.

"Oh, sweetie, if it was only that easy. You, my Bella, are a miracle to me. You understand and accept me, without reservation." Kira held tight, as if her life depended on it. "However, I can't for many reasons. I can't risk them trying to take you away from me, not ever. Besides, I'm positive when she regains consciousness, she'll still be pissed off at me." *And besides, she's way out of my league.*

Bella pulled back slightly. Kira sheepishly looked away. "What did you do? Oh God, I'm almost afraid to ask."

"Shit...I lied to her and told her I wasn't gay. Then..." Kira pulled away from Bella and sat in her chair.

Bella's facial features softened into a look of sympathy for Kira. "Oh, I see. That is why her father was here. She found you in P-town with a woman. Now she's hurt and you feel the guilt of the world on your shoulders."

Kira twirled the beer bottle between her fingers. "When and *how* the hell did you get so smart?"

"I'm your niece, that's how. As for when - it was the day you took a scared little girl in from the cold and gave her a home. You look tired." She sat on Kira's lap.

Kira closed her eyes, letting the fatigue seep into her bones. "Yeah, you could say that. I feel like I haven't slept in a year of Sundays. How about we both hit the hay? You have tests tomorrow that you are going to blow if you don't get some sleep."

Bella kissed Kira on the cheek. "And you have to go to the hospital to see how Remmy is doing. Don't even try to act like you weren't going there first thing." She put her forehead against Kira's. "She's going to be okay. I just know it." Bella stood, pulling Kira up from the chair. "Come on, old woman, off to bed with you. And I don't want to hear any noise coming from your bedroom in the night."

"Bella! We so are not going to have that conversation ever again. Is that understood?" Kira's face flushed red.

"Ah, come on, Aunt Kira, if I can't talk to you about sex, who then? Maybe I should talk to someone on the street about it?"

Kira chuckled, Bella was laying it on thick. She knew when she was beat and when to admit it. "Fine, I admit defeat. Damn, you are me, aren't you? If I didn't know better, I'd swear I was your mother."

Bella wrapped her arms around Kira's waist. "You may not have given birth to me, but you are my mother, in every other sense of the word."

✝

Taylor slept fitfully on and off, in the chair by his daughter's bed, until early the next morning. He was afraid she would take a turn for the worse if he left her side.

When Dr. Katz found Taylor still there, the doctor worried that soon he would have two patients. The previous evening, he and Jack both tried to persuade Taylor to go home, but they both knew he wouldn't.

Dr. Katz completed his exam and read over Remmy's latest vitals. He felt positive it wouldn't be long before she came around. She still looked ghostly white, but her color would return in a few days. Behind him, Taylor stirred, waking up.

"Taylor, I see you didn't listen to us. I want you to go home today and get some sleep, no arguments. Remmy is doing very well. Now it's just a matter of healing up. It's going to be a long road. She should be waking up soon but it will only be for a few moments at a time. Sleep will help in the healing process. I'll check back in a little while. In the meantime, I want you to go to the cafeteria and get some food in you. Then home." He slid the binder back into the wall pocket beside the door before leaving.

"I'll do just that as soon as Jack or Colin gets here to stay with her. I don't want her wakin' up alone." Taylor reached through the railing to hold her limp hand. "For now, though, I'll stay right here."

Jack met the doctor in the hall, and Dr. Katz informed him of Remmy's condition. Jack had tried as hard as he could to get Taylor to go home the previous evening, but the older man wouldn't hear of it. As he entered the room and saw the dark circles under Taylor's eyes, Jack wished he'd demanded that Taylor leave the hospital, even if it was home with himself and Patrick.

"Taylor, we're going to the cafeteria to get something to eat. Remmy will be okay alone for a bit."

Taylor tried to object.

"No, as I said, *we,* as in both of us. Come on, let's go." Pulling Taylor from the chair, Jack escorted him into the hall.

By mid-morning, Jack could tell Taylor's patience was wearing thin while waiting for Remmy to wake up. "I'm sure the doctor has done something wrong that's causing her not to wake. I just know it, Jack."

Jack called Colin to see how much longer he was going to be. "I'll be there as soon as I can. I just got off the phone with Mack, letting her know I would pick up the slack until Remmy was back up and ready to run the company."

Jack thanked him and turned to see Remmy slightly opening the eye that wasn't covered with a bandage. He ran to press the call button for the nurse while Taylor tried to soothe her.

Taylor held Remmy's hand and smoothed her hair that was sticking up. "It's okay, sweetie, don't try to talk. You're going to be okay." Taylor looked at Jack with tears in his eyes. "Go tell the nurse to call Dr. Katz."

"Daddy...where?" She seemed confused and unable to grasp where she was. Everything was muddled. "Fog..." Remmy slipped back into sleep within a few moments of waking.

"It's going to be okay, you're gonna be a bit foggy until you wake completely. Don't worry about anything right now. Everything is going to be fine." He soothed as Jack spoke with the nurse.

"The nurse said she would let Dr. Katz know Remmy woke up. She also said Remmy would probably wake up off and on for most of the day, but only for a few seconds at a time. Colin should be on his way up. When he gets here, you're going home to get some sleep."

The door to the room slowly opened, causing Taylor and Jack to turn. "Ah, speak of the devil. Now that you are here, we're leaving." Then Jack saw who was behind him. "Kira, good morning…"

Kira stood inside the doorway, afraid to go closer to the injured woman, fearful of breaking down. "Has she been awake yet?"

Wearily, Taylor sat in the chair by the bed. "Yes, only for a few seconds, just a little bit ago. Dr. Katz said she's doing well, considering what could've happened."

Kira nodded. Visions of what could have happened to Remmy if Colin hadn't arrived when he did had haunted her every moment since taking on the case. "I'm glad the three of you are here. Colin tells me Ronald is in North Carolina on business. I'd like him back here by tomorrow." All three were looking at her strangely.

Kira held her breath a moment then expelled it. "We got a lead this morning." She held out a hand to stop the questions. The bat had mysteriously showed up the previous evening on Charlie's desk. "As I said we have a lead. We found a match for the fingerprints that didn't belong there. They belong to a friend of Ronald's who has a record in a couple of other states. However, no one can seem to locate him and now I find out dear Ronald is not here either. I put out orders that I want both of them picked up for questioning. Unfortunately, though, that is all I have." Kira slid her hands in her pockets to stop herself from running them through her hair.

Colin stepped toward her. "What do you mean that's all you have? That's quite a lot. I'd bet anything that if you called the weasel and told him that Remmy had taken a turn for the worse, he'd come running back. For some unknown reason, he is under the assumption that he is inheriting everything if something should ever happen to Remmy. He keeps telling me the first thing he would do is fire all of us."

Kira thought about it a moment, liking the idea. "Colin, I want you to run with that idea. Call him and see if he'll take the bait."

"Good idea. It will be the easiest way to get him to come back. Okay, I'll call the little cockroach. He'd love the chance to gloat, thinking that he can soon rid the world of all of us."

Jack laughed. "As if...everyone would quit, never giving him the chance to fire them. I can tell you for a fact that he does not inherit one red cent from Remmy. She made sure of that. I have an even better idea. I'm going to call an old friend. She's gonna be pissed that I'm taking her away from her pregnant wife and child. However, once she hears what's going on, I'm sure she'll gladly drag the bastard back here. Plus, it helps that he's terrified of her."

What Jack didn't tell them was that he had already called Lillith and she was handling it. He had met Lillith when she attended Haley's funeral and Remmy had introduced her to him and Colin.

Kira was curious. "What's her name?"

Kira noticed the look that passed between Colin and Jack, and the not so subtle interruption from Taylor. "Also, while I'm thinking of it, does her will mention Ronald in it? The last time I met him he made it sound as if he knew she left everything to him."

201

Taylor stood. "I was there when she had her will done last year. I would testify in court that he doesn't get shit! Jack, why don't we go back to my place. I will rest for a spell while you cook us lunch."

Kira opened the door for them. "I need to get to the station to see what else I can dig up on these two. I will check in with you later. If anything changes, please call me. Jack, name please."

Kira saw Jack glance at the other two men. "Blackhawk…" Was all he said as he pulled Taylor from the room.

Colin waved goodbye to them, then settled down in the chair to try to get some more sleep. He hadn't gotten much during the night. Colin straightened the blankets covering Remmy. "I'll stay until Jack and your dad get back, then I have to head back to the office. Girl, I swear if he did this, I'll tear him apart with my bare hands. Of course, I may not get a chance if he pisses Lillith off."

†

Hours later as volunteers delivered the dinners on the fourth floor of the hospital, a woman's scream rang out and an alarm sounded from Remmy's room. As the two nurses and a doctor ran by the volunteers, they moved to the side of the hallway.

A panicked Jack and Taylor tried valiantly to calm Remmy down. Her terrified screaming was heard at the other end of the hospital floor.

The detectives had introduced themselves to Taylor. "I'm Detective Buttburn and this is Detective Nettles. We'll wait however long it takes her to wake up." Thirty minutes later Remmy woke up. When she did, the detectives immediately started hurling questions at her as if she were the suspect instead of the victim.

Jack and Taylor rushed into the room and the two detectives turned toward them. Taylor first asked them to leave and when they didn't, he buzzed the nurse to call for security.

The detective that Kira liked least of all, Detective Buttburn, ignored Taylor completely and took one last shot at the confused woman. "Ms. Garrick, we'll get to the bottom of this, so don't try to play the victim here. Also, don't try to tell me again that you don't remember anything."

Taylor approached the man. "Excuse me, detective, I think you should leave...*Now!*"

The detective turned to Taylor. "Listen here, old man, don't get in the way of my investigation."

"No, you listen. You are not handling this, Investigator Kirpatrick is. I really think you should leave now." At that, Taylor pressed the emergency button again for the nurse, wondering what was taking them so long.

Detective Nettles didn't like his partner's style. He stepped forward to say something but wasn't in time. Detective Buttburn turned his attention once more to Remmy. "Listen here, honey, when we find your boyfriend, we'll find out why he turned on you and tried to kill you."

He turned as the charge nurse rushed into the room, immediately taking over the situation. "Get out, both of you. Security will escort you out of the hospital."

Remmy tried hard to remember. All she knew when she woke up was she hurt all over. Then, here was this man, spewing all kinds of trash in her direction. All it did was make Remmy's head hurt more. He said something about a man trying to have sex with her and it triggered a memory. That, in turn, set off the current chain of events when all of what happened to her came crashing back.

As Taylor tried to calm Remmy and hold her down along with a second nurse, the first nurse and doctor spoke with Jack as to what happened. The on-call doctor turned to Taylor. "Sir, I'm Dr. Willis. Ms. Garrick is going to do more damage to herself if she keeps this up."

Taylor needed to hear no more. "Do whatever you need to do. Please just calm her down."

Taylor could hear just how furious Jack was with the detectives when he called Kira. The hospital rule of no cell phone usage meant nothing to either of them at this moment. Their only concern was for Remmy.

†

Kira answered her phone on the second ring as she drove away from the school after picking up Bella. At first, all she could hear was a woman screaming. Then she heard Jack's panicked voice over the confusion. "Kira, I'm at the hospital. We need you here. Hurry, please."

"Jack, what the hell is going on there?" Kira's internal alarm went off, especially when she realized the screaming was coming from Remmy.

Kira could tell Bella had heard the shouting through the phone as well by the worried look on her face.

Jack's frustration sounded through the phone. "Kira, we'll tell you when you get here, just hurry. Good-bye."

She threw the phone in the center console of her truck and glanced sideways at Bella. "Sweetie, I'm going to have to take you to the hospital with me. I want you to stay in the waiting room while I see what's going on, okay?"

Bella patted her Aunt's thigh. "No problem, Aunt Kira. You do what you have to do. I'll find some way to entertain myself."

Kira ran through the hallways from the parking garage and into the elevator with Bella hot on her heels. Remmy's room was located only a few doors from the atrium that also served as the waiting room. Kira pointed out Remmy's room to Bella just as the door opened and Jules walked out.

The two women glared at each other. "Jules…"

"Inspector…" Jules returned the icy attitude.

Bella defused the situation before one of them took a swing at the other. "Aunt Kira, Jack's waiting for you."

Bella turned to the other woman. "Jules, correct?"

Jules nodded.

"Why don't you join me in here and we can talk."

Jules figured she'd bite at the invitation to pick the young girl's brain about her aunt. "Sure, it would be an honor to discuss anything you have in mind." Jules pushed open the door so the two could enter.

As Kira entered Remmy's room, she knew exactly what the topic of conversation would be between the two women in the waiting room: her.

Chapter Ten

Kira opened the door to Remmy's room slowly and was shocked by what she saw. Jack and Taylor stood on the opposite side of the bed as a nurse strapped Remmy's good arm to the bed. She then noticed the other arm already had a strap over the cast.

Her anger soared once again at the bastards who had done this to the woman who, she realized, had captured her heart. Kira would catch him and, when she did, she truly believed he'd better have already prayed for forgiveness, because she was going to send him straight to hell.

Kira nodded to Jack, then her eyes landed upon Remmy. Kira couldn't tear her eyes away from her beaten body. "What the hell is going on? What happened? Why are they strapping her to the bed?" Her voice sounded on the verge of panic.

Taylor's throat sounded raw from crying. "Those damn detectives, that's what. They came barging in here. Buttburn told her to stop playing the victim, that she was lying about remembering things, saying it was her boyfriend that did this to her, which we know is pure bullshit. He yelled at her the whole time he was in with her. I told them to leave, but he just wouldn't stop..."

When Taylor faltered, Kira grasped his arm to steady him.

Kira looked to Jack for the rest of the answers. "Kira, we both want to file a formal complaint against him. The nurse had to call security to escort the bastard out of here."

Kira could see Taylor pulling strength from somewhere deep within himself and regained some of his composure.

"Kira, we need your help. Please keep them away from her."

"I'll call immediately and file complaints against him. I'll have Manny come and take statements from both of you, the nurse, and the security people." Her eyes still refused to leave Remmy's body.

"When he started yelling at her, I could tell by the look of horror and fear on her face that she started to remember what happened. She became hysterical after hearing the garbage he flung at her. None of us could calm her down. They had to sedate her, and then the doctor thought she needed to be restrained so she wouldn't hurt herself any more than she already is."

Remmy was aware of her surroundings despite feeling groggy and frightened by all she was remembering. She could hear the three of them as they stood talking about her in the corner of the room. She knew she had to tell them who was there with the man who beat her. "Kira?"

Kira needed to go to her but her feet felt rooted to the floor tiles.

Taylor motioned Jack to the door while he nudged

her. "Kira, talk to her. She needs your strength. Jack and I are going to the waiting room."

Kira nodded her head in acknowledgment. "Bella's in there."

"Good, I've been wanting to meet the young Annabella."

Kira grinned. "Yeah, so you can pick her brain about me, right?"

Jack put his hand on his chest, as if he had been insulted. "Me? Never! I would never do such a thing."

Taylor shoved him toward the door. "Let's go before the bullshit gets any deeper in here."

During their conversation, the nurse had quietly slipped from the room. Now with the two men gone, there was only Kira and Remmy left. Approaching the bed, Kira repeated in her head that she could do this... she could do this. However, when Remmy looked up at her with tears in her glazed over eyes, she faltered.

Kira removed the straps from Remmy's arms. No words were exchanged, none where needed. "Kira...I see it in your eyes. I know. Just like you must know how I feel. I...lo-"

Kira had to stop her from saying it. She couldn't take it if she heard the words aloud. "Remmy, don't. All that matters is that you get better. I'll catch the bastards and they'll never hurt you again. Don't be afraid. Take that fear and let it fuel your strength. Don't let any of what happened to you, defeat you."

Remmy smiled as best she could. "You make me feel special."

Kira sat on the edge of the bed. "You are special. Never doubt that for one second." She pushed the hair away from Remmy's face and let her fingers linger on her cheek. It was an unconsciously sweet and tender gesture that was pure instinct.

"Then why did you..." Remmy tried to hold back the tears.

Kira stopped her. "Please don't. You'll find someone who can return those feelings freely. Someone who deserves to be loved by you."

"And you can't..." Remmy's voice was laced with sadness.

Kira lowered her head, studying the tubes coming from Remmy's arm. "No."

"These drugs. Can't think. Where was I? Oh...Or you won't..."

Kira stood quickly from the bed. When had the conversation gotten away from her? When had she let her emotions take control? She stepped back and pushed her feelings into the furthest corner of her soul, forcing herself to be the ice-bitch they all thought she was. "I need to ask you a couple of questions, then I have to go."

Remmy sighed. "Ah, all business. Fine. Ask."

"Where's Ronald?"

Rolling her unbandaged eye, Remmy answered, "Don't know."

"I need you to make a statement. Do you remember enough to give Manny all the details next time you wake?" Kira wanted so badly to hold her, to take away the pain. She had to look away.

Remmy yawned. "Yes, I remember everything."

Kira studied the floor. "Good. Umm, one final question. Who's this Blackhawk Jack called to find Ronald?"

Instantly Remmy's head shot up, Kira could tell she regretted it immediately. She laid her head back onto the pillow. Kira could see drugs they had given Remmy were winning. "What! Why did he call Lillith? I need to talk to Jack, now. Oh my God, how could he have done that?"

Kira's senses went into overload. "Who is the woman?" The hair on the back of Kira's neck stood up.

If Remmy's brain wasn't muddled by the drugs, she'd never have said Lillith's name aloud, let alone volunteered information on her friend. "She's an old friend of Haley's. Didn't start out that way. She's a…liquidator…." Remmy closed her eyes. "…life." Remmy drifted off midsentence.

Kira was now even more confused. "What are you talking about?" She shook her head. "Oh well, as long as she gets Ronald back here. I want that bastard's skin on my office wall."

✝

She stepped into the waiting room and knew she was the topic of conversation when all of them became silent. Rolling her eyes, she walked over to the group. "Bella, we need to be going. Taylor, I'll send Manny over to take her statement later."

Taylor stood. "We were going to go grab some dinner. Would you like to join us?"

"Sorry, can't. I have some work to do at home that will take most of the night. Come on, Bella." Kira pushed her niece through the door.

Halfway home, Bella finally spoke up. "Aunt Kira, have I done something wrong?"

Sighing, Kira answered, "No honey, it's this case. It's getting to me." She ruffled Bella's hair. "What do you say to steaks on the grill for dinner?"

Bella's eyes lit up. "Oh, yes, please. I'll make the salad and potatoes. You start the grill." She loved steak, just like her aunt. It was how Kira sometimes bribed Bella.

†

Putting the last piece of steak in her mouth, Kira answered her cell phone. "What's up, Manny?"

Kira flew up from the table, knocking her beer bottle over. "What the fuck! Does the asshole know we're looking for him? We have a freakin' warrant out for him. Fine, I'm going over there."

Kira heard Manny slam his truck door. "I'll meet you there. There's no way you're going over there alone. Apparently, our boy wants to deal and give up Ronald. It's also not a good idea for you to be alone with Baby Huey."

"That bastard can kiss my fucking ass. It's not my fault Dad caught him being a dirty cop. I still don't know how the hell he got to where he's at. Captain? Please…he shouldn't even be cleaning a police station's toilets, let alone be captain. You don't need to meet me there. I'll be fine. I know how to control my temper if need be." Kira motioned to Bella that she had to go.

Manny sighed loudly. "Kira…"

"No, I'm fine."

"Sorry, but I'm meeting you in a few." Manny drove faster, needing to get there before Kira did something stupid.

Unfortunately, he was held up behind a traffic accident and arrived a moment too late.

He threw the truck into park and ran into the station in time to see two uniformed officers dragging Kira into the Captain's office.

Approaching the office, Manny pulled one of them

aside. "What the hell's going on?"

Out of breath, the officer told him what happened. "We were booking him, when the warrant popped up that you guys were looking for him. He wanted a deal as soon as he heard us talking. He told us about the video store and rigging the light. Then he rolled over on who hired him. That was when we called you. He didn't even want to wait for us to call a public defender for him."

Hearing a commotion, they both looked to the captain's office. "Okay, but what's that about?"

"Well…we were taking him from the interview room, when…"

†

Hearing the bastard boasting about tearing up the store and rigging the light had been bad enough. However, when he gave the details of beating Remmy and biting her breast, Kira almost lost her mind.

She saw the smug expression on his face as they escorted him from the interview room and Kira lost all reasoning. She stepped up into his face and whispered so only he could hear her words, "You aren't going to see your next birthday, you little fucker."

He looked around at the officers. "Police harassment! You guys heard her."

An inch away from his face, she said, "They'll hear what I want them to hear."

Kira didn't know the captain was behind her. "Kirpatrick, back off, he's ours."

"No fucking way. He's mine. I have a warrant on him for a case I'm working on." Kira turned to face the captain.

"You can have him after we're done with him,

Kirpatrick. It should be in about six months from now."

She knew he was baiting her but couldn't calm down, "No way! I have an outstanding warrant that takes precedence. I'm taking the piss-ant with me." Turning, Kira put a hand on the suspect's arm.

"Riley, Hewitt, bring Kirpatrick to my office, now!" Not waiting, he turned and stormed away.

The two officers behind him stepped up to Kira. She looked at them and frowned. "Oh, I don't think so. No way you're touching me! I'm taking my boy and leaving." She'd known Hewitt for years but the other was a rookie. "Come on, you know Baby Huey, he has it in for me."

Officer Hewitt took her arm. "Come on, Kira; let's not do this out here, okay? Please..."

"No fucking way, Hewitt. I don't have the time." Kira tried to push her way around him and the rookie.

"Kira... Damn it, don't do this. Don't dishonor your father like this."

Kira sighed. "You may have been my father's friend, but the only way you're getting me in there is dragging me." Kira turned her back to him to face her perp.

Kira's old friend quickly took her arm and twisted it behind her back. "Kira, please..."

Gritting her teeth, she pushed her ego aside. "Fine...let's go."

Slamming the door behind her, Kira screamed at the captain. "Fine, let's get this over with." Kira rubbed her arm. "You don't like me, I don't like you. You blame me because my Dad busted your ass fourteen years ago. You were crooked then and you still are."

The captain sat quietly, plotting revenge. "Are you

done?"

Kira smiled, then plopped down in the chair.

He smiled as he dialed the phone. He finally had her. Her badge would be his. "Good, because I've had enough of you messing with my cases. Mouthing off to me was the last straw."

The line picked up on the other end. "Yes, I want to talk to Mitchell right now! I want to file a complaint about one of his people who is currently sitting in my office." He grinned. "Oh, that would be Kirpatrick."

Henry quickly picked up the phone. "What's going on, Howard?" He decided to disarm the captain. "By the way, has she left with our suspect yet? I'd like to get this case wrapped up, because it's a biggie."

"No, she hasn't. I want to let you know she's mouthed off to me for the last time, Henry. She needs to learn respect."

Henry rolled his eyes, glad that Baby Huey couldn't see him. "I'll deal with her when she gets back here. Don't worry though; it won't happen again. Now, please tell her to get her ass back here. You can send our boy over with two of your officers. Our warrant overrules your charges, sorry."

The commander's door opened and Penny set a folder on his desk. "Thanks for calling me, Howard. Bye."

Captain Howard looked up at the smug investigator. "Get out! He wants your sorry ass back at the station. You'll be lucky if you have a job after this."

Kira stood and sauntered to the door. "No prob', Huey." She laughed as she shut the door behind her.

Walking up behind Manny, Kira yelled in his ear.

"Boo!"

Manny jumped from the chair. "Shit! Damn, Kira, you just took five years off my life."

"Good, you're catching up to me, then. Let's get out of here." She walked toward the door.

"What about our boy?"

"He's to be delivered to us. Apparently, I was a naughty girl and have to get back to the station ASAP. See you later, Hewitt." Kira chuckled.

Once outside Kira stopped Manny. "Stay here; make sure that prick sends him over to us. I don't trust him."

Manny nodded and turned to go back into the building. "Will do, I'll call you when they leave."

Climbing into her truck, Kira's cell rang. She knew without looking who it was. "Henry, I…"

"Kira just listen to me. I know he's a hotheaded dickhead. I know he's got it in for you because of your father. You need to stop baiting him, though. One of these days, he's going to call in favors again. I may not be able to save you.".

"I can't help it, Henry. He's a complete dickwad." Kira ran her hand through her hair.

"Kira… I know he is. You have to relax, though, or you're going to blow your career. Don't give him the satisfaction. Besides, your father would haunt your ass if you did. Now tell me something…"

Kira pulled out into traffic. "Yes…"

"Do you need some days off? You know, some personal time."

"No, why?" Kira honked at a car trying to cut in front of her. "Bastard…"

"Kira, focus. Well, I just thought you might. Kevin said something about going to Disney. Apparently it's pride week there."

"Henry, I hate Disney, you know that. Tell Kevin to have fun, though. Oh crap...tell him not to dare bring me back anything Mickey. I'll make him eat it this time." Last time he'd brought back mouse ears for everyone. Kevin then demanded someone take their picture.

Henry laughed. "Okay, will do. How's Bella doing?"

"She's good. I'm good. Everything's basically good. My concern right now is getting our boy under our roof. I want to know everything he knows by the end of the night. I'm stopping by home first. Then I'll be at the station." She pulled into her driveway and turned off the engine.

"Okay, see you in a few. Say hi to Bella for me."

✝

By the end of the evening, they had all they needed to charge Ronald with two counts of attempted premeditated murder. Kira couldn't wait to bring him down. They now had enough evidence, including Remmy's statement, to send him away for a long time.

Sitting in her home office early the next morning, Kira called Taylor. "Good morning, Taylor. I wanted to catch you first thing. How's Remmy today?"

"I just talked with her nurse. She didn't have a good night. Could you please go see her?"

Kira hesitated. "I um...I don't think I'll be able to get away today. I've got a ton of paperwork to process. I also need to call Jack and find out what's going on."

"Try to, Kira, and stop avoiding her. I know it would mean a lot to Remmy if you did. She needs to know people care about her. That we'll...we'll be there for her."

It was obvious to Kira Taylor was trying to guilt her

into seeing Remmy. She smiled. It had worked a little. "I'll try, Taylor. I'm not going to guarantee it, though."

Kira spent until late in the afternoon finalizing all the paperwork. She wanted to make sure all her ducks were in a row when the time came. She should have been done hours before but couldn't concentrate.

"Okay, I need food. That's the problem; my blood sugar must be low. I haven't eaten all freakin' day." She picked up her jacket and headed out for a sandwich. However, she changed her mind as she passed Penny, and decided to go to the hospital instead. "Penny, I'm going to the..."

Penny cut her off. "...to the hospital to check on Remmy. I know. Now go. You've putzed away most of the day already." Penny made shooing motions.

Rolling her eyes, Kira walked away. "Shit, does everyone here know my business? Damn busybodies."

†

Remmy woke in the late afternoon to whispers. She saw Taylor and Jack standing by the door, talking quietly. She knew immediately that something was up and sat up as much as she could. "Okay, you two, what are you talking about?"

She saw Taylor glance at Jack, who looked away. Jack always was a terrible liar. Remmy could always tell when he was lying.

Taylor took a step toward her bed. "We were talking about that new steakhouse. It's the first place we're going when we spring you from here."

Remmy didn't buy it for a second. "Dad, you're lying. You know I can always tell. Now what were you really

217

talking about."

Taylor straightened her blanket. "That's not important right now. How are you feeling, sweetie?"

"Dad, stop, I'm not a child."

"Okay, it's about Kira. We were discussing what a pussy she is."

Remmy snickered. "Jack! Stop! Fine, if you didn't want to tell me, then don't. Geez..."

Taylor shook his head. "Jack, sometimes I wonder if you were dropped on your head as a baby."

All three of them laughed.

Remmy looked at her father. "You know, Dad, I wonder the same thing sometimes. Now...when's dinner? I'm hungry. I also want to know what's going on. Have they found the weasel yet?"

"I just passed them in the hall with the trays. Your grub should be here soon," Mack said as she let the door close behind her. Shaking hands with Jack and Taylor, she rolled her eyes. Mack had heard most of the conversation as she walked in.

She kissed Remmy on the cheek. "I can't say how good it's going to be though." She laughed. "Jack, Taylor, why don't the two of you go grab something to eat. I'll stay here."

Jack nudged Taylor. "I could eat. How about you, pops?"

Taylor chuckled at Jack's antics. "Very funny, Jack... Okay, let's go."

Remmy questioned Mack as she sat down on the edge of Remmy's bed. "What's going on at the office? How's Colin handling everything?"

"Don't worry about work. He's on top of it all. You need to worry about you. When do you think they're going to give you parole from this place?"

Remmy smiled. "It can't be soon enough." Her door opened. "Ah, dinner time at the zoo."

The young volunteer placed the tray in front of her. "Here you go, Ms. Garrick."

Mack took the cover off. "Oh, it looks so yummy for the tummy. Thanks, I'll help her."

"Sarcasm doesn't become you. Oh, look at that. I wonder what species it was. Thankfully, I'm starving. Well, the smell is a little off of what a good steak would create. Oh well…"

"Here let me help." Mack helped her eat a few bites.

Remmy waved her off.

Mack sat down, taking Remmy's hand. "You okay?"

Remmy felt a little nauseous. "Yeah, just not as hungry as I thought I was. Can you turn on the TV and find some cartoons, please? I need a good laugh."

A few moments later a knock, followed by the door opening, interrupted the cartoon they were laughing at. Remmy wondered who would be knocking. "Come in."

Kira walked into Remmy's room and noticed two things immediately. The first was the uneaten food and the second was Mack holding Remmy's hand that wasn't covered in tubes.

Mack looked up at Kira and smiled. "Good afternoon, Inspector. How are you today?"

Totally snubbing Mack, Kira frowned at Remmy and said, "I'll come back later, Ms. Garrick, when you have some free time. Please excuse me." She abruptly turned and left.

Once in the hall, she verbally kicked herself. "Idiot! You have no right to be jealous of her. I can't believe that woman would be her type though." Pushing the elevator button once wasn't enough. Kira beat on it, willing it to hurry.

"Come on, damn it. Why is this thing taking so long?" Kira heard footsteps behind her.

"Kira, wait up a second. I want to talk to you."

"Fuck. I don't need this shit." Kira started for the steps, hoping to make a rapid exit.

"Kira, I said hold up." Mack caught Kira's arm. She tried catching her breath. "I'm sorry…I didn't know."

Kira pulled Mack's hand off her arm. "Excuse me? What are you talking about?"

Finally catching her breath, Mack explained. "I didn't know there was something going on between the two of you. I'm very sorry."

Kira froze a moment. "What? Uh, no. No, we don't. I'm the investigator working on her case. That is the extent of our relationship."

"No way, I can tell there's something." Mack wasn't going to be so easily swayed.

"Mack, I said no, never! Now please, leave me alone." Kira pushed the stairwell door open and headed down the steps, taking two at a time. She needed to run as fast and as far as she could.

"Damn! Fucking, damn!" *How dare she assume something is going on between us? I need to get out of this city.* Pulling her phone out, Kira punched in a speed dial.

"Penny, make reservations for me now. Yes, tonight…tell Henry I'll be gone for a couple of days."

Remmy glared at Mack as she sheepishly returned to sit beside the bed. "Okay, what was that all about? Care to explain why you tore off after Kira?"

"I'm sorry. I know you turned me down when I asked you out, but is there anything between the two of you? It's just that I think you can do better than her."

Remmy nervously laughed. "No, there is not. Let's leave it at that. Please, for me, drop it."

Mack was confused, but kept her mouth shut. "Okay, what are we going to watch now? Oh, Jules called earlier. She says she is on her way to London, then Cardiff. She'll be back in six days."

†

The helicopter touched down on a private airstrip outside of Raleigh. It remained only long enough for the tall, dark-haired woman to safely get out and step away. Her favorite mode of transportation was waiting for her, a Suzuki Hayabusa. The second vehicle would not be delivered until she requested it. Sitting next to the bike was a backpack containing everything she needed. Her personal phone vibrated in her pocket.

Smiling, she answered. "Hi, baby. Yes, I am here. How are you feeling? Good, please do not go into labor until I get back there. I love you."

She checked the pack to make sure everything she asked for was there. "Nik, I will be careful, I promise. It is only a retrieval, pure and simple. I have to go. Call me, though, if you need to."

Putting the phone in her pocket, she started the engine. "Ooh, this is going to be fun, Ronald old boy. Lillith is coming to claim her pound of flesh." She revved the bike, taking off like a rocket.

✝

Two hours later, Ronald had a gun at the back of his head but had no clue who was holding it. He had been sound asleep when, suddenly, he found himself thrown on the floor. He immediately realized what the object was that had been against his head. Eerily quiet moments passed. Then he heard a low voice he'd never wished to hear again in his life. He had no idea how Lillith had found him. Instead of checking into a hotel, he had found an old warehouse and crashed there for the time being.

What he failed to comprehend was that Lillith could find anyone, anywhere. It would not have mattered how far he ran or for how long, she would track him down. "Hello, weasel. I hear you have been a naughty boy. Whatever am I going to do with you?"

Her deep cruel laughter rang in his ears as he wet his pants. "Lillith, I can explain."

"I am sure you will try."

Ronald stuttered. "You can't kill me."

"True, for some reason, they want you alive." Lillith sneered. She hated this little man.

She pulled him to his feet. "Let us go. I am keeping my promise to Jack. So you can rot in prison."

Unfortunately, for Ronald, he just wasn't smart enough to keep his mouth shut.

He leered up at her. "Remmy says your whore's pregnant again. The two of you are an abomination, just as they were. Haley got what she deserved…raped and fucked into oblivion. Just as I'm sure that's what my friend did to Remmy."

Lillith's body tensed. "I changed my mind. Say hello to Hades when you meet him." She knocked him out and handcuffed him. Then she used his own belt to hang him like a side of beef. She pulled a satellite phone from the pack as she walked away. "I need a bonfire at these coordinates. I will pay triple."

She called Jack. "Sorry." No other words were needed.

Ten minutes later, she had the satellite phone and gun completely disassembled. She tossed the parts into the river at intervals as she rode out of North Carolina. Over the last years of her life, Lillith felt remorse for all the lives she'd taken. She had sought redemption, finding it when her heart was willingly stolen by a beautiful woman named Nikki.

This death was different though…it would bring satisfaction to all concerned. Now, it was only a matter of how would she tell her very pregnant wife that she had not kept to her word as she promised. Even though he would not die by her hands, she still held the responsibility for it.

†

Early the next morning, a burned rental car was located at the bottom of a ravine. When the vehicle was traced, it was deduced that the badly charred body in the driver's seat was none other than Ronald himself.

Kira's cell phone rang. "No! Damn it! I wanted him to stand trial for what he did. No…thank you for calling. I'll notify the next of kin."

Instead of calling Taylor first, Kira called Jack. "Good evening, Jack. I'm sure you know why I'm calling."

Kira's voice caused Jack to stutter. "Uh…. Hi, Kira, how are you?"

Kira sighed. "Jack…"

"Sometimes, Kira, I'm sure things just happen. He is a sick bastard who deserves anything that happens to him. I only wish I could be there to see him wet himself, 'cause I'm sure he will when he gets what he has coming to him. I, for one, will be very satisfied that he'll never hurt Remmy again. That is all that matters to me."

Kira could tell that Jack wasn't about to come right out and admit he knew. Kira ran her fingers through her hair.

"Well, since he's dead, he won't be able to hurt Remmy and I'm glad as well that she's safe. I have to go. I need to call Taylor to let him know it's over with. Please let her know she has my thanks and to let me know if she had any additional fees."

Jack laughed. "Ah, well, I'm sure it was her pleasure. Good evening, Kira."

Jack had been unsure how Kira would react to the news of Ronald's demise. Her response shocked him, yet it didn't. It confirmed her feelings for Remmy. Kira would never acknowledge it as anything other than an accident, therefore saving Remmy from further pain. Jack smiled. "I'd have to say our dear inspector is in love with her. She just doesn't have a clue how to handle it."

Chapter Eleven

Remmy patiently waited. It had been two days since Kira walked out of her room. By the end of the third day, she started taking it personally. Colin brought her a two-pound bag of her favorite candy, peanut M&Ms. They sat on the table unopened, as did the package of chocolate chip cookies. Mack told her stupid jokes, while Jack told her of his latest schemes to get her dates. No one could make Remmy smile or even laugh. Even the news of Ronald's death the night before did nothing to lighten her mood.

Remmy closed out Skype on her phone and slipped it into her pocket.

Jules pulled no punches. "I'm not sorry he's dead either, Remmy. He was a bastard. I hope to hell he suffered before he died. I am sorry, though, that I'm in Cardiff for another three days. I'd rather be there taking you home this afternoon. If I didn't already have these commitments, I would be, because I want to make sure you're okay. You're miffed about something. I can see it in your eyes. You're hurt because Kira's ignoring you, is that it?"

Sighing, Remmy stood slowly. "I'm doing well; don't worry about it. Jack and Dad will be here in a while. Then I'll just go home and sit for a month or so. I don't even have to worry about the office. Colin has everything under control for the time being. I'm so happy this whole mess is over with."

"You ignored my earlier question. Remmy, you're hurt by Kira ignoring you, aren't you? Have you tried calling her? I think you should. If you don't, I will. I don't want to get into the middle of it, but I will if need be. I care too much about you to see you continue hurting so much."

"Jules, don't, please. I can handle this. Will you drop it if I promise to call her?" Remmy slipped her feet into her slippers.

"Yes, gladly. Now tell me about what's going on with that loser friend of Ronald's. I want to strangle that man for laying a finger on you."

Shuffling to the windows, Remmy longed to be home in her own bed. "Kira was pissed because the DA accepted a plea in exchange for him telling them everything. She said he'll probably only do about five years at most, then get out on good behavior. Then he'll be out terrorizing little old ladies on the streets in no time. I wish they would've thrown the book at him. So, tell me what you're up to in Cardiff? Oh, are you going to the World Peace Concert tonight or tomorrow? The concert is supposed to be twenty-four hours long."

Jules stared at the bed. Laid out upon it were three pair of leather pants, three pair of jeans, twelve black t-shirts, two pair of black fingerless gloves, and a zippered black bag that contained twelve black special made masks that covered the upper part of her face. An additional mask sat apart from the rest of the clothes.

Running her fingers along the edges of the black fabric, Jules sighed. "I don't think so. Remmy, when I get back we need to talk about something."

Remmy gasped into the phone. "Jules, what's wrong?"

She laughed. "Nothing, babe...I...I just have something very interesting to tell you. After I get back, I'm going to crash for a couple of days, though." Maybe it was time she let someone into her life. No one knew, but maybe it was time.

"Okay, no problem, I won't push you. It's too bad you aren't going to the concert. I saw on that entertainment show last night that Phoenix, the one I go all fan-girl over, is going to be there. She's going to perform with most of the bands or singers."

Jules' heart stopped. "Really? You mean that drummer?"

"Yes, but she's no ordinary drummer. She's the best in the world. They say everyone wants her for their cds and tours. I saw her once a couple of years ago. It was incredible. All of her drums were on a separate stage in the back. It literally rose up through this blood-red mist. I tell you, it was awesome. I don't know how she's going to do it though. It means she's going to be playing for a long time."

Laughing, Jules started to pack her gear bag. She thought to herself that it would probably blow Remmy's mind if she knew that Jules was actually the person they were talking about. "I don't have a clue how she's going to do it either. This is the biggest undertaking she's ever done. I've read on-line in an article that she doesn't do drugs, so it's probably caffeine and adrenalin. You sound like you really enjoyed that concert." Jules smiled.

"Oh yeah… It was the best concert I have ever been to." Her door opened. "Well, the cavalry has arrived to facilitate my escape. I'll talk to you later."

Zipping her bag, Jules set it by the door. "Yeah, I'll talk to you later. Go home and do nothing but sleep."

"Okay, I will. Hope you find some great deals to bring home. Bye."

Remmy closed the phone slipping it into her pocket. "I know, I know. I'm not supposed to be using the cell phone in here."

Jack rummaged through the bag on the table by Remmy's bed. "Oh, who brought you chocolate? Yummy, yummy, you can't eat all of this, so I'll help you." He found his favorite and sat down, happily devouring it.

Taylor hugged his daughter. "When did Dr. Katz say you could get out of here?"

Remmy sat on the bed. "At three, if the rest of the tests come back okay." Sighing, she stared out the windows.

"Sweetie, what's wrong?" When Remmy didn't answer him, he laid his hand on her arm.

Startled, Remmy looked up at him. "I'm sorry, Dad. What did you say?"

She noticed Taylor exchanging glances with Jack. "When was the last time you saw Kira? Has she done something?"

Shaking her head, Remmy told him. "She came in a couple of days ago and acted really weird. Then she stormed out of here. That was the last time I saw her."

Taylor stormed, "I am so frustrated with the both of

you! Call her and just ask her. The direct route is best."

Remmy resigned herself to the inevitable. "I'll call her once I get home." She saw Jack digging in her bag of chocolate. "Hey, don't eat the whole bag. Save me a couple."

Jack smiled, sticking his tongue out at her. Remmy chuckled. "Oh, that's so mature, playing *lookie* at your age. How does Patrick put up with you?"

Jack popped another into his mouth. "Remmy, you should never act your age. Doing things like this..." He stuck his chocolate covered tongue out at her again. "...is what keeps us young. You should try it some time. It's been way too long since you did something childish."

Remmy rolled her eyes. "You're a trip, Jack. Now, where in the hell is that doctor? I want out of here."

†

It was after eight in the evening but Colin was still in his office at Garrick Construction. He was staying late to finish the close-out paperwork on Lee's jewelry shop project. He didn't mind all the paperwork in the least. He found he liked doing the job, even though it took him out of being in the field so much.

Colin picked up his ringing cell phone. "Hello, Kira. What can I do for you?"

Kira rolled the beer bottle between her hands. She'd finally bought a new Bluetooth for her phone. Seeing as she destroyed at least one Bluetooth every couple of months, Kira hoped the new one lasted longer. Especially considering the price she paid for it. The commander told her the last time that she'd have to buy her own for the next entire year if she destroyed her last one. Two days later, Kira had to tell him she'd lost it on the way back from a crime scene.

"I figured I'd give you a call since Remmy went home this afternoon. I'm sure she wants Mr. Bubbles back. I was thinking you could stop by tomorrow and pick him up." This was her last connection to Remmy. She needed to sever it in order to refocus her energy.

"Why don't you take Mr. Bubbles back to her?" He heard silence. "Never mind, I know. Because you're done with the case. So, you're washing your hands of her. You, Kira, are giving me a migraine."

Kira gritted her teeth. "Colin, you don't understand. Now, are you coming to pick him up or do I have to call Taylor? I even have a cat carrier for him so you don't have to touch him."

Colin sighed. "Fine, I'll be there tomorrow afternoon."

†

Opening her door, Remmy knew for sure her messages to Kira would go unanswered. Colin stood on her threshold with Mr. Bubbles. "I should have known."

Colin looked at her strangely as he walked in. "Known what?"

Waving him into the living room, Remmy put down her tea. "Nothing... Never mind." She took Mr. Bubbles from the carrier, hugging him tightly.

"It's so good to have you home, sweetie. I'll give you a special treat tonight. So, tell me, how's *Ms. Investigator* doing?" Remmy put Mr. Bubbles onto the floor. "Ah and there he goes in search of new play toys I might have bought him."

Colin set the bag of cat food down. "She looked like she'd been through a tornado. Who knows, though, that could be normal for her. How are you feeling?"

Remmy sat on the couch, pulling her blanket over her legs. "Tired as hell... I was almost asleep when you knocked. Before I forget, thanks for getting the house cleaned."

"No problem. I came by to drop him and his food off. I need to get downtown anyway. I have three permits to file for today. I'll need them tomorrow."

Remmy looked concerned. "Isn't that cutting it a little close?"

Colin waved his hand at her. "No big deal. It's all taken care of. This one was a last minute job that came up. Don't worry about it, I have it all covered."

"Okay, I trust you to know what you're doing." Remmy yawned. "Damn, how can I be so tired?"

He kissed her on the forehead. "It's your body trying to heal. Now, sleep. I'll check on you tomorrow."

"Okay, thanks. Can you push the lock on the door on your way out? Thanks."

Seconds after Colin left, Mr. Bubbles crawled onto Remmy's lap. He started kneading her thigh to make a comfy spot to lay.

Remmy reached down to pet him. "I missed you, boy." He meowed at her. "Oh please, I don't buy it for a second. I'm positive you were spoiled rotten. I do wish she'd return my phone calls, though." He meowed loudly.

Laughing, she slowly wiggled around to make both of them comfortable. Petting him, Remmy let her mind and body drift off. "I tried calling her twice yesterday and once today. What more am I supposed to do? I'm not begging. I'm not that pathetic."

Mr. Bubbles lifted his head to look at her. If she

didn't know better, Remmy would have sworn he gave her the evil eye. "Damn, boy, if looks could kill, you'd have just done me in with that one."

Closing her eyes, Remmy drifted off. "I'll try again tomorrow." Mr. Bubbles purred loudly and Remmy fell asleep.

Remmy woke up a while later, feeling relaxed. She was very glad she had thought to put the massaging/heating mat under her. "Oh nice..." Stretching, Remmy wasn't as stiff as she had been when she woke that morning.

"Okay, note to self, use massage mat thingie for the rest of my life." She moved the black furball aside. "Well Bubbs, let's go check our emails and see what Dad left us for dinner."

She opened the fridge and found a plate of chicken and broccoli casserole. She threw it in the microwave to heat up and booted up her laptop. A few moments later, she was devouring her dinner and sorting through hundreds of messages. Coming up on an email from Jules, Remmy opened it. She was curious about the pictures her friend had sent.

Opening the pictures, Remmy almost choked on the mouthful of broccoli. "Oh my God, look! She did go to the concert and she sent us pictures."

The next picture that popped onto the screen caused her to drop her fork. The noise startled Mr. Bubbles, who sat next to her plate begging for food. "Holy hell in a hand basket! Jules sent us a picture of Phoenix. Holy shit, she must have met her. Maybe the next picture is of the two of them."

It wasn't, though. It was a picture of a hotel room. Laying upon the bed were a pile of clothes and a black bag. Remmy went back to the text portion of the email. "Ah, she

says this is her huge suite they gave her. Wow, it's amazing."
Then she noticed something in the picture. Opening it
to full view, she looked closer at the bed. "Huh?" Remmy
then clicked on the picture of the drummer again. They were
the same clothes.

"Well, I'll be damned, Mr. Bubbles, it looks like she
got more than a picture. I think your Aunt Jules wasn't alone
last night."

Remmy replied to the email, saying… *Way to go,
Jules. I hope she was as hot as she looks.*

An hour later, Remmy put her dirty dishes in the
dishwasher and retired back to the couch. Turning the TV on,
Remmy quickly found her favorite cartoon channel. Within
moments, she was sound asleep once more, with a snoring
cat draped across her thighs.

†

Bella could hear her aunt's phone ringing. It wasn't
coming from Kira's office, which was where her aunt had
been hiding the last few days. Following the sound, Bella
found it buried in a kitchen drawer. She looked at the screen.

*What the hell? Twenty-four missed calls and eighteen
unplayed messages. Oh, Aunt Kira, what's going on?* Bella
walked down the hall to see her aunt.

Standing in the doorway, she found her aunt with her
booted feet on her desk. Kira's hands were clasped behind
her head, leaning back in the chair. "Aunt Kira, shame on
you. You always yell at me for putting my boots on the
coffee table…geez."

Kira smirked at her niece. "I can do it 'cause I'm
older."

Bella stood with her hands on her hips. "That's no

excuse."

"Shit. You really are a miniature replica of me."

Approaching Kira, Bella held out the phone. "Care to explain why you're not answering your phone? Or listening to your messages?"

When she didn't answer, Bella tried again. "Aunt Kira, I'm worried about you. You've been skulking around here for almost a week now. What's going on? I notice you avoid not only Remmy but Taylor and Jack as well. Several times in fact. You also haven't listened to their messages."

Kira growled. "Annabella…"

She waved the phone at Kira. "No, you always tell me to be honest. You say no matter how much the truth hurts, you should never lie."

Dropping her feet to the floor, Kira stood up. Flustered, she sat back down. "You're too young to understand, Bella. We've gone through this before, so just drop it."

Rolling her eyes, Bella sighed. "Yes, we've been through this before. We probably will again, unless you wake up, Aunt Kira. You're running away, as usual. I'm going nowhere. It's time for you to grow up."

Kira leaned over, resting her elbows on her legs. "It's not just that, it's other things too. My job is dangerous. I can't ask her to deal with that. She's been through way too much already."

Bella knelt in front of her aunt. "Aunt Kira, that's a cop-out. You know it and I know it. It's pure bullshit, as you would say."

"Bella…" Kira threw her hands up.

"Aunt Kira, talk to me. What else is going on? I've never known you to run from a fight. Why now?"

"Bella, she's way out of my league. She's rich,

beautiful, and way classier than I am. I could never give her all the things she's used to. I'll never have that much money. Compared to her, I'm a fucking welfare person." Kira was shouting. However, Bella knew her aunt wasn't shouting at her. She was shouting at herself for allowing Remmy to affect her so much. Kira dropped back into her chair.

Bella hugged her. "Has she ever made money an issue? Has she ever thrown it up in your face?"

"No, she hasn't. She's too classy to do that. It still doesn't mean that maybe she doesn't feel that way." Kira stood and picked up the empty beer bottles.

Following her aunt to the kitchen, Bella shook her head. "Aunt Kira, take a chance. Please do it for me. Taylor told me Remmy's birthday is in a few months."

Kira smiled. "He's a cool guy, huh. I know her birthday is coming up. Maybe…maybe I could do something nice for her. Now, mind you, I'm doing this so you'll stop harping on me."

Bella smirked knowingly. "Okay, yeah, whatever." Taking the empties from Kira, she rinsed them, then tossed them into the recycle bin. "Oh, my Aunt's going on a date."

"No! I said I'd do something nice. I, however, will not go on a date. No way, no how. Now, go finish your homework." Kira pushed her out of the kitchen.

"Aunt Kira, buy her something, then take her out to dinner."

Kira threw the dishtowel down. "I said no! I'm not going out in public with her."

Bella pleaded. "Please, take the chance. It'll only be dinner, no big deal. You need to stop hiding who you are. It's eating away at you. I'm not a stupid child, Aunt Kira. Please, don't treat me as one. You need to come out of the closet. You deserve to be happy." Bella put her arms around Kira, pulling her into a hug.

Kira held her tight. "You, Bella, are my lifeline. I'll try. It's so hard, though, impossibly too hard."

†

Taylor held back for the first week after they brought Remmy home. Over that time, she visibly became more withdrawn every day. Finally, Taylor had to speak his piece. But he hadn't been ready for Remmy's reaction.

The angry words still rang in his ears. He and Remmy had stood in her living room toe to toe. They argued about her trying to call Kira again. Taylor wanted her to, yet Remmy saw it as a waste of time.

He had just suggested that she call Kira, when she rounded on him fast, startling him. Remmy stood, with her face inches from Taylor's.

"Dad, get the hell out! This is my life. I don't feel like torturing myself any longer. I am done with this whole mess. Now…get out!"

He promptly turned and left. Taylor didn't try calling her, knowing Remmy would call when she was ready. When his phone finally rang, Taylor smiled. It had taken a little longer than he thought it would, but Remmy had finally called.

Remmy hesitated when her father answered. She was ashamed at how she'd acted. "Hi, Daddy, how are you doing?"

"Better now that you've called me. I hate when we disagree about something."

Remmy set her water bottle down. "Dad, let's just

236

agree to disagree on this one and move on. So that said, what are you doing for dinner tomorrow night?"

Taylor smiled again. "Cooking steaks on the barbeque for us, that's what. You know I like cooking on my grill year round. In my opinion, everything tastes better cooked that way."

"I was thinking of taking you out for a nice dinner. That way you don't have to cook." Remmy wanted to do something nice for him, considering how badly she'd treated him lately. "Okay, Dad, tell you what, I'll buy everything if you cook the steaks. We can watch the game later then, if you want." Remmy finished her bottle of water.

"Sounds good. How are you feeling?"

Remmy was surprised when he didn't ask that immediately. "I'm not feeling too bad. I'm going to start back into the office on Monday. Before you say anything, Dad, I'm only going to work a couple of days this week and next. After that, I should be good to go. I'll see you around four tomorrow."

"Okay, I'll see you tomorrow. Oh, can you bring some of that coffee you like? I only have plain."

Remmy laughed, knowing what he was doing. Her father was trying to bridge the gap a little himself. He disliked any flavored coffee, but for her, he'd drink it and call it good. "Sure, Dad, no problem. Bye for now."

✝

Colin entered Remmy's office, closing the door behind him. He'd been nervous since she called him earlier. Clueless as to why Remmy had asked him to meet with her, he assumed it couldn't be good.

He watched her pull a folder from a drawer. "Colin,

don't look so worried."

Colin chuckled. "That obvious, huh?"

Remmy laughed. "Yes, it is. Why I asked you to meet with me this morning is a good thing. You've really liked running everything while I was gone, haven't you?"

Sitting up straighter, Colin wondered what Remmy was up to. "Ah, yeah, you could say that. What's up?"

Smiling, she leaned back in her chair. "Well, I was thinking…"

Colin threw his head back with laughter. "I thought I smelled smoke." His grin filled his face. He loved teasing Remmy.

Remmy rolled her eyes. "Ha…ha, you're always so funny." Remmy laughed. "Okay, so I don't do sarcastic very well."

"No you don't. So what's up?"

"Answer me this. What would you say to my promoting you to Operations Manager? I'd like to keep Mack as my assistant, so we'll need to look for a new Project Manager. Everyone in the company would report to you, except Mack; both of you report directly to me. This way, if anything should ever happen again, I won't have to worry. You and Mack can handle everything and not have to worry about approval from anyone else."

Colin visibly relaxed. "It sounds good to me. It worked out great while you were out. This way it will also get a few things off your plate."

Pushing the opened folder toward him, Remmy tossed him a pen as well. "Yeah, like the union negotiations that are coming up. I'm not going to handle that shit on my own this time. So all you have to do is read and sign. Then you can have Mack get you new business cards, Mr. Operations Manager & Vice President." Remmy sat back and chuckled.

Colin looked up. "What the fuck?"

Laughing, Remmy leaned forward, resting her elbows on the desk. "Yep, thought you'd like that title. You earned it. You've been here a long time. You're a hell of a worker. Let me know if you have any ideas for a new PM. I also put an ad in the paper."

Signing the paper, Colin shook his head. "Seems so unreal. The shorter hours and less physical labor will be nice. If I think of anyone, I'll give you a call. Right now though, I've got to get over to Moe's."

Remmy grimaced. "How's it going with him? Do want me to talk to him also?"

Colin stood. "Nah, I'll handle it. He's not a happy camper. He still doesn't understand why we have to demo the remainder of the building. I can't get it through to him about the danger of the mold in it, let alone that it's not structurally sound. I'll work it out, don't worry."

Remmy put the folder in her drawer. "If anyone can do it, it's you. Call me later after everything's take care of."

†

Remmy called Mack's desk phone for the fifth time in the last two minutes. "Anything yet?"

"No, Remmy, he's not here yet, and no, Jules's flight has not landed either."

Remmy threw her pen on the desk. "Well, this guy is already fifteen minutes late for his interview. If he shows, call Colin, he's back in his office. He can tell him no thanks. As for Jules, how did you know I was wondering?"

"Cause I know you. Now relax, she'll get back safely. I'm worried as well. It threw me when Jules called saying her flight had encountered trouble mid-air and had to land right after takeoff. At least she was able to catch another flight and hopefully she's on her way home."

Closing her eyes a moment, Remmy sighed. "Yeah, I know, I'm totally predictable. Just like I know you rolled your eyes at me calling you every few minutes. Well, just let me know when you find out anything. I'm going over to scan in the Murdock plans that came in earlier."

"Ah, hold on, I just got a delivery for you. I'll be right in with it."

Colin was walking down the hall when Mack took the roses into Remmy's office. Wanting to know who they were from, he followed her. Flopping himself in the chair, curiosity got the best of him. "Okay, who are they from?"

"I agree with Colin, I want to know as well. It's about time someone took notice of you, Remmy. Ooh, I think someone has a secret admirer."

Colin smiled. "Yep, but it's not going to be a secret for long. Now open the card, woman, before I do." He reached for the card.

Remmy reached over and smacked his hand. "Do you freakin' mind? They are my flowers, not either of yours." Pulling the card from the envelope, Remmy blushed as she read it.

Happy Birthday
Will you have coffee with me in the morning?
K

Remmy's cell phone rang. Looking at the caller id, it was Kira, which caused her face to turn redder. Hitting the talk button, curiosity got the best of her. She wanted to know why Kira seemed to have done a complete turnaround. "Yes."

Kira announced, "I'll pick you up at your house at

eight-thirty. See you then."

Remmy sat looking at the phone. She was stunned that Kira had finally taken a step forward. Colin cleared his throat and reminded Remmy she still had company. "Uh...I'm going to be late in the morning."

Colin sat up, resting his arms on his knees. "Well, come on, who is it?"

Remmy's eyes twinkled as she smiled. "I'm having coffee in the morning with Kira."

"I'm shocked speechless." Mack muttered.

"Well, I'm not! What the hell?" Colin exploded. "She sent you roses and invited you for coffee? It's about damn time, in my opinion!"

Shaking her head in disbelief, Remmy stood. "I'm in a little shock myself. We'll see what happens. Back to business, though. Obviously this guy we were expecting is a no show. We've been looking for over a week now. Let's hire Andy and be done with it. Mack, get all the paperwork ready for him. Colin, go ahead and call him. Let him know to be here tomorrow morning. I'll be at the scanner for a while with these blueprints if anyone needs me."

Remmy's cell phone chimed that a new text message had arrived. "Okay, phew, Jules was able to get on the next flight. They're taxiing now onto the runway, waiting to take off."

Colin walked back to Mack's desk with her. "I'm dying to know what Kira is up to. So help me, Colin, if she hurts Remmy—"

He slapped her on the back. "Yeah, I hear you. I have a bad feeling about this; I know Remmy. She's going to get her hopes up and then get hurt all over again. I wish Kira would get out of the closet or just get out of Remmy's life for good."

Mack pulled up the forms to print off. "Me too, Colin, me too. I'll set these forms on your desk when I'm done."

Heading toward the door, Colin called back to her. "Okay, I'm off to do battle with Moe. Call me if you need me."

Chapter Twelve

The next morning, Remmy had a mini meltdown. After showering, she changed clothes six times before finally settling on comfortable jeans, red polo shirt, and black leather boots. Looking around the bedroom, Remmy saw clothes strewn everywhere. She'd made a royal mess without realizing it. This told her she was too nervous and needed to calm herself down. Cleaning the room helped, but what she really needed was coffee. Of course, that made her think of her coffee date with Kira.

She nervously looked in the mirror again and second-guessed her choice once more. *Damn, I want to appear casual and comfy, but I don't want to look like I don't care about my appearance. However, I don't want to dress up. It would make me look like a frigid bitch.*

She ran her fingers through her hair and settled for the tousled look. "Hell with it, casual it is. Or maybe…" The doorbell saved her closet from one more annihilation. She checked herself once more before opening the door.

She reached for the door handle and realized her hand was shaking. "Calm down, girl. It's only coffee."

She opened the door and found Kira standing behind the screen door, studying her boots. Smiling, Remmy opened the screen door for the investigator. "Please, come in. I just need to get my cell and bag."

Kira looked around. "No problem. Take your time. I'm a little early." She put her hands in her pockets. "Did you eat yet? If you haven't, we can have breakfast also."

Remmy walked back into the hall from the living room and smiled. She noticed that Kira seemed a little nervous, especially when she hid her shaking hands in her pockets. "No, I didn't. Usually I just grab a bagel on my way to wherever I'm going."

Kira opened the screen door for her. "I know of a café that has excellent bagels and coffee. Shall we?"

Nodding, Remmy closed and locked the door. "That sounds good to me. I don't have anything pressing until ten–thirty this morning. Actually, do you mind if we take both vehicles?"

"No, I don't mind at all. I want to do whatever is easiest for you." Kira smiled shyly.

Remmy smiled warmly at her. "Thanks, it would be a little easier."

Kira followed Remmy to her truck and opened the door for her. She waited for her to get in, then closed the door before getting into her own truck. When Remmy arrived at the café, Kira had already parked and was waiting for her. She opened Remmy's door, then the café door. Kira was acting like a gentleman, which reminded her so much of Haley.

She motioned for Remmy to grab a table while she went to order. Setting the coffees and toasted bagels with cream cheese on the table, Kira looked at her strangely. "Are you okay? How are you feeling these days?"

Remmy had been caught daydreaming. Her eyes misted over every time Haley came to mind. "Yeah, I'm okay. I was just letting my mind wander for a few. Um...really, I'm doing great. The body is still sore, and of course I'm stiff every morning when I get up. I'm glad I'm not as tired as I was, though. It seemed I couldn't last more than an hour without a nap."

Slowly Kira sipped her coffee. "I'm damn glad Colin got there when he did. If he hadn't..." Kira stuttered a moment. She cleared her throat. "Thank the gods for Colin."

Wondering what was going on in Kira's mind, Remmy looked her straight in the eyes. Not lowering her gaze, she quietly asked Kira what she had been wondering since the day before. "Why did you ask me out for coffee?"

"I...does there have to be a reason?"

Remmy could see in Kira's pained expression and her faltering voice that she had caught her off guard.

A look of fear washed over Kira's face. "No reason at all. Need to eat."

Remmy was concerned for Kira. She seemed to be having difficulties focusing. "Kira, is everything okay? Is something wrong?" Remmy sat up quickly. "Oh my God, has something happened to Bella?"

Laughing nervously, Kira touched Remmy's hand. "No, Bella is good. Maybe I just wanted to have coffee with you. That's all, nothing more."

"Ah, I see." Somewhat relieved that all was okay, Remmy took a bite from her bagel. She chewed while trying to think of something neutral to talk about.

Picking up her coffee, Remmy took a sip of the hot liquid. "What are your plans for July Fourth weekend?"

Kira swallowed her mouthful. "July Fourth is one of the two holidays I drew this year. I'll be working in a cruiser all weekend. We can always use all the extra hands we can get on the holidays. Actually, I'll be in the cruiser through next weekend. How about you, any special plans?"

"Nope...I have no plans at all. Well...other than staying at home with a good book. I don't care to deal with all the drunks on the road. I'll have Dad over for dinner day after tomorrow, but that's it."

Remmy had hoped that Kira would take another step and ask her to do something with her that weekend. Hearing that she was working the entire weekend saddened her. "Well, that and write. I want to get a few more chapters done this weekend." Jack was the only other person who knew about her writing and craving to be an author. Why she had told Kira was a mystery.

Kira looked up at her. "Wow, that's great. Did you get anything published yet?"

Waving her hand at Kira, Remmy blushed. "Ppfftt...not yet. I hope to one day, though. I've loved to write since I can remember picking up a pencil. I can hear the characters' voices talking in my head. Most of the time it's for the good, although some of them are very bad people." Remmy blushed. "Sorry, we already talked about that before." She was nervous.

"Wow, seriously, I'm still in awe of you." Kira picked up her coffee, then sat it back down. "So you're hanging at home, huh? No plans with Jules then for the weekend?"

Chuckling, Remmy ignored the jealousy she read in the question. "Nope, she's busy. Besides..." Remmy changed her mind. She wanted Kira to believe her once and for all. "Kira, Jules and I are only friends. That is all there will ever be."

Kira smiled for only a second. "So, no plans with Mack either? I'm sorry, that was crossing the line."

Rolling her eyes, Remmy laughed. "Kira, I have plans with neither. We are nothing but friends. They're not exactly my type." Remmy blushed.

Sitting up straight, Kira shocked Remmy. "So tell me, what exactly is your type?"

Remmy set her coffee down. Reaching across the table, she took Kira's hand. "You are..." She realized too late that she had pushed Kira too far.

Looking at their joined hands, Kira looked up at Remmy with a panicked expression on her face. Kira jumped up and bolted from the table. "No, no, no..." Kira didn't stop running until she was standing by her truck.

A few moments later Remmy exited the café. She'd taken her time clearing away their breakfast debris. Walking by Kira toward her own truck, she noticed the woman was ghost white. "Thank you for breakfast."

Kira took a deep breath. "Remmy, wait..."

Remmy held out her hand to stop Kira. "No, it's okay. I understand. Really, I do." She remembered the beautiful blonde woman she'd seen Kira with.

Opening her truck door, Remmy was on the verge of tears. "I'm very sorry for embarrassing you. I can guarantee you, it won't happen again." Quickly, Remmy got into her truck. She felt humiliated, having been sure Kira was reaching out to her. Remmy's cheeks were flame red as the tears were about to fall.

Kira caught Remmy's door with her hand. "Wait...please. Remmy, please wait. I'm begging please. Please, Remmy..."

Shaking her head, Remmy steeled her nerves. "There's nothing more to be said. I've embarrassed both of us enough for one lifetime."

"Please, you don't understand."

"Yes, I do understand. I know I'm not your type. You prefer beautiful, sexy blondes. I also refuse to go back into the closet. I can't be anyone but myself."

Kira's eyes pleaded with her. "You're wrong. You don't know...you can't possibly know." Kira looked down as Remmy touched her arm.

"Then tell me. Tell me why you seem interested one second, then in the next you're running away."

"Have dinner with me tomorrow night, in between shifts. I'll explain everything then." Kira gave her a slight smile.

"I don't know. Are you going to run away again, if the questions get too hard?" Remmy held her breath.

"No, I won't run. I promise. I hope you will listen and understand why it's a bad idea for us to date."

Remmy squeezed her arm. "Okay."

†

Kira loved spicy food. When Remmy mentioned Sabon was her favorite Thai restaurant, she knew where they were going for dinner. Over fresh spring rolls and jasmine tea, Remmy told Kira about the story she was currently writing.

When their main courses arrived, Remmy cleared her throat. "Kira, please talk to me. Tell me what yesterday was about."

Kira's fork stopped halfway to her mouth. Setting it back on her plate, she remained silent.

Remmy sighed. "Remember, you said you wouldn't run away. Now, please tell me what's going on."

Wiping her mouth, Kira agreed that honesty was best. "My brother and his wife were killed when Bella was very young. He'd made me legal guardian in case anything should ever happen to them. So I've raised her, I'm all she knows. Unfortunately, we live in a bigoted society. If the wrong person at child services even thought I was a lesbian, they might very well take her away from me. It's bad enough I have what they consider an extremely dangerous job."

"Oh, Kira..."

Kira picked up her fork once more. Chewing the food rapidly, she took a sip of her tea. "I've lived with the fear of losing her for so long. I'm all she has and I will do everything humanly possible to keep her with me. On top of that there is what I do for a living. Between my job and keeping our lives together, I would not have time for anyone in my life." Remmy reached for her hand.

"I'm positive they're more accepting now. I highly doubt you'd lose Bella. Plus, I think she's old enough now to make her own decisions."

Shaking her head, Kira pushed her empty plate away. "I can't take the chance. Maybe we could be...could be friends."

Kira loved Remmy. However, could she really be just friends with her? Every time she thought of her with someone else, her jealousy took over. A wave of panic struck Kira. "Actually, that might not even be a good idea. It also is a slight conflict of interest, seeing as you're part of one of my cases. Even though the case is closed, it would look bad." Kira motioned for the bill. "I know you think I'm being overly cautious but I have no choice."

Folding her napkin, Remmy set it on the table. "Kira, no one will take Bella from you. As far as a conflict, I don't see one. Like you said, my case is closed. Why don't you take me home and we'll discuss it more? I have excellent coffee and fabulous Turtle Pecan Cheesecake at home."

Kira's eyes lit up at the mention of cheesecake. "Uh, okay. Let me just pay this." Seeing Remmy was about to object, she pulled her card out and handed it to the waitress. "Nope, I invited you to dinner, my treat. No arguments. You don't always have to pay."

Remmy sighed. "Okay, I know when not to argue. Thank you for dinner."

Signing the receipt, Kira left the waitress a hefty tip. "Okay, shall we?"

"Wow, you really do want that cheesecake, huh?"

"Guilty as charged." Kira had Remmy's birthday gift hidden in the glove compartment in her truck. Putting her card back into her pocket, she stood.

Picking up her bag, Remmy started for the door. "Dessert it is, then, and then you need to get back on the road."

†

Kira sat on the sofa in the living room, sipping her coffee, Remmy having gone to the kitchen a few moments before to cut their dessert. *Ah crap, the gift. I left it in the truck.*

Setting her mug on the end table, Kira yelled out to Remmy. "I forgot something in the truck. I'll be right back in."

"Okay, just watch out for Mr. Bubbles. He likes to sneak out on the porch once in a while."

"Will do."

Quickly, Kira retrieved the gift and she was back waiting on her treat. When she sat down, Mr. Bubbles flew onto her lap. He'd taken an instant liking to Kira and she to him when she had watched over him.

Kira and Mr. Bubbles were having a love fest, when Remmy walked into the room. Mr. Bubbles was purring so loudly it echoed across the room. Kira flipped him on his back and rubbed his belly. "Wow, I'm shocked he lets you do that. He never lets anyone muss his fur up. Haley was the only one... He must like you quite a lot." Remmy handed Kira her plate then curled up in the recliner. "Just be careful or he'll try to steal a bite off your plate."

Kira laughed. "Yeah, I found that out the hard way before. He seems to like coffee ice cream. I set my bowl on my desk and went for a drink. I came back to find his face buried in it."

"Oh my God, I'm so sorry that happened. He can be quite a pisser sometimes. I'm afraid he's been spoiled his whole life."

Kira pushed a little piece of the cheesecake to the edge of the plate for him. He greedily sucked it up. "That's okay, he's a sweetie."

Remmy watched, trying not to cry. Kira looked like she was right at home. Remmy cleared her throat. "Mr. Bubbles, you've had enough. Naughty boy."

Kira had been about to share her last bite with him, when Remmy called him naughty. "I guess that makes me a naughty girl for giving it to him, huh?" Popping the last bite into her mouth, Kira looked up. She tended to eat fast when she was nervous.

Smiling, Remmy shook her head. "Yes, it does."

While Remmy finished hers, Kira went to get them more coffee. After handing Remmy her full cup, she retrieved the gift from the corner of the sofa. Kira had it hidden behind the pillow since going to her truck for it. Shyly, she handed the oblong box to Remmy. She was about to do something that scared the socks off her, but she decided to try. "Happy birthday. I'd like to try for us being friends."

Remmy had a look of shock upon her face. She took the gift from Kira. "You didn't need to give my anything."

Kira took a gulp of her hot coffee, burning her mouth in the process. "Damn, that's hot."

Remmy laughed. "Uh yeah, hot coffee." She opened the box to find an engraved pen. "Wow, thank you. It's beautiful."

Kira picked at an imaginary spot on her jeans. "I thought it was something you should have."

Remmy was speechless for a moment. She just sat staring at Kira. "Thank you."

Nervous, Kira thought for a moment that Remmy didn't like it. "If you don't like it…"

"Oh no, no, I do. Thank you. It's beautiful. This is perfect because I write everything on paper first. Then I transcribe it into the computer."

"It's something special for you…for your writing."

"Seriously, this is fantastic. I've always wanted a fountain pen." Remmy opened the pen. "Oh, cool. It takes cartridges. That makes it so much easier."

"I figured it would be. That's why I opted for that instead of the refillable." The alarm on Kira's cell beeped. "Oh shit. I need to get going. I had a nice time tonight." Kira stood, stretching her legs.

Remmy set her gift on the table by her notebook. "I'll walk you to the door. Thank you for dinner. I agree, it's been a nice evening."

Kira followed Remmy to the front door. When Remmy stopped too fast Kira crashed into her. "Oh, sorry…" Remmy laughed. "No it's me that should be sorry. I stopped too fast. Thank you once again for dinner and the pen."

Kira looked down at Remmy's hand on her waist. *When did that happen.*

"You're welcome. I need to pick Bella up then head back out. I'm on duty tonight. Uh…thanks for going to dinner with me." Kira bent over to kiss Remmy on the cheek. Kira's lips touching Remmy's cheek caused an electric spark.

"We can't have you late, so you better get going. Tell Bella hello for me and if she needs anything to call me or Dad. Please have a safe night."

"Will do. Hopefully, it will be a quiet night. I'll try to call you next week. Night…"

✝

Remmy was impressed. Kira was making an effort. Shutting the door, she called Jack. When he didn't answer, Remmy left him a message, then she called Jules.

Jules picked up on the second ring. "Hey, babe, how's the week been? I'm currently in a taxi going into Manhattan. I'm on the way to my hotel to crash. I'm just contemplating what to have for dinner later tonight"

Taking a cleansing breath, Remmy relaxed. "Crazy. I just had dinner with Kira. She gave me a birthday gift, a beautiful fountain pen. How have you been?"

Jules was shocked. "You what? That's fantastic. It sounds like maybe you're finally getting through to her. I'm doing good, even great, I always like coming back to New York City."

Curling up in her recliner, Remmy picked up the pen. Twirling it between her fingers, she grinned. "Wicked, are you going to be able to do any shopping while you're there?"

"Ah, no, it's all business this time around." Jules looked at her kit bag sitting next to her. "We still need to talk when I get back."

Remmy didn't want to pry, knowing Jules would tell her what she needed to, when she could. It was killing her not knowing, but Remmy kept telling herself that she'd live. "Whenever is fine."

"Okay, I've got to go, the taxi just got to my hotel. I'll talk to you later."

"Okay, call me when you get in on Monday." Remmy laid her head back and was asleep within seconds.

✝

Kira knocked on the door, expecting Mrs. Tibble to answer and invite her in for coffee. What happened threw her for a moment. The door opened and Bella flew onto the porch and past her to the truck. "What the hell? Bella...Bella, wait up." Kira pulled the house door closed, then chased after her niece.

Bella climbed in the truck, slamming the door. Kira followed suit, only carefully closing her door. Turning on the ignition, she waited for Bella to say something. When nothing was forthcoming, Kira pulled out of the driveway.

Long moments of silence passed until Kira could take no more. "Okay, what was that about?" Bella started crying.

Kira pulled a napkin out of the center console and handed it to Bella to blow her nose. "What's going on, sweetie?"

"Freddy…" Bella hiccupped from crying.

If Bella was this upset, it must be bad. "Okay, what about Freddy? Aren't you two best friends?"

"I thought we were too. I was wrong, though. He's a cruel and ignorant pig." Bella stared out the side window.

"Okay, some people are. What's happened to make you say that?" The warning hairs on the back of Kira's neck stood up.

Bella sighed deeply. "I'm so sorry Aunt Kira. You've always put your trust in me and I messed up. I never want to do anything to hurt you. He asked if you had a boyfriend. I said no, that you didn't have a *girlfriend*. That you were single."

Kira gasped. "Bella…"

"I know. I thought I could trust him. He started screaming horrible things. He said all you needed was to be screwed by a man and it would cure you." She started crying again. "I trusted him and he betrayed both of us."

Kira tried to speak as calmly as her emotions would allow. Her hands were clenched around the wheel as she pulled into their driveway. "Bella, this type of thing is very private. You shouldn't be talking to anyone about it."

"I'm sorry, Aunt Kira, I didn't mean to cause trouble. I just don't understand how people can be so cruel anymore. I really thought we'd come a lot further than that." Bella got out, closing the door gentler than before.

Turning off the ignition, Kira wondered when Bella had grown into an adult. Walking around to the other side of the truck, she pulled Bella into a hug. "Sweetie, humans are generally assholes. I know I sound jaded. Maybe I am because of my work, I don't know. What I do know is there are a few good ones out there. You just have to search for them. You'll find a new best friend."

Kira unlocked their front door. "You never know, he or she could be moving into the neighborhood for all we know. Now, let's get you settled, 'cause I need to head out on the road. Tell you what, there's ice cream in the freezer. Why don't you have a huge bowl of it? Better yet…eat right from the carton of the smaller one."

Bella looked up at her aunt. "But that's yours."

Kira ruffled Bella's hair. "I know and you can have it." Kira threw her keys on the table and headed toward her room. "I need to change shirts. I spilled coffee on this one. Then I need to get going."

Strapping her gun belt back on, Kira picked up the ringing phone. "Hello?"

Kira pulled the phone away from her ear. "Who the fuck is this?" She couldn't believe the filth that spewed across the line, all of it to do with her being a lesbian. It had been many years since she had been personally subjected to such an attack. Kira slammed the phone back in the cradle.

Bella yelled down the hall to her aunt's office. "Who was that, Aunt Kira?"

Walking out of the room, Kira fastened the last buckle on her belt. "No one, sweetie. Just do me a favor tonight, okay?"

Bella looked at her aunt strangely. "Sure, anything."

"Make sure the door is locked and don't open it for anyone. Also, don't answer the phone. Okay?" Kira was nervous about leaving Bella alone considering the call she'd just picked up.

"Aunt Kira, is everything okay? Who on the phone?"

Hugging Bella, she put it out of her mind. Kira didn't want to worry her. "Wrong number is all. You know me though, always nervous leaving you home alone."

Bella swatted her aunt's arm. "I'll be fine. Don't worry. Now go, before you're late."

Kira laughed. "Okay, okay. Geez, when did you get so pushy? I can't imagine where you get it from."

Rolling her eyes, Bella pushed Kira out the front door. "Neither can I, now be careful tonight. There'll be a lot of drunks out there. Call me when you're on your way home in the morning. I'll have breakfast waiting on you."

Hugging her niece tightly, Kira kissed her on the forehead. "Will do, now lock the door."

Chapter Thirteen

Nightmares of every form of punishment invaded Kira's dreams. Finally, after waking for the third time, she gave up all together. Looking at the clock, Kira found that only an hour had passed.

Sitting up, she swung her legs out of bed. Stretching like a panther in the afternoon sun, Kira stood from her bed. "Fuck this shit. I'm never going to get any sleep."

Wiping her hands over her face, Kira worried she'd disturbed Bella with the last dream. She was sure she'd been screaming out in her sleep. *Damn, how can one phone call affect me so much?*

Peeking into Bella's room, Kira found her laying on her bed with headphones on, tapping her foot to the music. Gently, Kira closed the door, heading downstairs to the kitchen for coffee. "Yes, that's what I need to clear out the mind. A good strong cup of coffee will do the trick."

Minutes later, while pouring her first cup, Kira automatically picked up the ringing phone. Again, just as the night before, vulgar bigotry filled the line.

"Okay, that's it! You do realize I'm a cop, you asshole? I can and I will trace this call. Then I'm going to arrest you for harassment, just for starters. I'll also throw in hate crimes for another. With the new tougher law that just passed last month, you'll be sharing a cell with the big boys for a very long time. So listen here, you stupid little shit, never ever call here again and I'll forget the whole thing. Got it?"

Silence greeted her. "I thought as much." Hearing the other person hang up, Kira did the same. Then she slammed the phone on the kitchen counter.

"Damn little fucker. I'd love to wring his scrawny neck. I'll be damned if Bella's going to find out about this." Sitting at the kitchen island, Kira rested her head on her hands. "Shit, I don't need this crap."

Kira was bone tired. Knowing she needed some sleep, Kira shuffled into the living room. Relaxing on the sofa, she flipped to a talk show. *Yep, these always put me to sleep.*

Just as Kira was dozing off, her cell phone rang, causing her to jump from the sofa. "Shit! This better be good." Not bothering to look at the caller ID, she barked into the phone. "Kirpatrick…"

"Uh, Kira, is everything okay? Did I catch you at a bad time?" Remmy had agonized about calling Kira, ever since waking in the early morning from the most erotic dream she'd ever had. Now Remmy was sure it wasn't a good idea. She had had such a wonderful time the previous evening that she decided to see if they could do it again. Remmy called Kira, intending to ask her to dinner; now she second-guessed herself.

When Kira didn't answer immediately, Remmy became concerned. "Kira? Is something wrong?"

Shaking the cobwebs out, Kira focused on the phone. "Uh, yeah. I'm okay. What can I do for you?"

Picking at the bottom of her sweatshirt, Remmy took the plunge. "I had a great time last night. Thank you once again for the pen."

"You're welcome."

Remmy noticed Kira didn't comment on their previous evening. "I was wondering if you would like to have dinner with me tonight or tomorrow night."

The memory of the belligerent caller sounded through Kira's head. She now knew having dinner the previous night had been a mistake. It had given Remmy a false sense that they could have a relationship. Kira had to stop it right then.

"Actually, I'm sorry about last night. I led you to…" Kira pinched the bridge of her nose. Her head was starting to pound.

"I don't understand the complete reversal from last night."

The phone calls had put Kira on edge, causing her to withdraw. "I'm sorry. I made a mistake going to dinner with you and that is all there is to it. Now, I have to go. My date is going to be here soon and I don't want to keep him waiting."

Kira's heart broke into jagged pieces as she lied to Remmy. Cold tears streamed down her face to match the ice forming around the shards of her heart. Kira had trouble breathing. Silence greeted her. It was followed by the sound that brought Kira's world crashing down upon her—the dial tone. Remmy had hung up on her, without responding.

Kira berated herself. *What the fuck did you expect?*

You've lied to her, treated her like shit…now this ultimate insult. She deserves better than that.
Kira looked at the clock. "Shit. I need to get moving. I'm working a double again on the roads."

✝

She hung up on Kira. For a rare moment in her life, Remmy was speechless. Hearing Kira's words through the phone, Remmy's mind went into survival mode and did the only thing it could - shut down.

She thought of nothing but numbing the pain as she pulled a bottle of tequila out from under the island. Not bothering with a glass Remmy sat in the chair on her deck, drinking from the bottle. Sitting in silence, she let the alcohol work its magic.

A short time later, Remmy heard the patio door open and close behind her. She could smell his aftershave. She associated the scent only with her father. "Hello, Daddy."

Taylor looked at the almost empty bottle, then at his daughter. He had not seen her in that condition in several years. Taking the bottle from her, Taylor set it on the patio table. "Hi, sweetie, want to talk about it?"

Remmy looked up at him with unfocused eyes. "'Bout what…"

"About why you're out here, drinking from the bottle by yourself and obviously having a pity party about something." Sitting down across from Remmy, Taylor pulled no punches.

Remmy laughed. "Always smooth talker…aren't ya."

"Sweetie, nothing is worth doing this to yourself

261

again. Now, what's going on?" Taylor sat waiting, knowing she'd open up soon. When Remmy started crying, he was tempted to pick up the bottle and have some himself.

"Daddy, what's wrong with me? First, I lose Haley…now this."

"Remmington, there is nothing wrong with you. You're a fine woman. Any woman in the world would be lucky to have you. Now what exactly is this about?" Remmy in pain hurt Taylor more than anything in existence.

Looking off into the blue sky, Remmy told him. "Kira's dating a man. She won't be who she really is. She's letting them make her something she's not. Saddens me most…she's going to let them win. Nothing I do would make difference. She doesn't have the courage. Hell…she has no fucking balls."

"Remmy—"

"No, Daddy! I've fought too hard to be me. How can she hide? She's lying to herself and everyone. It doesn't matter…none of it matters."

Taylor reached over and grasped Remmy's hands. "Honey, she has more courage than both of us. Someday you'll understand it. I know you're hurting like hell. You have to hang on and have faith. Do you remember one of our talks many years ago when you met a very brash hellion?"

Remmy smiled. "Yeah, I do."

"Well, you need that same faith and courage now. Kira is doing the best she can at this moment in her life. You have patience, 'cause I just know some day she's going to come out of the fog she's in."

"I talked to Jules. She says I deserve better. Told me I need to find someone who treats me like a goddess." Closing her eyes, Remmy leaned her head back. "Tell me, Dad, how do you unlove a person?"

"You can't, sweetie. Once they are in your heart, that feeling never goes away no matter how hard we try to rid ourselves of it or how hard that person tries to push us away. I do agree with Jules, at this point Kira is not ready. Have that faith in her, though, that she will someday, somehow be the one. In the meantime, try to be the best friend you possibly can to her. Be supportive. If you feel you need to step back then do so, but don't give up on her. She may not say or show it, but she needs you. needs your strength to find her way."

Standing, Taylor held out his hand. "Now, let's get you cleaned up. I'll cook us some steaks on the grill for dinner."

Remmy roared with laughter. "Yes, food...the cure-all."

✝

Her stomach filled with steak, potato salad, and corn, Remmy relaxed on the sofa to watch a movie. The remaining alcohol in her system caused her to fall asleep within minutes. Mr. Bubbles curled up on her lap, kneading her thigh until he was pleased with the result. He too was fast asleep, after cleaning his face of the steak juices.

As the sun rose, Remmy awoke in a panicked state. She tried focusing on the TV. Realizing she had slept through the night, she saw the early morning news blaring away at her. Flashing upon the screen was a breaking story: *Local State Trooper hit by drunken driver.*

Remmy sat up quickly, causing her head to pound. Turning up the volume, she jumped from the sofa. The anchor with the horrific toupee delivered devastating news. Remmy's knees felt as if they were Jell-O. The newsman delivered the story in his nasally voice.

"While working this July Fourth holiday weekend, State Investigator Kirpatrick was approaching a vehicle she had pulled over when she was struck by a drunk driver."

Remmy heard no more of the story. She was already in her truck, backing out of the driveway when Kira's picture flashed on the screen. Driving to the hospital, she quickly called Jack. Remmy hoped Patrick was working. He would know how Kira was.

Jack started talking right as he answered. "Yes, she's at his hospital. She was hit on the expressway and they still have her in the trauma center. That's all I know right now."

"I'm on my way there." Remmy tried not to cry. She had to be strong.

"I'll call Taylor and let him know."

Arriving in the emergency room, Remmy found it filled with officers, firefighters, and EMTs. The scene resembled a well-rehearsed fire drill. Finding Maddie, Remmy caught her attention.

"Sweetie, they won't let you in. It's family only." Maddie liked this young girl. When first witnessing the chemistry between Remmy and Kira, she had been impressed. Maddie told her husband that night that there would be plenty of fire, brimstone, and warfare before they would finally get together. Looking back, Maddie realized how right she'd been.

"Bella's in there now. I'll have her come find you in a bit, okay? Go to the lounge at the end of the hall." Maddie shooed her in that direction, then went back through the doors leading into the trauma center.

Not meaning to, Remmy fell asleep as soon as she sat down on the sofa. A sixth sense once more told her to wake. Walking out of the bathroom into the hall was Bella.

Bella turned toward her. "Bella…"

The young girl ran down the hall and slumped into her arms. Holding the sobbing girl, Remmy looked at the clock on the wall. It was late morning already. "Shh, sweetie… I have you. Shh…I'm not going to let go."

Together, they sat on the hallway floor and cried. Bella sat on Remmy's lap just as she had her aunt's so many times. Remmy feared the worst had happened. Holding Bella tightly, she let the young girl purge her grief. "It's okay, sweetie. When you're ready, tell me everything."

Bella hiccupped. Her crying slowed. "Her pelvic bone is fractured, collar bone dislocated, knee torn up, and leg broken in three places. She's covered in bruises already. She also has a severe concussion. The doctor says she's lucky. The car only grazed her. Oh my God, Remmy, what if it had hit her full on?"

Remmy kissed Bella's forehead, then held her tightly again. "It didn't, Bella, and that's all that matters…okay?"

Bella snuggled into Remmy's arms. "Would you like to see her?"

Nerves caused Remmy's heart to skip a beat. "Yes, I'd like that."

"Come with me, then. They won't give you a hard time that way." Bella led Remmy to her Aunt's room. "They have her on lots of painkillers, so she's not awake."

Entering the room, Remmy held her breath. She had to fight to put one foot in front of the other; both felt as if they had turned to lead. There, sitting by Kira's bed, was a very good-looking man. Gasping, Remmy withdrew back into the hallway. *Oh my god, maybe Kira wasn't lying.*

"Remmy, what's wrong? Are you okay?"

Remmy remained silent.

"Remmy, it's all right, they said she'll be okay."

"Good, I'm very glad. I really shouldn't be here."

Bella closed the door behind her, joining Remmy in the hall. "I'm confused. What are you talking about?"

"Her boyfriend is here. So, I *really* shouldn't be here." Remmy was exhausted.

Bella took a deep breath. "What are you talking about?"

"That man in there. Isn't he her boyfriend, the one she told me she's dating?"

"Wait, Remmy, I'm trying to make sense of what you're talking about." She looked to the door leading into Kira's room, then back to Remmy. "Do you mean Paul? Paul is Manny's husband. What exactly did Aunt Kira say?"

Remmy felt a migraine starting. "When I talked to her yesterday, she said she was dating a man."

"No, she's never dated a man."

Fury replaced the fear in Remmy's face. "So, she lied to me again." Remmy turned just in time to see her father walking toward them.

Bella put her hand on Remmy's arm. "Remmy, give her a chance to explain. My aunt can be pigheaded sometimes. She's scared to death and does stupid things, trying to do what she thinks is right."

Remmy shook her head. "No, I can't see her right now. This isn't something for you to worry over. It's your aunt's issue, not yours, okay?"

"Bella, girl…I sense a storm brewing with her, let's let her work off some of her ire. I'll try to talk to her later." Taylor pulled her into a tight hug. "You look exhausted. How about you come home with me, okay? I'll make you some lunch, then you can sleep for a while. No arguments either."

"Okay, let me tell Paul." Bella slipped inside Kira's room.

Taylor turned toward Remmy. "Remmy?"

Remmy heard her father calling her. Not wanting a confrontation, Remmy kept going. Once home, she curled into a ball in the middle of her bed and cried herself to sleep.

Later that evening, after calling hours had ended, Remmy went back to the hospital. Patrick was working a double shift and would pretend not to see her. Sneaking into Kira's room, she placed a crystal vase containing a single red rose onto her nightstand.

Attached to the vase was a note that simply stated:

You own my heart & I will love you until the end of time...There will never be another in my heart.

Chapter Fourteen

Five Months Later

The winery would be harvesting the grapes for their famous icewine, which was Remmy's favorite, on the first of December. She had been working since July without a day off. When Jack and Jules suggested a mini vacation to visit some of her favorite wineries and antique shops, she jumped at the chance. Not only was she exhausted, but also she had lost a good deal of weight. Looking in the mirror the previous day, she found her clothes were at least two sizes too big.

Remmy used the hour in the truck to catch up with Jules on what had happened over the past week. Jules was currently giving her a strange look.

Pulling up to the winery hotel, Remmy was telling Jules about her new adventure. "Yep, I sure did. I called yesterday and joined."

Jules chuckled. "You mean the gym over on Fifth Street?"

Handing the valet her keys, Remmy grabbed her bag from the back. "Yeah, it's the closest."

"I'm excited for you…it means you'll get out more. Hell, maybe you'll even meet someone."

Remmy scowled at her. "Oh please, that's the last thing I want."

"Yeah, well, you never know. Love will find you one way or another."

Approaching the front desk, Remmy tried not to sound sarcastic. "Well, I'm not holding my breath. Okay, let's check in, then go meet Jack for dinner."

Jules bumped her hip into Remmy's. "Then, Remmy my dear, we're going dancing. I know the perfect place."

Remmy rolled her eyes. "Oh please, it's not some trendy dyke bar, is it?" Remmy gave their names to the clerk.

Shaking her head, Jules laughed. "No, it's just a nice bar. I would never do that to you again. How did I know taking you to an upscale lesbian leather bar would be such a big mistake?" Jules shuddered. "Nope, never again…"

Remmy signed the credit card authorization slip. "I'm wondering how many shops Jack's already been to since he arrived yesterday."

Jules took her passkey from Remmy. "Yeah, and how much has he already bought? Remember, Patrick said not to let him overdo it. They will only have to move it all in a month when they settle into their new house."

Pushing the elevator button, Remmy smiled. She liked seeing Jack happy. "I know, he told me the same thing. I still can't believe it, Jack married and the two of them buying a cute house together. Who would have ever thought?"

Jules slipped her passkey into the lock. "I know what you mean. Okay, I'll freshen up and be ready in about twenty minutes."

"Okay, see you in a few."

†

They were lucky to have found a table when they did. Minutes after their arrival, the bar started filling up. There were women, and a few men, from all walks of life, mingling and dancing to the loud music. Jules stopped a server and ordered their drinks.

"See, I told you it was a nice place."

Jules laughed as Remmy looked her up and down. "Yeah Jules right, luckily no one's going to notice me with you looking so...well, damn. Sexy doesn't even begin to cover it. I know I've seen your outfit before, I'm just trying to remember when."

Jules threw her head back in laughter. She'd worn her black leather pants, black tank, and black leather boots that she wore on stage. It was time Remmy knew, and Jules was hoping her friend would figure it out on her own.

Even for someone as outgoing as Jules was, she was still shy in some respects. No one knew who she really was and, until recently, Jules hadn't cared. "Uh, yeah, you've seen the outfit if you really think about it. Was it Cardiff, perhaps?"

"I've never been there, you have. Remember, you sent me..." Jules watched as Remmy's face lit up. "Oh my God! You're..."

Jules grinned. "Yes."

Throwing her arms around Jules, Remmy hugged her tightly. "I take it no one knows who you are, right?"

"Nope, only you."

Jack's eyebrow raised. "Okay, you two, why the love fest?"

Remmy visibly blushed. "Ah, no reason, just happy to be with good friends. Ooh, our drinks have arrived." She downed half her bottle of beer in one gulp. "Whew, I was parched." Before the server got far, Remmy called her back and ordered another round.

Looking around, Remmy watched some of the women having intimate conversations, while others kissed and groped each other. Observing this made Remmy realize she truly did wish she had someone to go home to, even though she had denied any such thing to Jules.

Finishing her third beer, she watched a good-looking blonde butch approach them. Remmy's stomach flipped when the woman stopped in front of her.

Leaning over, she whispered in Remmy's ear. "Would you like to dance?"

Before Remmy could reply, Jules pushed her out of her chair, toward the woman. "She'd love to."

The other woman took the lead through two fast songs. When the third one started, Remmy recognized it as one of her favorite songs. She didn't like too much rap, but this one was very sensual. Between the beer and the loneliness creeping in, Remmy let the woman draw her close.

Kissing Remmy on the neck, the woman next moved her lips to Remmy's ear. "You're very sexy. May I kiss you?"

Remmy's panties were instantly damp. Unsure what made her so bold, she ignored the nagging warning in the back of her brain. Remmy needed, at that moment, to feel the comfort of another body next to hers. "Yes, please."

When their lips first met, it was light, as if each was afraid to hurt the other. They became bolder and the kisses harder. Within seconds, Remmy had to pull away to breathe. She was about to do something naughty with a stranger and it excited her. Remmy's erect nipples pushing against the fabric of her bra became torture. "Walk me back to my hotel room?"

The woman pulled Remmy forcefully against her own body. "Gladly, baby."

Halfway across the lobby, Remmy asked her what she did for a living.

"I'm a homicide detective."

Remmy stopped dead. Mumbling, she looked away for a moment. "Figures..." The reality of what was about to happen set in, and so did what had attracted Remmy toward the tall butch. It was the swagger. It was the same as Kira's.

"Shit, I'm sorry. I, uh...I really can't do this. This isn't me. I'm truly sorry."

The other woman shrugged. "Okay, well, if you change your mind I'm in room 414." She kissed Remmy on the lips and walked away.

Remmy was far too wired to sleep. Needing to relieve the tension, she headed to Jules' room to wait for her. It was mutually beneficial for both of them. Neither of them was in a relationship and not looking for one, so the friends with benefits worked perfectly.

†

Moments after Remmy left with the blonde butch, Kira watched Jules scan the room. Her eyes fell upon Kira sitting in a dark corner of the bar.

Kira's heart hurt to watch Remmy dance and then leave with someone else. Never did she think Remmy was the type to have one-night stands. Realizing too late that she'd been seen, Kira watched Jules storm out of the bar.

Over the past couple of months that Kira had been off-duty due to her injuries, she had lots of time to think. The reality of her life had hit home when she saw that singular rose sitting by the bed. Planning on calling Remmy when she arrived home from her mini vacation, Kira was now not so sure. "Shit, I have no right to be jealous. Damn, now I'm talking to myself."

Kira wished now that Jack hadn't laid on the guilt, eventually wearing her down. Trying to get out of meeting up with him, she had told him Bella had the rest of the week off. Jack, thinking quickly, had told her to bring Bella with her.

Kira watched Jack walk toward her. *Shit. I don't want to listen to him right now.*

Jack sat quietly next to her.

"I blew it, didn't I, Jack?"

Jack shrugged. "Maybe...maybe not. She's hurting over you lying to her. She's also lonely. Kira, Remmy's a good woman. The two of you would make a perfect pair. She would never hurt you."

She smiled. "I know. She left me a rose that first night I was in the hospital." Kira didn't tell him what the card said. It was private; meant for her heart only.

"We're going to the Golden Dragon for lunch tomorrow. Just in case you're wondering. By the way, where's Bella?"

Kira contemplated what Jack had told her. Could she just show up and expect to be welcome? She'd have to give it some thought. "She's in her room watching a movie and reading. I'm not sure, Jack, if I should go tomorrow."

Jack glared at her. "What? Why the hell not? You've come this far."

Embarrassed slightly, Kira bowed her head. "I've changed, Jack. I'm not sure if I want to be with someone who would sleep around."

"You're joking, right? Aren't you calling the kettle black? Her leaving with that butch meant nothing. Leaving that rose for you, though, meant everything. She's in love with you; it's just a matter of getting her to forgive you. If you have to, get on your knees and beg."

"That's asking a lot of her, Jack. I've hurt her quite a bit. Maybe it's not possible for us." Kira looked out into the crowd of women. Not one of them interested her. There would be no one but Remmy in her heart. Standing, she put her hand on Jack's shoulder. "We'll see about tomorrow. I'm just not sure."

†

Arriving back at her room, Jules opened the door to find a naked Remmy in her bed. She smiled. Jules had known Remmy wouldn't sleep with the other woman. "I see you sent her on her way. Why?"

Remmy laughed sarcastically. "She's a cop. I don't need another one fucking me over, so to speak." She eyed Jules up and down. "So do you happen to have it with you? Since I picked you up at the airport and we came right here, I'm guessing yes."

"Yes, I do." Jules walked over to her kit bag. Pulling out a smaller black bag, she pulled out one of the masks. Putting it on, Jules became someone else. "Phoenix would like to come out and play. It would be her honor to fuck you senseless."

Remmy threw back the covers and spread her legs wide. "Oh, yes, please. Oh, I decided we're going to Billy's tomorrow because I'm getting the dragon tattoo on my arm. Now come play with my body."

✝

That night Kira made a hard decision. Hoping she didn't regret it, the next afternoon she and Bella walked into the Chinese restaurant. Scanning the room, Kira found her friends toward the back on the left. "I see some people we know, we might be joining them." The hostess waved them on.

"Aunt Kira, it's Remmy, Jack, and Jules. It doesn't look like they've ordered yet." Bella was excited to see the three.

"What the fuck is she doing here?"

"Jules, please play nice. Jack, you too."

Remmy stood to hug Bella, who practically fell into her arms. "Hi, sweetie."

"You look good, Remmy."

She ruffled Bella's hair. "Thanks, kiddo." Remmy turned to Kira. "Hello, Kira. Why don't the two of you join us? We haven't ordered yet."

"Hello, Remmy. If it's okay with Jack and Jules, it would be our honor to join you."

Remmy was more than a little curious how all of them ended up in the same town at the same time, not to mention the same restaurant. She looked over at Jack and immediately knew. He'd called Kira. *Well, damn.*

Looking back to Kira as she sat down at the empty place across from her, Remmy just had to ask. "So, what brings you here?"

Kira visibly flinched at Remmy's words. "We've been here a couple of days. We, uh, did some shopping and stopped at a couple of wineries. Nothing very interesting really." Kira sighed.

There was something different about Kira. Remmy couldn't put her finger on it at first, then it hit her. Kira was sad. Her shoulders were slumped and she had a defeated look upon her face.

Everyone kept the conversation light through lunch. When their fortune cookies came, only the cracking of cookies could be heard. Bella looked around the table. "All right, everyone. We each take turns reading them." Everyone laughed.

The last to read hers was Kira. "Mine's not any good. So let's skip it."

Bella nudged her with her elbow. "Come on, Aunt Kira. Don't be a chicken-shit."

"Annabella - such language!" Kira smiled even though she was scolding her.

Bella poked her again. "Oh please, I've heard a hundred times worse coming out of your mouth."

Kira blushed. "Okay, fine. Mine says – 'It takes courage to grow up and turn out to be who you really are.' Like I said, it's garbage."

Silence filled the air. "So, Remmy, Jules and I are going to hit some of the antique shops today and wineries tomorrow. Which direction should we head in first?"

Kira set her napkin on the table. "Head east, right up the main street. You'll hit some really good ones. Sorry to cut this short, but we must be going. It was good to see everyone."

Jack stood as well. "We need to head out, too, if we're going to get anything done today. It was good to see the two of you. Try not to be strangers, okay?"

Remmy watched as Kira and Bella left. Looking at Jules she smiled. "Jules, you look tired."

"Actually I am. Would you two mind if I just go back and sleep for a while? This jet lag is catching up."

After kissing Jules on the lips, Remmy opened her door. "No problem. I wondered how long you were going to last. If I find something you might like, I'll write down what store it was in. That way you can go back."

"Thanks, sweetie. Jack, don't spend too much money."

Jack looked indignant. "I suppose Patrick told you to keep an eye on me, right?"

The two women laughed. Both answered, "Yes."

Jules turned and headed back to the hotel three blocks away.

When Remmy started the engine, Jack reached over and turned off the radio. She quickly looked over at him. "Okay, I'll bite. What?"

"So, how was last night? Was she any good?"

Remmy sighed. "Actually, I got to the hotel and sent her on her way. It's just not me. Besides, she's a cop. Just my luck, huh, a freakin' cop."

Jack patted her thigh. "I'm sorry, sweetie."

Turning into the driveway of the first shop, Remmy lowered her head. "Jack, please stop. What if her fortune was correct? Personally, I think it suited her. Maybe she is all she can be, already."

"Remmy, you need to forgive her. She did what she had to do. I think it's possible she might have changed. Coming close to death will do that to a person. Why don't you call her when you get home? Ask her out for a beer."

Opening her door, Remmy caved in. "Okay, fine. I'll think about it. Now drop it, please."

†

Kira knew it was coming, "Go ahead, Bella, get it out. I know you're dying to."

Bella raised her eyebrow. "You know me so well."

"Yes, all mouth."

"Yep, that's me, all mouth and attitude. I really think your fortune was very interesting."

Sighing, Kira pushed the number for their floor. "Bella, I am who I am. I've made quite a few mistakes in my life, some of which I regret. Others, well, those couldn't be helped." She leaned against the wall of the elevator. "Everyone has regrets. Now, let's just forget that piece of paper and relax for a bit before we have to head out to the holiday festival."

Bella shook her head. "Aunt Kira, I really feel you should heed your fortune. It's never too late to do a little butt kissing."

Ruffling Bella's hair, Kira then flopped on the bed. "Some things are best left alone."

Making one last effort, Bella said, "Aunt Kira, I love you. Please open your heart and try. I really think today was some kind of karma for you. It's saying that no matter how hard you try you can't outrun what's meant to be. I truly believe you are meant to be with Remmy. I just know it, here." Bella placed her hand over her aunt's heart.

Kira smiled inwardly as she mulled over her niece's words. Knowing she had to change the way she lived her life, but actually doing it, was what scared the hell out of Kira. "We'll see, sweetie." Kira closed her eyes and let her mind wander. "Let's see what the next few months bring."

Kira contemplated her lonely life, realizing it matched the eerie silence of the room. Opening her eyes, she found Bella staring at her. The two looked at each other for several moments without a word. Kira finally broke the tension. "What?"

She didn't mean to shout, it just came out that way. Watching Bella shrug her shoulders, then turn around to look at her laptop, Kira felt guilty. Worse was that she had disappointed Bella.

"Shit. I'm sorry, sweetie, I've done the one thing I never wanted to do." Bella started to speak, but Kira cut her off. "No, hear me out."

Bella nodded and moved to sit on the bed opposite her aunt.

Kira rubbed her hands over her face. "I know I've disappointed you and I'm sorry. It seems I've been screwing up a lot lately with everyone. I've made a right fuck up of my life." Sighing, she stood and walked to the window.

Kira knew she could talk to Bella about anything. Her niece was much wiser than the teenager that she was. "I know nothing about relationships, that much is obvious. It seems every time she and I are together, I totally one hundred percent fuck up. Let's face it, I don't think I would have the first clue on how to romance her...or do you call it putting the moves on someone? I only know the three f's."

"Oh my God, Aunt Kira..."

She turned and glared at Bella. "Hush now." Kira turned back to the window. "See I'm completely clueless. I really like Remmy. Ah hell." Kira laid her forehead against the glass.

"Aunt Kira?"

Kira heard the worry in Bella's voice. "I'm okay. I love her, Bella, and I don't have a fucking clue in hell what to do about it. I just don't want to mess up anymore with her."

Sitting back down on the bed, Kira took Bella's hands in hers. "I need to get my life and feelings under control before ever considering having someone else sharing it. Bella, I know it's asking a lot but, if you're patient with me, and maybe with a little help along the way, I can do it."

Tears streamed down Bella's face. "Oh, Aunt Kira, you can always count on me. I love you to pieces and know you can do it. I'm positive it will take some time, though. So, no rushing off and making a jackass of yourself again."

"Annabella!"

"Oh, please, remember, I take after you. So anyway." Bella started putting on her leather ankle boots. "We need to go and polish off a couple of lobsters and work on your sex appeal. That way you can rock Remmy's world and get her into bed. Yes...lobster, here we come. I was so happy when I saw that on the menu for the festival."

"Annabella Kirpatrick! That is one thing we will not discuss."

Bella turned toward Kira. "What? Your sex life? Or lack of it at the moment? Oh, please, Aunt Kira, I know all about sex and it's nothing to be ashamed about. It's a wonderful thing with the right person. For you, that would be Remmy. So, let's work on you while you decide on all the places you're going to take me in Italy after I graduate. We need to start making plans now."

"I still can't believe you'll be graduating a whole year and a half early. You've grown up too fast for my liking." Kira put on her own boots.

Putting her jacket on, Bella smiled. "Yes, but I've turned into a wonderful young lady, just like you raised me. An honest, caring, loving one who knows her aunt will end up with the love of her life and they will be happy together."

Kira patted Bella's shoulder. "Yes, my dear, you are all of those and more. Let's take it one day at a time, though, 'cause any more than that scares the shit out of me. Now, let's go do our favorite pastime."

"Eat," they both said in unison, walking out the hotel door laughing.

†

Jack and Jules checked out Remmy's new tattoo that covered her left bicep. The tattooist who did it was a true artist. Remmy had given him a photograph of the dragon tattoo that had adorned Haley's left bicep and he was able to recreate it perfectly.

Remmy smiled. "I think he captured exactly what I wanted. I decided to do this because I know it's time to truly live my life again. Haley will always be in my heart but I can hide from reality no longer. She wouldn't want me to. It's time to start the next chapter in my life. I must thank the two of you and a few others for sticking by my side and never giving up on me, even when I felt like the world was crashing in on me."

Hugging both of them, Remmy felt better than she had in so long. It was as if the ground under her feet were once more vibrating with love, inviting her to feel its power, the power to live.

Chapter Fifteen

Valentine's Day

Remmy watched Jack look around her office at the mess. "Really, it's not a disaster like you think it is. Everything is organized. The nineteen projects we're bidding on are all on the left side of the office. The seventeen we've been awarded are in order by the start date on the right. Then these eight here on my desk, all rolled up are ones we are currently working on."

Jack shook his head. "Damn, woman. No wonder I haven't seen you since Christmas. So, I guess business is good, by the looks of it. Especially since you are here twenty-four seven. It's Saturday and you should be home relaxing."

Sitting behind her desk, Remmy was curious. "Okay, I'll bite. Why are you here?"

Flipping through a set of the blueprints, Jack turned his back toward her. "Just wanted to stop by and say hi since it's been so long. Does there have to be another reason?"

"Jack, why don't you turn around and try that again?"

Remmy knew Jack was unable to pull off lying to her when they were face to face.

Turning, Jack faced her. "I just came to see you and to take you to lunch."

Sitting in the chair in front of Remmy's desk, Jack wiped his sweaty palms on his jeans.

Remmy laughed. "Bullshit. Jack, my old friend, you can't lie to me. Your palms are sweating like crazy. Did Dad send you?" She was amused by his nervousness.

Jacked rolled his eyes. "Okay, fine. We're all worried about you. You've been hiding in this office since we came back from the wineries. No one has seen or heard from you."

She raised her right eyebrow. "All?"

"Yes, all of us, your father, Colin, Jules, and me, even Bella. Don't give me that look, either. Bella comes to hang out with Taylor every couple of days. She's interested in becoming an architect. He's become a mentor for her. I think she also looks at him as a kind of grandfather figure."

"I love all of you, but you worry too much. I'm fine, really, I am. As you can see…" She waved her hand around the office. "I've been swamped. Projects are coming out my ears. So by the sounds of it, Bella is doing pretty good."

"Why don't you ask what you want to? Don't you miss having someone in your life?"

"Don't, Jack. Just don't." Remmy glared at him.

He remained silent.

"Yes, all right, I admit it, I miss coming home to someone being there. Haley is gone…and, well, no one can replace her." Remmy's eyes misted over.

Jack leaned forward putting his hands on her desk. "Sweetie, we know that no one can replace her. But Kira is a wonderful woman. She's different from what Haley was, and maybe that's what you need."

Remmy sat back in her chair. "Kira has never called me or made any attempt to see me. Besides, I've been on a couple of dates with someone." She wouldn't admit that Kira had indeed called her, but she had ignored the voicemails. She detested lying but she just didn't want to open the old wound that had Kira's name on it.

Jack sat with a shocked expression on his face. "What? Who? As for calling you, the phones work both ways, you know. You really should call her. She's really changed and you need to see her."

Closing her eyes, Remmy sighed. "Fine, I'll think about it. That's all I can guarantee. Don't ask any more of me, please."

"Well, who's this person you've been out with?" Jack frowned. "I don't like not knowing everything."

"She's just someone who has asked me out to dinner."

Jack stood to leave. "Okay for now, but I want to know everything soon. Also...please call Kira." Jack held his hands up. "Okay, okay, I'll keep my mouth shut."

Remmy watched Jack heading toward her office door. "Hey, I thought you were taking me to lunch?" She laughed.

"Well, I promised Patrick I would meet him for lunch. I'll talk to you later." He left her office in a flash.

Remmy laughed some more, only louder. She watched Jack sprint from the room. The second he was gone silence filled the room. *Oh Jack, I knew why you were here the second you arrived. I wish it were as simple as all of you think.*

†

Kira paced back and forth in her home office. She had already left Remmy two messages since the beginning of the year. She knew her pacing was making Bella nuts when her niece sighed and left the room. Flopping down in her chair, she put her booted feet on her desk. "Damn. Damn. Damn."

Bella shouted from the kitchen. "Would you just go over there? Jack called and said she was in her office."

Kira mouthed sarcastically, "Why not just go over there? Yeah, right, and get shot in the ass with a nail gun?"

Bella put the two teacups in the microwave. "I heard that! Don't you dare mock me, Aunt Kira. You march your stubborn ass right over there and ask her out to dinner."

Taking the tea out, she handed one to Taylor, who sat at the kitchen table, snickering.

Kira could hear them from the other room.

"You are so bad, young lady," Taylor said. "I wonder where you get that attitude from. Is she still pacing?"

"Gee whiz, I can't imagine where it comes from. Could it be someone tall, dark, and cranky perhaps? Yes, and she's going to wear the finish off the hardwoods." Rolling her eyes, Bella took the other tea to her aunt.

Taking her drink from Bella, Kira gulped it without thinking. Scalding her throat, she slammed the cup on the desk, causing it to spill onto the desk. "Shit, that was hot! Damn. Bella bring me a towel." Kira knew it was her fault for not paying attention. She had been so distracted lately that everyone around her was suffering.

Taking the towel from Bella, Kira said, "I'm sorry for shouting, sweetie. I just seem a little on edge lately."

Bella put a hand on her aunt's arm. "Aunt Kira, go see her. Please?"

Cleaning the spilled tea, Kira said, "Okay, you win. You stay here with Taylor and decide what you want for dinner. See if Taylor wants to stay as well." Kira didn't want

Taylor grilling her on where she was going. Kira threw on her leather coat, grabbed her keys, and left.

Taylor watched amused. "Sit, my dear Bella. Is she going where I think she is?"

"Yes, finally. She's as stubborn as a mule."

Taylor sipped his tea and laughed. "As is Remmy. They are a match made in heaven. They just haven't come to see it yet. Now, did Kira say something about dinner? I'm feeling like a good steak dinner, how about you?"

At the mention of food, Bella giggled. "Mmm...that sounds wonderful to me. Since it's Saturday, we'll need to make reservations."

Taylor smiled. "Well, hopefully it will only be the two of us for dinner. If everything goes well, we might be celebrating with those steaks."

Bella slapped her forehead with her palm. "Oh shit, I wonder if Aunt Kira remembered today is Valentine's Day. I hope she asks Remmy out for dinner tomorrow night. Maybe if they go out tonight and Aunt Kira sees all those romantic couples she...well, let's just say she's not progressed that far yet."

Nodding, Taylor handed Bella the phone. "I agree. Kira has come a long way but still gets spooked easily."

Bella's call to her aunt went right to voicemail.

†

Kira sat in her truck, gathering her courage. Opening her door, she saw Remmy locking the front door of her office. "Well, it's now or never. Shit, woman, why the hell are you sweating, you're just asking her out for a drink,

possibly dinner. Both of which you've done together before."
Letting out a deep breath, she walked over to Remmy.

There was a puzzled look on Remmy's face. "Hello, Kira, how have you been?"

Kira did something that startled both of them; she hugged Remmy.

"I've been okay, taking each day as it comes. How've you been?" It was small talk but it was a place to start.

After placing the rolled up blueprints in her truck, Remmy turned back to Kira. "I've been swamped. Business has *gone wild* as Colin would say. I'm glad to hear you're doing well; you look less stressed than usual."

It was true; Kira had come to realize all the stress she put herself under was going to kill her. "Yeah, well, I've changed a bit over the last few months. Being told repeatedly that I'm a stubborn, pig-headed ass might have had a little to do with it. I want to say I'm sorry for the way I have acted in the past and to ask if you could possibly forgive me." Kira smiled at her.

Remmy stepped closer to Kira. "Wow, uh…that must have taken a lot of courage. I'm proud of you. Thank you for saying that, it means a great deal, not just to me but to you as well."

"Myself?" Remmy puzzled Kira.

Smiling, Remmy touched Kira's arm. "Yes, to you. It means you've grown to realize you can be who your heart tells you to be. And yes, I forgive you."

It was now or never for Kira. "If you have no plans, I'd like for you to have dinner with me."

"Well, I have nothing planned. What about Bella?"

Kira thought for a moment. "Taylor was at our place when I left. I'm sure they're already planning dinner without me."

Remmy laughed. "Okay, sure, let's go grab a bite to eat. You call Bella and tell her, though, that way they're not possibly waiting. I'm feeling like Italian, how about you?"

Kira's stomach growled. "It sounds good to me. Let me call her real quick. Do you want to meet me there? That way you don't have to come all the way back here?"

"Yeah, that would probably be a lot easier. I'll meet you there then."

†

Bella's cell phone rang. "Aunt Kira. What are you up to?"

"Remmy and I are going to dinner. So, it's going to be just…"

Needing to tell her aunt what day it was, Bella tried to interrupt her. "Aunt Kira, you do know what day…"

"Yes, it's Saturday and everywhere is going to be packed. I need to go. We'll talk tonight when I get home."

Bella heard the dial tone. "Damn." She looked over at Taylor. "Oh well, she wouldn't let me finish. It'll serve her right for cutting me off. It will do her some good to shake her up a bit."

Taylor sighed. "Yes, but for the better or worse? It could go either way."

Picking up the car keys, Bella look back at Taylor. "I agree, but it's out of our hands. Now, let's go get those steaks. I'm starving."

Bella's stomach growled and they both laughed, knowing what took priority…food.

†

As Kira sat down, she wondered about the smiling, giggling hostess. Their waitress approached and she forgot about it, but only for a moment.

"Hi, my name is Amy and I'll be your waitress tonight. Since it's Valentine's Day, all couples get a free bottle of wine this evening." She opened the bottle and poured each of them a glass. "Can I start you off with an appetizer?"

Remmy spoke before Kira had a chance. "Could we each get water as well?"

The waitress looked at Kira, who was losing a little color in her face. Kira quickly came up with something to say. "We're not sure what we want yet. We'll need a minute."

Kira turned and looked at Remmy. "I'm sorry, I didn't realize what today was. I do have a question though." Kira took a deep breath. "Are we just two friends having dinner or is this possibly a date?"

The arrival of their water and a basket of bread, left the question hanging for the time being.

Remmy's mind was reeling. After ordering, Remmy knew she had to confess to Kira that she was possibly seeing someone. Yes, she still had feelings for Kira, but she wasn't sure if she wanted to chance getting hurt again if Kira once more decided to do an about face.

Kira took a drink of her wine. "So, how have you really been?"

"I've been good. No more nightmares about what happened. Once in a while the broken bones ache, but that's to be expected I'm told." Remmy placed her napkin on her lap.

Kira jumped in with both feet. "Sounds like all you do is work. So, no social life then?" It was Kira's subtle way of asking.

Remmy blushed slightly. "Yes, I work a lot. I've been out on a couple of dates with someone. Kira, I want someone I can come home to. A woman who will be there for me, kiss me in public. That special one who would take me to the ball and dance with me."

Silence fell at the table, creating a tension between them. Kira looked up to see Remmy staring at her. What was Remmy trying to tell her? Was Kira too late? Saved from further thinking, their salads arrived. They each thanked the waitress and set about picking at their food.

Remmy was pushing her half-full plate away when Kira took one last bite and gagged it down. She, too, then pushed hers to the edge of the table.

The waitress approached. "Was everything okay? Would you like boxes for your leftovers?"

"No." They said in unison.

She looked from Kira to Remmy. "Okay, would you like dessert or coffee then?"

Remmy looked over at Kira. "No, thanks. I'm all set."

Kira shifted in her seat. "Just the check, please, thanks."

Feeling sick and unable to stop the words, Kira tried again. "So, do you think this woman might be that special one?"

"I'm not sure. So, how have you really been? Like I said you look good."

Kira finished her wine. "Bella has been great. She's the top student in her class. One of her class friends has really stepped up to the plate and been there for her since her best friend turned out to be an asshole."

"That's fantastic. She's a terrific young lady

Any time Kira thought of her niece, she smiled. "Bella is one hell of a good kid. Problem is, she's not a kid anymore. I'm going to take her to Italy for her graduation."

"Wow, that's great. I'm sure the two of you will have a good time. I hear the food is to die for." Remmy was silent for a moment. "So, you didn't answer me about how you've really truly been."

Kira deflected the conversation from herself once more. She wanted to know about the woman Remmy was dating; she wanted to check her background. "What's she like, the woman you've been dating?"

Remmy gasped slightly. "Her name is Maggie and she's the manager of the local gym where I go. She's nice."

Remmy's description sounded too clinical. Was she so afraid of being hurt again that it wasn't possible for her to fully give someone her heart? Had Kira hurt her so badly that Remmy didn't want to give Kira any real details?

Kira pulled out her wallet, counting out enough cash to cover the bill and tip. She had a gut-wrenching need to run as fast as she could from the restaurant. Laying her napkin on the table, she stood, took a step back and looked around her. At the other tables were happy, loving couples. Something Kira had told herself time and again was probably never possible for herself. Now she knew for sure that it wasn't. Remmy was lost to her. Nothing else mattered now.

Kira's crushed heart told her that Remmy was the only one for her and she had blown it. Unable to stop the tears, Kira turned away from the table. "I'm sorry, Remmy. I can't do this." She took a few steps then looked back at Remmy. "I can't sit here and pretend that it's okay that you might be with someone else. Have a good life with Maggie; you deserve to be happy above all else."

Remmy sat and watched Kira leave. She didn't try to stop her. To Remmy, it was the detective's choice to walk out and not stay to fight for her. "At least now I know." Remmy barely made it to the restaurant door before the tears hit her. She loved Kira and that would never change. There was something in the woman that drew Remmy to her no matter what. Remmy took Kira's words to mean she was setting her free to see someone else.

But what did Remmy want? Even she wasn't sure of that any longer.

Chapter Sixteen

Valentine's Day

2 Years Later

The world continued to spin around without a care. Two years was a long time to hide from life, but Remmy did just that. She hid.

After arriving home that night two years ago, Remmy shut out everything except work and the occasional dates with Maggie. She made Taylor and all her friends swear to her they would never mention Kira's name again. Most tried the first several months to talk sense into her, but this resulted in her not talking to them for weeks after that. Remmy worked day and night building her company until it was bursting with projects.

Her television went untouched and her newspaper was cancelled. Remmy's philosophy was that if she didn't watch it or read it, she would never have to deal with the knowledge in case Kira was ever to be hurt again. She had very effectively cut Kira from her life. Remmy went so far as to never go to her father's place, always making him come to hers.

She knew Taylor, Jules, and Jack feared for her well-being. They were positive if she didn't deal with reality soon, it was going to come up and slap her in the head.

Fate almost took a hand when, eight months previously, Kira and Manny were asked to help with the investigation of a dead woman found in the woods not far from the deceased's home. Three days of tracking down clues and statements of a nasty ongoing quarrel between the victim and her spouse brought the investigation back to the distraught husband. Rather than being taken into custody, he pulled a weapon on them. As the gun was fired, Kira jumped in front of Manny, taking the two bullets in the leg.

Many grueling hours and lots of steel later, Kira's bones had been rebuilt from the fragments that were left. Now, almost a year later, Kira walked with a cane and had yet to return to work. One specialist told her that she would always need the cane and another told her right off to retire.

When Kira was shot, first Taylor then Jules tried to tell Remmy. Each time she hung up or would not answer the door at home. Finally, Jack decided to go to her office to try to see her. Remmy assumed he was there for the same reason the others had contacted her and she had Mack send him away.

✝

It was now Valentine's evening, two years after their last words together. The Fates decided to smack Remmy's and Kira's heads together one last time.

Maggie, the woman Remmy had been dating, had picked her up earlier and they now sat in the same restaurant Remmy had been at two years previously. Remmy had been reluctant about dinner but Maggie had convinced her to go.

Remmy was sure Maggie was going to ask her for a commitment, one which she was not ready for. Remmy fidgeted and gulped down some wine.

Remmy noticed that Maggie was suddenly distracted by something behind her. Not wanting to appear rude, Remmy didn't turn to see what she was staring at. She sat waiting for Maggie's attention to come back to their table.

Maggie continued to look at a couple who had just been seated across the room. "Wow, that woman's daughter looks exactly like her. The mother must work out to keep her body that muscular."

Curiosity finally got the better of her and Remmy turned. She couldn't believe her eyes. It was Kira and Bella. Seeing the cane in Kira's hand, Remmy's heart stopped and tears came to the surface. Remmy gasped. "Oh my...oh, Kira, baby, what happened?"

"Do you know them?" Maggie had the ring box ready to set on the table.

Remmy turned back toward Maggie. "Yes, she's an old friend whom I've not seen for two years. I wonder what happened." The cane in Kira's hand clued Remmy into what the others had wanted to tell her, but she wouldn't allow it.

Sitting down carefully, Kira looked across the restaurant after hooking her cane on the chair beside her. Her eyes landed upon the woman who held her heart having dinner with a very butch-looking woman. "Fuck. Uh, Bella, are you sure you want Italian?"

"Yes, why?"

Kira was frowning.

"Aunt Kira, what's wrong?" Following Kira's line of sight, she had her answer. "Ah, I see. Don't get mad at me. I knew she'd be here. I know you still love her. You haven't been to P-Town in the last two years. Why don't you go say hello? If you don't, you'll regret it."

"Bella, she's with someone." Kira picked up her menu.

"Aunt Kira, at least go say hello. It will be rude if you don't."

"Fine, I'll go." Standing, Kira grabbed her cane and gathered her inner strength. "Order me a beer and the veggie lasagna."

Kira approached Remmy. Seeing no ring, Kira's stomach suddenly had butterflies. Could it be? Was Remmy still unattached? *Am I being given a second chance.* Remmy was smiling as Kira drew near, which was a good sign.

"Hello." They both said in unison.

"Okay, let's try again. Hello, Kira, this is a friend of mine, Maggie."

Remmy's dinner partner corrected her. "Girlfriend."

It was obvious by the look on the woman's face and the tone of her voice that she was upset at Remmy calling her just a friend.

Kira watched in fascination as the *girlfriend's* face turned into a scowl. Kira extended her hand. "I'm Kira, nice to meet you." Releasing the woman's hand, Kira turned back to Remmy. "I thought I would just come over and say hello for Bella and me."

"Tell Bella I said hello also and that I'll talk to her soon. I might have an internship open for her."

"I will. She'll be very excited to hear that. Well, I guess I should leave you two to dinner then. I'll give you a call next week, maybe we can do lunch or dinner." Smiling, Kira walked back across the restaurant.

Kira smiled for the first time in so very long. She was happy. She couldn't stop. Sitting down at her table once more, Kira was almost giddy. "Well, I think I pissed someone off."

"Aunt Kira, what did you do to Remmy?"

Kira's head tilted a little. "Nothing, I think the woman who is with her doesn't like me. You know what, though? Remmy started smiling as soon as I approached the table."

Bella's eyes rolled. "Aunt Kira, she still loves you. You need to go get what's yours, before you lose your chance."

"You know what, sweetie, you're right. Enough is enough. It's time, as you told me a long time ago, to grow a pair and take what's mine. Sweetie, I'm sorry it took me so long to do it." Kira's mind was set on talking to Remmy once more and doing the right thing once and for all.

Kira watched as the woman Remmy was with pulled a small ring box from somewhere under the table. Kira knew her last chance was at hand. As rapidly as her cane and leg would allow her, she made her way back to Remmy's table.

She saw several patrons at tables around Remmy's start to notice something was going on. As Maggie set the box down, Kira approached them.

Kira arrived as Remmy's dinner partner took her hand. "Remmy, I have something to ask you."

Remmy looked up and Kira saw in her eyes what had been left unsaid for so long. Being in public didn't stop Kira; nothing would. Bending over, Kira took Remmy's head in her hands and kissed her. It was no ordinary kiss, though.

It wasn't gentle; it was filled with passion and hunger. Kira poured every last ounce of courage she had into the kiss.

"Excuse me, what the hell do you think you're doing? We're having a private dinner and I was about to ask Remmy something when you rudely interrupted us. Now, I'm really trying not to cause a huge scene, but please leave. Remmy and I have something to discuss."

Kira as well as everyone around them waited for the answer. Those who would have been aghast at seeing two women together were anxious as well to see the outcome. The onlookers all had another thing in common—they were waiting for the fight to begin.

Remmy looked at the ring. There was only one answer. "No. I'm sorry, I can't. I like you but I don't love you." Kira made as if she was going to say something. Remmy shook her head no at her, stopping Kira cold.

Gathering her purse and coat from the chair beside her, Remmy stood and walked away from the table. At the hostess' counter, she asked the woman to call her a cab.

†

In the main dining room of the restaurant, the dejected woman gathered her items to leave after laying cash on the table to cover the bill. "So, you're Kira, huh? Well, she may have said no to me, but I'm sure if you went after her, the answer would be different."

A Cheshire cat smile spread across Kira's face. "I think I'll have dinner with my niece then go grovel afterwards. I'm sorry things didn't work out."

The woman shrugged her shoulders. "I knew she was holding back. Then when I saw how she reacted to your presence, I knew what it was. Good luck to you."

299

The two women parted ways. Kira arrived back at her table to a giggling Bella. "Well, I saw what happened. Now, what are we still doing here? Aren't you going to go after her?"

"Yes, I am, after we have dinner. I know where she's going. This will give her a little time to relax. Now let's eat, I'm starving. Then I need to drop you off at home and drive over to see Lee at her shop. I'm hoping she still has that piece in the window." Kira dug into her food, making quick work of the meal. "Yep, let her just sit there for a bit and wonder." It was now Kira's turn to giggle.

"Oh. My. God. Aunt Kira, you mean the Celtic ring with the Russian Chrome Diopside in it?"

Kira giggled again.

"Nice choice, really nice. Let's go, I'm done."

Epilogue

And so now, I have my ending...

Why was tonight so important for the ending of my novel, you ask?

It seems that without meaning to, I wrote a novel that mirrors my life. I was waiting to see how it would end. There are a lucky few who get that second chance at a happy ending in life. I plan on taking it and making it my own, in life and on paper.

The sun has set now and most likely, my neighbors are now clearing away their dinner dishes as I realize my doorbell is ringing.

I open the door and smile.

Then I cry because my heart feels so full.

Here, my soul stands in my doorway.

She holds a bouquet of purple roses and a ring box.

My eyes travel to the top of her head and I laugh. She is wearing a pair of those silly Halloween devil's horns on her head.

I cry more, yet I laugh.

She bows. "I'm the little devil, My Lady, and I am at your service."

"Yes...but you are my little devil, are you not?" I laugh.

She holds the box forward.

"Care to be the Little Devil's wife?"

I grab her neck and pull her down for a kiss. "Ask me in the morning, after you've spent the night loving me."

After gently pulling her in the door, I lead her to stand by the corner of the sofa. She looks down at me and I see uncertainty in her eyes as I take the cane from her hand. Setting the cane on the sofa, I take her hand in mine. "Do you trust me to never let you fall?"

Kira smiles at me and I see any misgivings that she might have had vanish. "Yes, I do. I trust you with my heart and soul as well."

Pulling her down, I gently kiss her lips then her neck. When my lips touch the spot on her chest in the opening of her polo shirt, I feel her shiver. She moans softly as I start to pull her shirt out of her jeans.

Smiling up at her, I tilt my head toward the bedroom. She nods her head.

"Don't worry, lean on me if you need to."

Two steps down the hall toward the bedroom, I stop and back her up against the wall. Putting my hands on the hem of her shirt, I start pulling it off her. As I have the shirt halfway up with her arms in the air, I'm presented with breasts covered with a black satin bra.

"Beautiful. How did you know black satin is one of my favorites?"

"Lucky guess?"

Not wanting to wait for me Kira pulls her shirt the rest of the way off and drops it to the floor. As she puts her hands on my hips, I pull down the bra cup covering her left breast. Licking the nipple before me, it jumps to life and seems to grow before my eyes.

"Exquisite…"

Licking it again, I then wrap it with my lips and suck. I feel Kira put her left hand on the back of my head to hold me in place. As I continue to suck, she starts moaning.

"Oh God, baby. That feels so good."

I trace with my tongue the Celtic design that runs from the top of her breast to her shoulder. Pulling her away from the wall, I start to walk backwards down the hall toward the bedroom, bringing her with me. I continue to kiss and lick her chest as we go.

Almost to the bedroom door, I reach around and undo the clasp of her bra completely freeing those delicious breasts. "These are so perfect." I drop the bra and reach for the top of her jeans.

Now in the bedroom I back her up against the bed. I undo the buttons on her jeans and pull them down her long legs. As I do so, I push her carefully down onto the bed. "Sit, darling."

On my knees in front of her, I grasp her booted foot and come face to leg with her. In front of me are her battle scars. I've heard tell that scars define who we are. To me they tell a story of how strong she is, how she can conquer all, just as she conquered my heart.

A lone tear slides down my face. "I should have been there. If only I had listened to everyone and not pushed them away. Oh, baby, if I could take the pain from you I would."

Kira reaches down and wipes the tear away. "No more should have's or if only's or what if's. This moment starts a fresh time in our lives where none of those exist. Love me and any pain they caused will go away."

Pulling her boots and socks off, and then her pants, I can feel her watching me. Looking up, I see that she has reclined a little, leaning back on her elbows. I leave her laying there clad only in her black satin panties.

I slowly run my eyes up and then down her body as I stand, taking in the tattoos and scars. "You, Kira, are the most beautiful woman I've ever laid eyes upon." I kiss the inside of each of her thighs.

"Rem...you're killing me here."

I chuckle. "Oh really? I'm not even undressed yet. Shall I remedy that?"

Kira moans. "Yes, please do."

Reaching down I run my index fingers along the rim of her panties. "I think these need to come off first please."

Slowly, teasingly, I pull them off her as she lifts her hips a little. Where the crotch of the panties was is now a patch of midnight black hair that is already glistening with wetness. "Mmm...looks like someone is a little wet already."

Kira parts her legs to give me a better view. Now it's my turn to moan loudly. "Ooh lordy..."

I shake my head no. "Not yet."

She smiles wickedly at me. "I agree. I think you have too many clothes on. Why don't I help you get them off?"

Backing up, I shake my head no at her. "Nope! You get to watch, baby."

Reaching down, I unzip my jeans, but I don't take them off. Luckily for me I had taken my boots and socks off earlier. Not bothering to unbutton my blouse I pull it over my head, uncovering a crimson satin bra that hooks in the front. I decide to have a little fun and tease her some more.

Instead of undoing my bra I cup my satin covered breasts with my hands and squeeze them. I feel my hardened nipples pushing against the fabric. Closing my eyes I squeeze again. "Mmm…"

This time as I squeeze them I look at her. Lust covers her features and her legs are farther apart.

Leaving my bra on, I then pull my jeans down revealing panties that match my bra. After kicking the jeans aside, as I straighten back up, I run my right hand up over my satin covered center.

"Oh my God, Rem…you are wicked."

Undoing the clasp on the front of my bra, I lick my lips. "I've only started, baby."

Pushing the cups of my bra aside I grasp my hard nipples and pull on them. "Ooh…" As I pull, I twist them. "Do you like what you see so far?"

Kira chokes out, "Yes."

I step up to the bed wearing just my panties. She sits up and grasps my hips.

I feel her hot mouth close over my left nipple and begin to suck. As she does so, her right hand moves to my ass and starts to massage my ass cheek. Kira then reaches up and pinches my other nipple.

I can't help but push my body into her. "Oh, baby, yes. So good. Harder."

After pinching my nipple hard several times, I feel her bite down on the one she has been sucking. As she bites it, she lets go of my nipple that she has been pinching and I instantly miss the contact.

She reaches down and pulls my panties down. Just as quickly as she started she pulls away from me. Moving her long body up the bed, she motions a finger at me to come up onto the bed.

I was extremely glad at that moment I have a king size bed. Kira is so tall she needs the extra leg room it provides.

Slowly I make my way onto the bed and straddle her hips. Both of us gasp as our wet centers touch.

Kira's voice is even lower than usual. "Up here now!"

I moved up so that my knees are on either side of her head. Grabbing the headboard, I held onto it like a lifeline. Slowly I lower myself onto her waiting mouth. The second her tongue hits my clit I think I am going to explode. "Oh no…no…not yet."

She licks my clit again. "Come for me, baby. I know you need to."

"Oh, please, not yet. I want it to last."

"Don't worry, we've only just begun."

Taking my right hand off the headboard, I grab my right nipple and start playing with it. "Oh God Kira. Your mouth…it feels so good."

"Come in my mouth, baby. Come for me."

I pinch my nipple hard. "Suck my clit. Please."

She sucks it gently at first. "Mmm, I can feel it growing in my mouth as I suck on it."

I am so wet now I can feel it running out of me. Just as I am about to beg her, she takes my clit into her mouth and sucks hard.

"Yes! Kira…yes!"

It's starting, I feel my stomach muscles contract as it travels through me. "Oh God, baby, bite me. Bite my clit!"

Just as she bites down, I felt myself coming and gushing into her waiting mouth. "Oh fuck! Oh baby, yes! I'm going to come again."

Pushing my center down hard against her mouth, I come again.

Moving back a little from her, I look down at her as she licks my juices off her lips. I have to have her. I want to taste her. "I want you now!"

As quickly as I can, I turn around so that my head is over her center and mine is once again against her mouth. I have to move down a little more because she was so tall compared to me.

Spreading her legs, I bury my face between them. I forgo licking her and go right to sucking her clit. "So wet."

Feeling her run her fingers over my opening urges me on. Bringing my right hand up I, too, start to trace the opening to her flood of wetness. As I feel her finger enter me I thrust my tongue into the hole.

As she moves her finger in and out, I cannot help but move my hips with her. She then adds another finger and then a third. I then slide my thumb into where my tongue has been, and her hips buck as I move it deeper.

I can feel her body start to shake. I let go of her clit for a moment. "Come for me."

"Please Rem...please."

Biting down hard on her clit, I hear her scream as she pushes her fingers deep into me.

She's panting. "Oh fuck, baby, that's it. Eat me! Bite it...harder!"

I obey her wish as she comes hard against my mouth and thumb. Kira coming so hard only excites me more. After she thrusts into me, I pull away and then push back into her as she again and again rams her fingers into me. When she adds a fourth it is all I can take. I push myself hard against her fingers and come.

Needing to kiss her, I move myself around so I am stretched out on top of her. Looking down into her eyes, I see more than lust. There is love and trust in them. "I love you, Kira. I have since I met you."

She leans up and kisses me hard. I can taste myself on her. "Rem, baby, I'm so sorry for not waking up sooner. I love you with all my heart and can't imagine my life without you in it. Tonight, at first, I was afraid that I would need you too much and scare you off. I can see though that we truly belong together in every sense of the meaning. I get extremely excited just thinking about you. Now seeing you, every nerve in my body is screaming."

I smile down at her wickedly. "Kira, my love, this is only the beginning. Something tells me your tastes run as mine do."

Reaching over, I pull the top drawer in the nightstand open. I pull out a wide, long, double-headed dildo and harness. Sitting up I lay them on her abdomen. I then roll off her as she sits up.

With the harness in her hand, she stands up beside the bed smiling down at me. "Yeah, they do. Anything but vanilla."

I watch as she puts the harness on and fits the shorter end into herself so that the ring on it fits perfectly into the harness. As it enters her, I watch as her eyes close.

"I take it that feels good?"

"Yeah, baby, but I know what will feel better."

I try to act innocent. "Oh my...what would that be, my darling?"

She grabs my legs and pulls me to the edge of the bed. Spreading my legs, she lifts me slightly off the bed. "Fucking you, that's what!"

In one swift motion, she rams into me then pulls back out. "Do you like? Is this what you want? Or maybe I should..."

The next thing I know she has flipped me over and pulled my hips up and is entering me from behind. "Oh fuck, yes. Oh my God yes. Fuck me. Please, Kira..."

Pulling her pillow toward me I bury my face in it as I continue to scream for her to fuck me. Just when I think I can't take anymore she rams inside me and stays there. I hear her pull the drawer open a little more and wonder what she is doing. Then I know.

Reaching back with my left hand I pull my ass cheeks farther apart. I feel the lube drizzle down over my ass opening. "Oh yes..."

She then slides the short dildo into my ass. Oh yes, it's the one with the vibrator in it. She doesn't bother turning it onto low, she goes right to high as she starts thrusting into me once more.

As she pushes into me, I know it is pushing into her as well. She is feeling every sensation that I am feeling.

Kira's breathing changes, it is coming in short gasps. She is as close to coming as I am. "That's it baby, fuck me."

"You feel so good. I'm so close."

"Harder, baby. Fuck me harder. Your cock feels so good in me."

Then she does what sends me over the edge. As she fucks me harder, she pulls the one in my ass almost out and starts fucking my ass too.

Raising my head completely up I can't stop the scream that tears from my lungs. "Fuck...I'm coming. Oh God, Kira..."

My body shakes as I come. "Kira...come inside me, please. I need you to."

As the words leave my mouth she thrusts harder and deeper than she has before, tearing a scream from her lungs as she comes. "Rem…you're mine. All mine as I am yours. Oh fuck, babe… Oh fuck!"

✝

Several hours later, I wake to the moon shining brightly through the window. I hadn't realized the blinds were open. Luckily that window faces the woods.

Rolling over, I look up and find Kira grinning down at me. "You're so gorgeous. When you sleep you look so peaceful."

I snuggle into her side. "Mmm… That was the best sleep I ever had in my life. You make me feel safe."

Kira pulls me up so I am laying stretched out on top of her. "You, my love, will always be safe with me. Today starts a new chapter in our lives, and I'd like for you to be a permanent part of mine."

Reaching under her pillow she pulls out the ring box. "How did you?"

Wiggling her fingers up at me she giggles. "Magic."

I smile again and hold my left hand out.

She slips the ring on my finger.

I look deep in her eyes. "Welcome home, love, I see you finally listened to your fortune cookie."

She draws me down and whispers into my ear. "That I did, love…that I did."

About the Author

Alane Hotchkin

If anyone knows where the birthplace of oil is in North America you will know exactly where I am talking about. I was born in Oil City, PA and later lived in Pittsburgh. You say do not know where Oil City is. Well, imagine a tiny town, population "two," directly between Pittsburgh & Erie, PA. I grew up with family always around (mostly male) and all with wicked senses of humor. One cousin one day decided to see if his father's (my uncle) car would float in the retention pond.

Okay, so now you also know where I got my sense of humor. My earliest childhood memory is driving to the store with my favorite uncle to buy his cigarettes & booze in his HUGE Cadillac with the top down, while listening to an eight-track of Dolly Parton's *Coat of Many Colors* and so a little girl's education was started. LOL

Side Note: Finally, in 2005 I had to admit to myself and, unwillingly, to others that, well...I'm a country hick even though all my life I tried to be a city girl. LOL

Alane Hotchkin

Went to college and majored in Accounting/Business Law/Economic Engineering and guess what, I ended up in the accounting field. Now tell me, how many people actually end up working in the field they studied for? The accounting led to working at a bookstore for five years, a local television station for ten years, and then onto where I am now. What can I say, I love numbers.

Contact Alane at Lillithblackhawk121@yahoo.com and visit her website at www.ahotchkin.wix.com/mysite.

Other Books from Affinity eBook Press

Captivated by Annette Mori
Juliet Lewis has one too many quirks for her own well-being. Snooping was bound to get her in trouble. Sexy police officer Tanner Sullivan gets Juliet's attention and she wants to know more. Will Tanner turn out to be her jailor or savior? Sparks fly when the obsessive-compulsive Juliet and the paranoid Tanner cross paths in this quirky thriller with a new twist around every corner.

Pausing by Renee MacKenzie
Jordy Chapman is the Emergency Service Coordinator at Cypress Haven mental health facility in Naples, FL. Keira Yeager's family owns an upscale furniture store in Naples and orchestrates a generous donation of furniture to Cypress Haven. When the two meet, they hit it off immediately. Will a Yeager family's anguish and misunderstanding threaten their new relationship?

Breaking the Silence by JM Dragon
Still grieving five years after the death of her father, Dilana Sterling is a shadow of the woman she once was...a successful author with a string of best sellers, and a longer

string of women. Rachael Alderman, a teacher at the local orphanage, lives a quiet, yet satisfying life. When Dilana and Rachael meet, they develop a friendship that leads them on personal journeys of self-discovery. Will their memories of the past prevent them from moving toward each other, or will they find a path that leads to each other so they can experience life together?

The Termination by Annette Mori
Codee is having a bad day and it's only going to get worse. Sawyer, a compassionate young woman, is resigned to her fate. Her only question is what fate is that? After slipping on ice, Codee wonders if she is hallucinating and fallen into an Alice type rabbit hole. The only thing she knows is that she needs to save Sawyer. Enjoy this satirical romance, with all of its twists and turns, that just might make you go hmm...

Next Time by Erin O'Reilly
What if you had the chance to make history stop repeating itself? Would you sacrifice today for a chance at a better tomorrow. There is a moment in everyone's life that defines their future. For Jac and Carol, that time is now. Jump ahead twenty-five years and meet Carol's granddaughter Livvy. She is ready for a challenge and is fleeing the nest and getting on with her life. Read this wonderful love story that spans several lifetimes.

Open Your Heart a Sensual Collection by Ali Spooner
Excite your senses, rejuvenate your memories and best of all flirt with the edge of eroticism. Allow us to help you relive that first kiss, flirting with young love, your dream come

true, surprise encounters, and your wildest desires... Enjoy these stories of love, sweet seduction, and steamy encounters. Open Your Heart...a sensual collection.

Secret of Stone Creek by Natalie London
Jennifer Cameron arrives in Stone Creek, Wisconsin to sell her grandparents' large Victorian home. While there she is intrigued by a twenty-four-year-old never solved murder. Her attraction to the lovely and mysterious librarian, Diana vies for her attention. Follow this suspenseful whodunit to its conclusion.

The Promise by JM Dragon
An accidental meeting with Melissa Grant, leads to an unexpected offer for Kris Lake—refurbishing a beach cottage, with the help of Melissa's granddaughter Claire. Do outer imperfections prevent them from reaching the beauty that lives inside and the chance of a happy new life? Find out in this lovely romance that will fill you with heart-warming sensations throughout the story.

Christmas at Winterbourne by Jen Silver
The Christmas festivities for the guests booked into Winterbourne House has all the goings-on of a traditional holiday. The only difference is that this guesthouse is run by lesbians, for lesbians. Join the guests and staff at Winterbourne for a Christmas you'll not soon forget.

The Review by Annette Mori
Silver Lining, a successful lesbian romance writer, has the

crazy idea to sponsor a contest where the first reader who posts a review wins a home-cooked meal with an offer to fly the winner to Washington State. Jasmine, the winner, has engaged in subtle flirtations with Silver. Bizarre messages from the unknown fan has Silver questioning the wisdom of a relationship with Jasmine.

South or Heaven by Ali Spooner
Kendra Drake has taken over as Captain of her father's shrimp boat. As a favor to her father, Kendra has agreed to give fellow shrimper, Lindsey Bowen, a chance to work on the boat but first must prove herself to Kendra and her crew. Lindsey finds a way into Kendra's heart. Will it only last for the summer?

Catch to Release by Lacey Schmidt
On the verge of success, lesbian folk-rock star, Shay Greenaura, finds herself caught up in more than just her music. Threats have her manager hiring a security firm for protection. Addison Weller, a former Diplomatic Security Services agent is called in to assess the threats against Shay. Their undeniable attraction, brewing silently between them, could prove to be a fatal distraction. Follow this fast-paced adventure to its surprising romantic conclusion.

Ready for Love by Erin O'Reilly
Kylie Wilcox's life dramatically changed with the death of her husband. Dr. LJ Evans, a renowned archaeologist, needed and wanted nothing but her work for her happiness. Their worlds are about to collide and lives will be altered forever.

Neptune's Ring by Ali Spooner
In the sequel to *Venus Rising*, Nat and Liz, owners of Venus Rising, invite Levi and Vanessa to join them in a venture for a new club on another island. They find the perfect place in an unfinished resort, Neptune's Ring. While on the island, Levi is drawn into a mystery involving secret compartments and a murder. Join the characters in this page-turning adventure, filled with steamy romance, intrigue, and an unsolved murder.

The Ultimate Betrayal by Annette Mori
Lara is a successful, beautiful, charming, financier. She is also a total control freak, so whatever Lara wants, Lara makes sure she gets. Rachel is Lara's fun-loving, charming, irresistible wife. Sophia's surprise visit to see Lara sets in motion a number of life changing events for them all. Hell has no fury as a woman scorned.

It's in Her Kiss by Various Affinity Authors
A collection of various holiday stories dedicated to anyone and everyone that reads it. Young, old, lesbian, gay, bisexual, and transgender. We are all the same inside and want the same things outside…love, happiness, and that special someone to spend all of our holidays with.

Keeping Faith by TJ Vertigo
You loved them in the previous novels, Private Dancer, Reece's Faith, and Reece's Star, now join the antics of Reece, Faith, Cori, Vi, and even The Animal, one last time in *Keeping Faith*.

E-Books, Print, Free e-books

Visit our website for more publications available online.

www.affinityebooks.com

Published by Affinity E-Book Press NZ LTD
Canterbury, New Zealand

Registered Company 2517228